I0666709

The Lion of Farside

Volume 1

John Dalmas

Sky Warrior Book Publishing, LLC

©2014 John Dalmas, Second Edition

All rights reserved.

This novel is a work of fiction. Names, characters, places and incidents are either the product of the author's imagination, or, if real, used fictitiously.

No part of this book may be reproduced or transmitted in any form or by an electronic or mechanical means, including photo-copying, recording or by any information storage and retrieval system, without the express written permission of the publisher, except where permitted by law.

Published by Sky Warrior Book Publishing, LLC.
PO Box 99
Clinton, MT 59825
www.skywarriorbooks.com

This is a work of fiction. All characters and events portrayed in this book are fictitious, and any resemblance to real people is purely coincidental.

Cover Art by Jay Larsen
Cover Layout by M. H. Bonham
Editor: Carol Hightshoe
Publisher: M. H. Bonham

Printed in the United States of America
0 9 8 7 6 5 4 3 2 1

This book is for
Jerry Simmons and Sarge Gerbode
and for the
Spokane Word Weavers

My thanks to (alphabetically) Eileen Brady, Mary Jane Engh,
Jim Glass and David Palter, for their perceptive critiques. And
most especially to Hank Davis at Baen Books, for a critique
which will prove of lasting value to me as a writer.

PART 1: *To Waken The Lion*

Chapter 1: Varia

None of my family knew where Aunt Varia really came from. Evansville, we figured—that's what she'd let on. Uncle Will had met her in Salem, at the Washington County Fair, and it was love at first sight, he told me once. For him, anyway. "And at second sight and third," laughing when he said it. He claimed she was the best wife a man ever had.

Sometimes she seemed a bit peculiar, but of course she wasn't the only peculiar one in Washington County. Not even the only peculiar Macurdy. Fact is she had to be a little strange to have married Will. For one thing, from his eighteenth birthday on, the only time he stuck his nose inside church was for his own wedding. Unless you count his funeral, and I don't think he had any nose then. Of course, Ma and Gramma were the only ones in the family who were really churchy; most of us were semi-churchy.

Plus he'd get strange notions from time to time. One time Max tells about, before Varia came on the scene, he and Will were helping Dick Fenton butcher steers, and Will caught some hot blood in a tin cup and drank it down like milk. Said it was good for the muscles and glands. Dick said considering how Will didn't have any girl friend, his glands weren't doing him much good anyway, unless he was servicing the livestock. Strong as the Macurdies are, especially Will, we had a reputation as easy going, which no doubt was why Dick figured he could get away with saying that. But just then Will took another notion: He punched Dick right between the eyes, which also broke his nose.

But whenever the family gathered on a holiday, or Ma and Gramma would be feeding a harvest crew, Aunt Varia would be in Ma's big kitchen, or sometimes Julie's in later years, helping do the things women do when a big feed is getting fixed. Fact is Gramma and Ma both said Varia was a magician in the kitchen. And she was always easy to get along with. When folks were gathered around the table or in the sitting room, Varia would sit there not saying much. Not shy; only quiet and watchful. She'd just sit there, the really really pretty one, listening and smiling.

She had two smiles, actually. The usual one was purely friendly and cheerful, but the other one, which I'd only see now and then, seemed kind of spooky to me. As if she knew things other people didn't, and sometimes I wondered what they might be.

I wasn't the only one. I remember Ma saying once she wondered what Varia thought about behind those peculiar eyes. Not the Bible, she'd bet; Aunt Varia didn't go to church any more'n Will did. She did read a lot of books, though. Library books about history and science, Will said. I remember once he laughed and said if he died, she could go off to Bloomington and be a professor, after all she'd read. He told me she'd even read Darwin's book on evolution, but not to tell Ma or Gramma or he'd kill me.

Another thing about Varia—she wore her hair long. Not braided, but in two bunches like a pair of shiny copper-red horses' tails, only kind of out to the sides. That was a time when women hardly ever wore their hair long. Some old ladies Gramma's age let theirs grow long, but they tied it up back of their head in a bun. Ma wished she'd wear it different; the way it was showed her ears, which were kind of pointy. I always thought it looked pretty, though I didn't say so, and her ears went with her eyes just fine.

When I was young, I always thought what was oddest about Aunt Varia was how she'd laugh, now and then, when no one else did. I remember once we had a new preacher over for supper, and he was standing up saying the blessing when Varia laughed like that. First thing he did was look down to see if his pants were unbuttoned or anything. Most of us saw him look, and Frank and me laughed. Couldn't help it. Threw the reverend off his prayer so bad, he just sort of limped on through to the amen. A lot quicker than he might have, which was fine by Frank and me.

Varia was still pretty young then. I mean actually, in years.

But what folks noticed first about her was her eyes. She had two, just like the rest of us, but they were different. Big and leaf green—leaf green!—and tilted up at the outside corners. Made her look foreign. She was a pretty woman though, the prettiest around, and those eyes were part of it. They suited her just right, as if any other color or size or shape would have spoiled her looks.

Along with her eyes, her build was what caught the eye most, even among women I think. A little slim, maybe, for some tastes, but not where it counted. When I was thirteen, fourteen years old, sometimes I'd get a hardon when I looked at her. Whenever I did, she'd look at me and laugh, as if she knew. That killed it every time.

Not that it was a mean laugh. There wasn't any meanness to Varia at all.

I said earlier she had to have been strange to marry Uncle Will. As a farmer, Will was seriously short on judgment, though otherwise he seemed reasonably smart. He'd take a notion to do the darnedest things. His place was right next to ours, with his northeast forty up against our northwest forty, and right in the middle of the two forties was a thirty-acre clay pocket too heavy and wet for growing anything but hay. So that's what we'd always used it for, a hay meadow. Anyway, this one spring day I was fixing fence and saw Will out there plowing his half of it, turning over that nice stand of grass. His team had all it could do to pull the moldboard through it.

Naturally I was curious, so I went over and asked how come he was plowing it. "Gonna plant potatoes," he told me. Potatoes in clay! Was it anyone else, I'd have thought he was fooling.

What he ended up with was a worn-out team, busted up harness, and twelve acres of ground that, when the top dried out, was like a cobblestone pavement. Afterward, when he tried harrowing it, the disks just hopped along the top. I was only fourteen at the time, but I sure as heck knew better'n to do something like that. When Pa saw it, he just shook his head. So far as I know, he never said anything to Will about it. Wouldn't have done any good.

But if Will was a little short sometimes between the ears, he made up for it further down. The Macurdy men were well known for their strength, but Will was almost surely the strongest man in Washington County, and fast-moving. He could outwork most two men. Even if he didn't have hair on his chest, or any whiskers beyond a little peach fuzz. That was typical of Macurdy men, too, and a little embarrassing when I was a teenager.

Anyway he got so he did a lot of work off the farm, which was just as well, considering the kind of farming decisions he sometimes made. Most of his land he rented to Pa, and didn't keep much stock to tend to. A few pigs, a couple of cows that Varia milked, and a team of horses he used logging. He worked for the barrel works a lot of the time, logging white oak cooperage, and cutting up the tops for the Barlow brothers' brick kiln.

And it wasn't just Will's muscles that were big. The Bible says you mustn't show yourself nekkit to folks, but we all figured that rule didn't hold down by the Sycamore Bend. That's where us boys used to swim. And Harley Burton used to have easily the biggest one of all the kids that swam there. (Course, I was only nine, ten years old then. By the time I turned fourteen, and seemed likely to beat him out, Harley was off to France in the Army, helping teach the Kaiser a lesson.) Anyway, when I was about ten, I mentioned to Pa how big Harley's was, and Pa said he'd be surprised if Harley's was near as big as Will's. Said there was someone like that in every generation of Macurdies, but Will had outdone himself. After that I was always a little curious to see what Will had, but of course I never did.

Will was the youngest of three boys, Pa being the oldest. (The Macurdies had always been cursed with what folks around there considered small families; I'd find out more about that later.) I was a little kid five years old when he married Varia. Will was about twenty-five at the time. Even then, I wondered why such a pretty girl would marry someone strange as Will. Some months later she got with child, and when she was supposedly about five months along, Will took her into town. She'd take the train to Evansville, she said, to get cared for and midwifed by her gramma on her mama's side. Some folks thought that was an insult to the Macurdy clan, and to Doc Simmons, and it seemed awful soon, only five months along. But Will was content, so no one in the family said anything. Us Macurdies have always been easy going; let folks pretty much be what they are. And Varia'd said the women in her family had a lot of trouble carrying to full term and birthing, so she wanted to be with her own gramma.

She was back about six weeks later, her belly down to normal, which on her was flat. And didn't have any baby with her. No one was surprised at that, of course; she hadn't carried it long enough. Miscarried, she told Mamma, like she'd been afraid she might. No one troubled her to tell more; didn't want to grieve her.

Melissy Turnbuck told Julie she wondered if the baby hadn't been the victim of an orangewood knitting needle. Julie slapped her face for that; I saw her do it. The only one more surprised than me was Melissy. Years later, Julie told me Varia having an abortion at five, six months wouldn't make sense anyway. Julie worked for Doc Simmons then, and explained that five months is too far along for that.

Afterward, Varia got with child about every other year—pretty remarkable in our family—and always went off to her gramma, and never came home with anything more than her suitcase. After about the third time, we came to expect it, but she and Will kept trying.

By then we'd come to know she was strange in other ways than her miscarriages, her tilty green eyes, and laughing at odd times. Because us kids were growing up, and Will didn't look all that young anymore—but Varia didn't look any different. In fact, when I was twenty-five, she still looked twenty, though she had to be around forty by then, at least.

That's the year a big old white oak barber-chaired on Will—split up from the stump, kicked loose about ten feet up, and fell on him. White oak's treacherous that way; the main reason folks log it is, it's the only tree that's much good for wet cooperage, so it's worth a lot. The one that got him had a butt better'n three feet across. He'd chained it and all before he ever picked up the ax, and tightened the chain with wedges, but the grab hook broke off! Ed Lewis, on the other end of the saw, said all he could see of Will was his left boot and right arm; the rest of him was under that big oak butt, squashed flat as pie crust. It shook Ed so bad, he quit logging; got a job at Singleton's, delivering coal and hogged stovewood. After they got the tree off Will, Byron Haskell, the undertaker, said he never before saw anything looked like that, and hoped never to again. The casket was kept closed, of course.

Pa said one thing about it was, Will died too quick to suffer.

Ma commented on how brave Varia was, what a strong front she put up, though she did look a little pale and drawn for a while. Afterward a couple of fellas around there tried paying court to her. Pretty as she was, the prettiest woman in Washington County, you might have thought there'd be more, quite a few more, but there was only the two. Unless you count old Lennox Campbell drooling on his vest. Could be they were scared off by how young she looked for her age, plus when it came to giving birth, she seemed sterile as a freemartin.

Or maybe they knew, without knowing, she wasn't shopping for a man.

She stayed on the farm for more than another year, all by herself. Didn't seem right, even when you knew she was forty or whatever. A new Watkins man was going around, and when she answered the door to him, he asked if her mother was home. She did her own milking, dunged out her barn, gardened, fed her cows and chickens—stuff like that. Sold her team to Pa, though, and her hogs, and Pa agreed we'd farm her land for her on shares. She helped with things like shucking corn and oats, the way she'd always done. Even slim as she was, she was strong, and no one ever knew her to get sick, not even a cold.

At first Frank and I took turns going over and doing whatever heavy work there was to do; it was less than forty rod from our place to hers. But after a little, it seemed like it fell to me to do most of it, which I didn't mind. It was all family. We kept expecting her to get tired of being alone like that. Figured she'd either marry or go someplace she had blood kin. Evansville, probably.

Finally, after more than a year, she asked Pa if he'd like to buy her place. If the terms weren't too hard, he said, so they sat down together and worked out an agreement. That was in February; she figured to leave in April. And suddenly the whole family realized how much we'd miss her—Ma, Pa, all of us.

Right after that, I was over there with the spreader, getting her manure spread before plowing. I was pitching on a load when she came out to the barn and told me she was driving into town. (Will'd bought a Model A truck.) She said if I wanted to take a break, there was half a peach pie in the pantry; eat all I wanted of it. Then she left.

That sounded all right to me. Matter of fact, I got so excited; I couldn't hardly hold myself till she drove off. And it wasn't the pie I was excited about, it was the house! I didn't even finish loading the spreader, just put the pitchfork aside and went out with half a load. Soon as I got back with the empty spreader, I went to the house, left my barn boots on her porch, and went in. I didn't know what had got into me, but I was practically shaking.

I'd lived just down the road from it all my life, but never seen much of the inside; I'd hardly gotten farther than the kitchen. Our house was a lot bigger, so all the family get-togethers were held either there or at Max and Julie's over on the Maple Hill Road, turn and turn about. Now, alone inside, I asked myself why in the world I was so shaky-excited about a chance to snoop around Varia's house. I walked all through it, just walked through it looking around, and I realized what I was looking for was pictures: family photos. Not of the Macurdy family, but *hers!* Seemed to me there ought to be some, and I wanted to see what they looked like. Wanted to see so bad, my chest felt all tight.

I didn't find any on the walls, so I started looking through dresser drawers and closet shelves for albums, or maybe boxes that might have pictures in them. Not mussing anything up; what I surely didn't want was for Varia to know. And when I didn't find anything downstairs, I went up in the attic.

The first thing my eyes hit on up there was a chest. Un-locked. I opened it, and right on top was this big brown envelope I knew had to have pictures in it. I went over by the window with it, and took out what was inside.

On top was what looked like a letter, a letter I couldn't have read if I'd stood there all week. Could have been Chinese for all of me. Under it was pictures, snapshots. And if I hadn't thought before Varia was peculiar, the pictures would have done it for me.

They were of children. The first showed four little boys alike as twins—looking a bit like Will, but with Varia's tilty eyes. The next was of five little girls, like twins again, and there wasn't any question who the mother was: Varia. In fact there was five—lit-ters, I guess you could call them, the youngest of them looking about two years old. And written under each child, real small, was what might have been a name.

I didn't have any doubt at all that they were Will's and Var-ia's kids. Twenty-three little Macurdies, except I doubted they thought of themselves that way. Five litters. But Varia'd gone off pregnant probably eight or nine different times—more than five, anyway. So all told, it seemed to me she'd given birth to some forty. Having litters and a short term explained why she'd started to swell so early, but even so, they couldn't have been much bigger than squirrels when they were born. I was amazed they'd lived. Seemed like with Varia, Will was more fertile than all the Macurdy men since God knew when.

And if all that wasn't enough, they were dressed strange, in little coveralls about half snug, like they were tailor-made. Tucked into little black, pull-on boots coming not much above the ankles. Looked like they were dressed for Sunday, but not at the Oak Creek Presbyterian Church. The little girls had Varia's long hair, fastened like hers in twin horse tails that hung down over the front of their shoulders. The boys' heads were just about shaved, and they stood there at attention like grinning little soldiers. All of them, boys and girls alike, would have their mamma's green eyes, I had no doubt, and they looked to be standing in front of a low building with white stone pillars. Didn't look like any studio backdrop, either. Looked real. Those pictures—kids and building—gave me chill bumps like a plucked turkey.

And there was one other picture, which I took one glance at and covered up quick as I could. Then I put them all back in the envelope in the same order they'd been in, and put the envelope back in the chest the way I'd found it. Closed the lid, and went back downstairs, all of a sudden scared to death Varia might come back before I got out of there. Because she had a big big secret, and I'd found it out.

I went right back to spreading manure; didn't have the nerve to stay and eat any pie. When I heard the eleven-forty train whistling for the Ramsey Road crossing, I unhitched the team and drove them home. Halfway there, Varia passed me in the Model A. I didn't even wave; I was afraid she'd stop to talk. When she drove by, I could feel those bright green eyes right on me, and it seemed to me she knew what I'd done, what I'd found out. My mouth was drier'n dust. I didn't know how I could ever face her again.

* * *

That night I dreamt about Varia. I dreamt I was over to plow her garden patch and couldn't get the plow in the ground, which was all paved over with brick. Then she came out to me wearing only a shirt, one of Will's, the tails scarcely halfway to her knees, and unbuttoned down far enough at the top, I could see the roundness of her titties. I was sure she wasn't wearing anything underneath it. She invited me in for pie. Her tilty green eyes were bigger than ever, and smiling, she asked me what the trouble was. I said I couldn't get it in, that it was too hard, meaning the plow and the ground. She laughed and put her fingers on my cheek, and said it couldn't ever be *too* hard. My face got hot as a depot stove, and somehow we weren't in her garden patch anymore, but in my bedroom. And I wasn't asleep anymore, it seemed like. Nor was Varia there, really, but only her ghost, so to speak. I could see right through her. But I could still feel where her fingers had touched my cheek.

"Haven't you ever wanted to be a daddy, Curtis?" she asked. Her voice was soft when she said it, not at all like a witch.

I swallowed and told her I'd never thought about it.

"Well then, have you ever wanted to be in bed with a pretty woman?"

I couldn't more'n nod. Frank and me'd been to see the Linzler sisters a couple times, on their farm outside Salem; they charge two dollars. And I screwed Maudie Hodge a few times in her daddy's hayloft. Wearing a French safe, except the first time with Maudie. I didn't want to have to marry anyone, surely not Maudie Hodge, and you couldn't know but what the Linzler sisters might have the clap, or worse. None of them were really pretty; nowhere near as pretty as Varia. Of course, they didn't drop whole litters of strange, smiling little kids, either.

Anyway she took me by the hand and we walked out of the house together, her transparent in the moonlight. And somehow I didn't have my pajamas on, but my regular pants and shirt, and my barn boots. Which about three-quarters decided me I was still dreaming. I've looked back on that night more times than I'd care to count, and I'm still not sure.

When we got to her house, another her was waiting on the back porch, this second Varia not transparent at all. She wore what looked like the same shirt, plaid flannel. The first Varia stepped up to the second Varia and they melted right into one another, while I found myself taking off my barn boots. Then, chuckling like she does, she opened the storm door. And the hinge squeaked, making me start like someone waking up.

And there I was, really on her porch, like I'd sleepwalked there. I mean *really on her porch.* No way was this a dream any longer. "You didn't eat your pie," she said softly, and chuckled again. I walked through that door like I was bewitched—I couldn't have stayed out any more than I could have flown by flapping my arms—and she closed it behind us. Then, in the kitchen, she put her arms around me and kissed me like nothing

I ever imagined, and led me by the hand into her bedroom.

"Curtis," she said softly, "since Will died, you're the strongest of the Macurdies, and you're smarter than Will. A lot smarter; you have no idea yet how smart, how able. Perhaps you never will. Although your uncle was more intelligent than people gave him credit for, and a nice nice man. I became very fond of him."

I only about half heard what she was saying, because she was unbuttoning my shirt while she talked. "You'll give us fine children, Curtis. More than fine. They'll be pleased about that." *They?* I thought. Then she kissed me again, and stepped back and smiled at me. "Will and I did have children, you know. The ones you saw in the pictures this morning."

I stared at her. She knew all right, just like I figured. Then she stepped around behind me and pulled off my shirt, put her arms around me and unbuckled my belt—and felt around inside while she kissed my back. Now she knew what I didn't—how I sized up with Will. I couldn't hardly breathe, and my knees like to have buckled. When she'd finished undressing me, she shucked out of Will's old shirt, and I'd never seen anything like her. So sweet and pretty, it made my throat hurt just to look. Then she pulled me onto the bed, and after that—no way could I describe what it was like. Between times, she told me she wanted me to marry her. I told her that's what I wanted, too. At least part of me did, no doubt of that, but I wasn't so sure about the rest of me, and I guess she knew what I was thinking, because she said there wasn't any hurry. Then she chuckled again and said next week would be soon enough, and started wriggling around on top of me and eating my face.

After another hour or so, I washed up and got dressed, and the transparent Varia led me back home. I was worried that someone would see us, but she said there wasn't any danger of that. That's the first I ever knew of invisibility spells.

* * *

The next day I finished off her manure pile, and while I was forking manure that morning, I got to worrying. She hadn't aged for more'n twenty years, while I'd gone from a bitty little boy to six-foot-one, and two-twenty-four on the creamery scales with my clothes on. In twenty more years, I'd be forty-six and she'd still be twenty. And in forty years…Folks already talked; some were even a little scared of her. That was one reason she didn't go into town any more than she needed to. First Will and then Ma had done most of Varia's shopping in recent years. They even went to the library to get books she wanted.

No doubt about it, being married with her would be somewhat more than just thrashing around on the bed together. And by the light of day, riding behind a team of Belgians spreading cow manure, it seemed to me we needed to talk about that. So when I heard the eleven-forty train whistle, I left my pitchfork there and went up to her house and knocked. She let me in, then cranked up Ma on the phone. Asked if I could stay for lunch and help her eat leftovers before she had to throw them out.

Ma didn't answer right away; there was half a minute there I couldn't hear her voice. Maybe she wondered if I'd started doing more at Varia's than just work. But she said that'd be fine. Anyway I sat down at the table, and we began talking while Varia rustled up a meal. I told her what was bothering me, and she just smiled. "We won't stay here," she said.

"Where—Where would we go?" I wasn't sure I wanted to hear the answer to that. Because suddenly I wanted to be with Varia the rest of my life, and was scared her answer would be something I couldn't live with.

"Where would you like?"

I thought for a minute. "Since the Depression hit last fall," I reminded her, "lots of folks are out of work. It's hard to get a job nowadays."

"We'll get a farm," she said, reasonable as could be. "Somewhere well away from here; maybe some black land in Illinois."

I shook my head. "That'd cost a lot of money. Especially that Illinois black land."

"Land prices are way down. I talked to them at the bank before I sold out to your father. And my grandmother's got money that belongs to me."

Her grandmother. I supposed I'd meet her. I wasn't sure I wanted to.

"She looks a lot like me," Varia said without my asking.

"Just as young?" I was a little scared of what the answer might be.

Varia laughed. "A little older. Maybe twenty-one." Light danced in her eyes when she said it. She was so bright and lively, I couldn't help thinking she'd be a wife like no one ever had before, except Will. But still—

"How about when I'm fifty," I said, "and you still look twenty?"

She looked at me a long time before she answered. "You won't need to look fifty, if you don't want to. Not you. You can look just as young then as you do today."

The first thing that hit me was, I'd have to sell my soul to the devil. I've never actually believed in the devil, but that's the thought that came to me. I set it aside. "Will aged," I reminded her.

"Will never had the choice. I tried. He was a nice man, a gentle man, and he had some unusual genes we need. But not the talent; not enough. I planned to stay with him till the situation here got dangerous—from my not aging, I mean—have sixty or seventy children by him, then disappear. I'd leave a note that I was afraid to stay, because I wasn't aging. That I was going somewhere where people thought I was twenty."

I guess I must have looked troubled, because she put her hand on my cheek again, soft as goose down, and said: "I never actually loved Will, as fond of him as I came to be. It's you I've loved. For a dozen or more years now, since I realized what you might be. Or who."

For a dozen years! That was a stopper. But she wasn't done. "And in the Sisterhood," she said, "we learn self-control." Her mouth twisted a bit. "Self-abnegation, really. It's not always easy, even though we're from selected stock. There's a lot about a person that's not genetic."

It's funny how much I remember of what she said, considering I didn't understand half of it then. The biggest puzzles were who this *we* was she talked about. And Will's jeans? I never knew him to own a pair of jeans. He'd always worn overalls, like most farmers.

Anyway, the upshot of it was, we'd tell Ma and Pa we planned to get married and go somewhere else to live. And when we got there, we'd tell folks I was twenty-five and she was twenty. Then, in twelve, fifteen years we'd move again. Might be interesting to live different places.

* * *

We got married ten days later. The family didn't announce it beforehand; Varia asked them not to. We just got the blood tests and license, and one evening after supper, my folks went with us to the parsonage. Took Reverend Fleming totally by surprise. I suppose he thought I'd got Varia pregnant. Anyway he took us next door to the church, turned on the lights, and married us in our coats, it being cold out and no fire in the furnace. When it was over, we all went home—Ma, Pa, Frank and Edith to their house, Max and Julie to theirs, and me and Varia to ours. Varia Macurdy. She didn't even get a new name out of it, nor much in the way of wedding gifts. The ring was the one Will gave her.

I said something about it when we went inside. She said none of it mattered, that she'd got me, and that was what counted. Then we went upstairs to bed. We hadn't been to bed together except that one night, but we made up for it before we went to sleep.

We'd already packed most everything she wanted to take with us—not a whole heck of a lot. The week before, I'd hammered together sort of a shed for the back of the Model A, with stakes for the stake pockets, that we could use to move. So by ten the next morning we were sitting in the cab together, headed south for the Ohio River, happy as two worms in an apple.

We didn't have a notion of what we were getting into.

Chapter 2: Idri

Evansville actually was where her gramma lived, except her gramma wasn't her gramma. More like her cousin. And almost as good-looking as Varia. The big difference was their personalities; I could see that right away. Idri's eyes were mean and hard, not laughing like Varia's. As if she held grudges; I recall thinking that. She didn't seem to be married—didn't wear a ring, anyway—but I smelled and saw cigar butts in an ashtray. Maybe a brother, I thought. Not knowing Idri at the time.

After Varia introduced me as her new husband, Idri looked me up and down and scowled. The first thing she said was, "You'll have to take him through! He's needed there right now!" Not "It's nice to know you," or "Welcome to the family," or "I suppose you'd like to meet your stepchildren." Just giving orders: "You'll have to take him through." Whatever that meant.

Varia's eyebrows shot up. "I have no intention of taking him through," she said. "We're moving to Illinois. I just came here to let you know, and draw five hundred dollars from the contingency account."

Idri raised more than her eyebrows; she raised her voice. I don't know what she said, because they started talking in some foreign language. But she sounded as mad as anyone I'd ever heard, ripping Varia up one side and down the other. Varia looked shocked at first, but after a minute she snapped something sharp and hard at Idri that stopped her in mid-snarl. Called her something, I suppose. Then she took my sleeve and dragged me out the door, and right on out to the truck. When we'd got in the cab, she started shaking, and I asked her what was wrong.

"There's a lot I didn't tell you," she said. "It didn't seem important. Now it is."

I didn't say anything, just nodded and sat listening, my eyes on that beautiful face.

"Idri and I are not—Americans. And not from some place in Europe. We're from another world entirely, a world called Yuulith." She looked at me as if begging me to believe. "It's as if it's right beside this one, and now and then, in a few special places, openings develop between them for a few minutes. We call them gates. We can go through them from one world to the other. The nearest is across the river in Kentucky; that's the one we use."

I'd heard or read some strange things in my life, but this was the strangest. Yet somehow I believed. For one thing, the name Yuulith gave me chills. No, she was telling the truth, and she knew I knew. "I can't tell you everything about it all at once," she said, "why we're here, why I'm making babies here—except it seemed very important. In our world, there's a land with very bad people—soldiers, and lords of magic—evil, and very powerful. But recently—recently they sent an army into our country and killed most of us."

Her voice was quiet while she told me all this, but her face was drawn up tight. "Idri and I belong to a Sisterhood that over the past three hundred years has worked to develop our power. But when the gate opened, the time before last, Idri learned what the enemy had done. The ylver, they're called. They'd captured our Cloister—our town—and destroyed it, taking most of our Sisters captive."

Varia'd cried the edge off her grief a couple months earlier, though none of us knew it then, but the tears were running again. "Then they killed the children," she said, "and their soldiers raped the Sisters over and over, making the people watch. Finally they set their war dogs on them, on the Sisters that is, to tear them apart."

I sat staring at her. "And Idri wants us to go *there*?"

She nodded, and her voice took new strength "But I'm not. It's over with there, it's all turned evil, and this is my world now. You and I are going to Illinois and make babies, beautiful babies, one or two at a time, and bring them up ourselves, and love each of them. And each other."

What could I say? I kissed her right there in the cab in broad daylight, then put the truck in gear and headed out of Evansville, bound for Illinois.

Chapter 3: The Blackland

Within a week we'd moved onto 120 acres of blackland in Macon County, Illinois, north of Decatur. And it was ours as long as we kept making the mortgage payments. Varia made the down payment, $600, from money left her by Will, and what Pa had paid down on Will's place. And had enough left over to buy a team and harness for $80, and equipment we hadn't brought with us, plus seed and some house furnishings. Everything secondhand, of course, but lots of people were selling stuff, good stuff, to keep food on the table. We weren't bad off, compared to them. We still had money for potatoes and beans, bacon and oatmeal, and salt and sugar and flour. Buying livestock would have to wait though. Except for pasture and hay, I figured to plant most of the ground to corn—corn and a big truck garden—and enough oats for the team next winter and for the cow I figured to buy when I'd made a crop. In the barn there was already hay and oats enough for the team a few months, while the woodshed had wood and cobs for the stoves awhile. Even a couple sacks of coal for the kitchen.

The buildings were pretty decent, and the house was more than big enough for the two of us. They all needed paint, but that'd have to wait. The five hundred dollars Varia hadn't been able to get from Idri would have made a big difference—except it wouldn't have, the way things turned out. But anyway, it seemed to me we'd get by in good shape.

You never know entirely what to expect, working a new team, but when I brought them home, Varia talked to them awhile, and they worked out real well. She was always good with horses, riding or handling them. I started plowing that same day.

I even got a job milking eight Brown Swiss cows for a neighbor, morning and evening. Given the hard times, it paid pretty decent—fifty cents a day—and each morning I took home a big jar of milk and some fresh butter, worth another twenty cents or so.

It also meant I got up at four every morning, to eat before going to Morath's to milk, and finished up there at seven or so in the evening. Between milkings I walked a furrow behind the team all day, keeping the plow where it belonged. So I made a point of being in bed before nine, and I'm talking about in bed for the purpose of sleeping.

Nonetheless, we had time to sit around a little before bed-time, and the very first night, Varia told me she wanted to lay a spell on me. Naturally I kind of backed off from that. "What for?" I asked her.

"So you'll understand me better."

"Hon," I said, "I understand you pretty well already."

She didn't say anything for a minute, just sort of chewed on her lower lip as if she was thinking. Finally she said, "Why do you suppose the Macurdy family was chosen to father my children?"

I stared at her without knowing a thing to say.

"Where do you think the Macurdies came from?" she asked.

"What d'you mean? From Kentucky, way back when James Madison was president."

"And before Kentucky?"

It seemed to me right then I was going to learn something I didn't want to know. I shook my head. "Grampa said we're Scotch-Irish. In school they told us that means from Scotland by way of Ireland."

"Let me put a spell on you, and afterward I'll tell you. It will make it easier for both of us."

I squirmed in my chair. "Will it take long? I thought maybe the two of us could go to bed early."

She laughed, the same young-girl laugh I'd heard since I

was a little boy. "It won't take long. And it's as good as an hour's sleep anyway."

It took me half a minute to say yes, but I knew right away I'd do it. I mean, I'd trusted her so far, and she'd trusted me, and we'd bound ourselves together till death us do part. And what was I scared of? She'd never do me any harm. Besides, it seemed to me she'd spelled me that night she'd taken me to her house, and that had worked out just fine. "Okay," I told her, "I'll do it."

"Thank you, darling," she said, and pulled her chair up closer. "Now look in my eyes."

That was always easy to do, but this time was different. It was like they drew me right in, and I went limp, but after what seemed like ten, fifteen seconds I came back to normal again. "Sorry it didn't work," I said, thinking she'd be disappointed. But she laughed.

"Look at the clock."

I looked, and my mouth must have dropped open. We'd sat down at ten to eight, and now it was a quarter after. "What happened?" I asked.

"You and I did what was necessary. Told your body not to get old; that it's got the ylvin genes. And got you ready to start learning." She came over and knelt down beside me, and kissed me sweeter'n honey. Old Junior started to swell up right away, and Varia began to purr. "Do you still want to go to bed early?" she asked me.

We both of us stood up then, her laughing, and off we went. I didn't get to sleep by nine that night, but I felt fine when she woke me up at four. I'd been dreaming up a storm, and none the worse for it. Part of the dream was being a hundred years old and still young. Strange dream, but not near as strange as it would have been if I wasn't married to Varia.

The next evening we did something different. She laid a lighter spell on me that left me awake but relaxed. Then she taught me to do what she called meditate. I'd always thought "meditate" meant to think about something, but this was different. She told me afterward she hadn't thought it'd go that well, first time. The spell had helped, but she told me my breeding was showing itself. It turned out we'd sat like that, straight-backed in two kitchen chairs, for half an hour.

When we were done, she began telling me things. I listened, but I didn't really believe. I mean, part of me said she wouldn't lie to me about things like that, but what she told me was flat-out unbelievable. My great-great-grampa had come from her world, she said, where her Sisterhood was breeding up strains of people for special purposes, like we breed up hogs and cattle and horses. This was because they were always in danger from "the ylver," who had a lot more power than the Sisterhood, and the only way her people could survive was to get stronger and smarter, and be better at magic.

Anyway, Great-great-grampa had been an experiment, and it'd worked real well. Except for one thing: he hadn't wanted to do what they told him. He was to breed a lot of different sisters, but he'd fallen in love with one of them, and her with him, and he didn't want to keep on living as a stud horse. So the boss sister took her away, sent her off somewhere.

To make a long story short, he ran off to the nearest gate and went through it into Kentucky, coming out in Muhlenberg County. Afraid of being followed and caught, he headed north and crossed the Ohio River into Indiana, where he got work deadening timber long enough to make a stake and get married. Then he went on north again to Washington County, where he homesteaded the land our family's worked ever since.

They'd bred up other studs besides him, but back in Yuulith where'd he'd come from, his progeny proved out specially good, so they tracked him by following his trace in what Varia called the Web. That was something they'd just learned to do; only a few knew how. Then they sent her to bear children by Will.

That's what she told me, and knowing what I know now, I know it's true.

Only now, she told me, it had all gone to waste. Most of the Sisters had been killed and the rest scattered. She didn't know if any of her children were alive. The whole story seemed a little more real to me when she said that, from the way her eyes welled up. She'd never seen her children beyond a couple weeks old, except in the pictures I'd found, but they were hers, all she had.

* * *

After that she spelled me often, and did drills with me, twenty or thirty minutes at a time. To open up my magical powers, she said. I told her that'd be a waste of time, that I didn't have any to open up, and anyway I didn't want magical powers. I had my brain and my two hands and my muscles, and everything else I needed. She was magical enough for both of us.

She looked at me long and seriously. I'd never seen her more serious. "Darling," she told me, "you do have them. They showed up more when you were little. Do you remember once when you were seven or eight, and you looked up at the corner of the ceiling, where I'd looked? Before Idri, my Evansville contact was my favorite sister, Liiset, and now and then she'd look in on me. Something Idri couldn't do.

"She wasn't there physically, but you sensed her spirit and translated it to her physical appearance—her face. You couldn't have done any of that if you didn't have the talent."

I remembered, for the first time since that day. It'd been too spooky. "Seems like I've lost it since, though," I said.

She shook her head. "How did you find the pictures? How did you even know enough to look?"

"But what if I don't want magical powers?" I asked her.

She didn't answer right away. Then she said, "If you were blind, and didn't entirely believe in sight, you might be uncomfortable if I said I wanted to open your eyes."

I didn't have anything to answer, so I nodded and told her fine, let's do it. It would make her happy, and I figured she wouldn't do something bad for me. My problem, I told myself, was I was scared of what I didn't know. I'd been scared that night the transparent Varia took me home with her, too, and look how much I'd liked that after we got there! But I still felt uncomfortable about "opening my magical powers."

* * *

Over several weeks, I couldn't see we were making any

progress. Varia said it was a little like putting a pot of water on the stove to boil: You wait and wait, and nothing seems to be happening, and suddenly there it is boiling. I couldn't help wondering, though, if maybe the wood in my firebox was piss elm, and wouldn't burn.

One evening when we'd finished, her eyes didn't have their usual steadiness, and I asked her if anything was wrong.

"Not with you," she said.

"With what, then?"

"I guess I'm just tired."

"Looks like more than tired. Looks like worried."

She smiled. "See? Your powers are coming back. I was thinking about my children; all forty-one of them."

Yeah, I thought to myself, *maybe my powers are coming back, 'cause I can tell you're lying to me.* I really didn't believe they were; just a look at her face told me. But I wasn't going to badger her. "I'll have the plowing done tomorrow morning," I said. "Maybe you and I ought to take the rest of the day off. Go in to Decatur and walk through the stores. Buy some ice cream, and celebrate. Maybe Morath will even divide my cows up between his daughters to milk in the evening, and we can blow twenty cents on a movie."

She came over and kissed me, tears in her eyes. "Curtis, you're so nice, I love you more than you know. If anything ever happens to me, I want you to remember that. Regardless of anything. And tomorrow—tomorrow I'd love to go to Decatur with you when you're done plowing."

That's Varia for you, always thinking, always trying to do the right thing. I still didn't realize how well I'd married. A good good woman.

* * *

Anyway, when tomorrow got there, and I'd milked and had breakfast, her tune had changed. "Before we blow any money on ice cream and a movie," she said, "there are things I need to do to this house. Let the plowing wait till this afternoon." She handed me a list. "I want you to get these things for me right now. I need to civilize this kitchen."

I stared at her. She was standing there kind of like Ma did in front of Pa sometimes, when she didn't want any argument. I looked at the list: red and white checkered oil cloth, paint, and eight or ten other things she had every right to want, or even have. But none of it seemed very important, and I'd have to chase all over town to get it. "Okay," I grumped. I'd never been grumpy before with Varia; I didn't even give her a kiss, sad to say. How many times I felt bad about that.

I went out to the truck, gave it a crank, and drove off to Decatur. It was almost noon when I got back. By that time I'd convinced myself she'd gotten pregnant; I'd heard how women can get notional when they're pregnant. When I walked into the house, she wasn't in the kitchen, and I felt a little pang. "Honey!" I called out, "I'm back! I got your stuff!"

She didn't answer, and I got a sick feeling. Two weeks before, I'd have told myself I was scared she'd gone off and left me because I hadn't given her that kiss, but now I hardly glanced at the idea. It was something a lot worse. "Maybe she's out in the privy," I muttered, but didn't believe that either, not even enough to go out and call to her. Instead, somehow or other I went into the pantry, and there on the counter was some folded tablet paper held down by a stove-lid handle. I unfolded it and started reading, though somehow I knew what had happened— not the details, but the main thing.

Sweet darling Curtis, the gate is going to open again soon, and they are coming to take me away, Idri and some men. The Sisterhood still exists. It's been butchered and forced to flee, but it still exists. Idri must have tracked me, and then gone back to Evansville for help.

I sensed them coming yesterday, and this morning I felt them again while I was cooking breakfast. They'll be here very soon. It wouldn't do any good for us to run away. They would only follow. That's why I sent you to town. I'm sure she's supposed to take us both, but she'd find an excuse to kill you. I know her too well.

Don't forget to take the money out of the honey jar. It's yours. Darling, it hurts so much to leave you like this. But you'll get over it. It was beautiful to be your wife this short time. I'll remember you and love you forever.

Reading it, it was like I'd been there watching her write it, tears running down her face like mine were, and for a minute, when I was done, I felt helpless, like a wooden man. But only for a minute.

Chapter 4: Conjure Woman

I stopped at Morath's long enough to tell Miz Morath I wouldn't be able to milk for them awhile. That my wife's relatives had come and stolen her away, and I was going after them. I left my team there; Morath could use them or rent them out, to pay for their keep. Then I headed south on Route 51, and before I got forty miles, the truck quit on me. I figured it was the carburetor—I'd had trouble with it before—but fooling with it didn't help, so I gave up and hiked on into Assumption, where I hired myself a tow. The fella at the garage there fussed with it awhile, and I ended up getting a new one put on. All in all, it cost me more than three hours. I didn't know whether to swear or cry.

I'd never before felt the way I did then: dangerous. Never knew I could. I didn't feel at all like the Curtis Macurdy folks knew back in Washington County.

Then I drove on. North of Vandalia it threw a rod, and there wasn't a thing in hell I could do about that. Not in the time I had. I wondered if Idri'd cast a spell to keep me from following them, and told myself if she had, it wasn't going to work. Leaving the truck by the road, I started walking. Each time a car came along, I stuck a thumb out, and after a while a moving van went on by me a little way and pulled over. I took off running and climbed in.

"Where yew a-headin'?" the driver asked me. A southerner by the way he talked.

"Kentucky," I told him. "Muhlenberg County."

He laughed and slapped his leg. "Talk 'bout bein' in luck! I'm deliverin' this load to Central City; that's in Muhlenberg

County." He reached under the truck seat, took out a clear glass bottle three-quarters full, and handed it to me. "Have a swig," he told me.

I handed it back. "Thanks," I said, "but my family's all tee-totalers. Been that way as far back as anyone remembers."

He didn't take offense like some might. Just pulled the wooden stopper with his teeth, raised the bottle, took a big swig, and about strangled. "Good stuff," he said with his eyes watering. "Not like most of the rotgut folks sell these days. My uncle makes it hisself."

He started the truck then and drove on, talking about how he wished he was headed for home instead of Kentucky. After a while I started dozing, off and on. Woke up when he stopped the truck for gas. It was beginning to get dark out.

"Yew gonna git a crick in yore neck, yew sleep like that," he told me. "I'm figurin' to drive all night, if I can, but I'm apt to git sleepy. Can yew drive a truck?"

I told him I could.

"I put a sofa crosst the back of the load, so's I can go back there and sleep if I need to. Why don't yew go back there? Then if I git too sleepy to drive, yew'll be all rested, and we can change places. Git there quicker."

Anything to speed things up. I went around back, opened the doors and climbed in, latching them behind me. After a minute the truck started again. The sofa felt good enough, but laying there, I didn't feel sleepy any longer. I kept wondering how in the world I'd find the gate, once I got to Muhlenberg County. Finally I told myself, *same way you found the pictures.* However that was. Anyway it settled my mind enough I got to sleep.

* * *

When I woke up, it seemed like I'd slept a long time. A long time full of dreams. Dreams with Varia in them. Laying there, I felt them slipping away, and they were gone, just like she was. The truck wasn't moving, so I got up, felt for the latch, and opened the doors. It was night out, moonlight, and a little spooky feeling, but nothing bad. I hopped down.

We were on a country road, stuck in a mudhole. I went to

the cab; the driver was inside, laying against the steering wheel asleep. The door was locked, which surprised me, and so was the one on the other side, but moonlight on the seat showed the whiskey bottle laying on its side without the stopper. I decided he'd finished it off after he got stuck.

There was a little field across the road, but otherwise it seemed to be all woods around there, and a big big hill on the other side. Didn't look like any place I'd seen in Illinois or Indiana, the hill was too big, so I decided I was in Kentucky.

The moon was full and low in the sky, which meant it was near daybreak. I set off down the road with the moon at my back, not liking to leave the driver like that, but I needed to find that gate. I felt pretty optimistic. I'd made it to Kentucky in under a day, even though I'd lost my truck.

Right away I left the field behind, woods crowding the road on both sides. The night was mild, and in a little bit I started enjoying the hike. The leaves were coming out, and it smelled like spring. I must have walked a mile or more before I came to another cleared field, not more'n six or eight acres, with a little shack at the far end, just back from the road. By that time, morning had started lightening the sky a bit.

The whole shack turned out to be made of shakes, walls and all. I heard a dog woof inside; a minute later the front door opened and an old woman looked out.

"Who's out there?" she yelled.

"Name's Curtis Macurdy," I told her. "I'm lost. I'd appreciate if you could tell me where I am."

She cackled like a hen. Her old hound came out past her and down the steps, to sniff my legs without making a sound. "Yew ain't from nowheres 'round yere," she said.

"No ma'am. I just left Illinois, headed for Kentucky."

"Kentucky?!" She cackled again. "Yewr in Missoura!"

Now I realized who she sounded like. Her accent was like the truck driver's, only thicker. He must have drank enough, he decided to go home, and these hills must be the Ozarks. From what I'd heard and read of the Ozarks, it could be a month before the van company found out where their truck was, if they ever did.

"How far to Kentucky?" I asked.

"Don't rightly know. But yew ain't goin' to walk there to-day. Tell ya what. I got to go fetch water. If'n yew'll tote it fer me, I'll feed ya breakfast."

She didn't have a well, but across the road just three, four chains, was a spring in the hillside, with a wooden trough for the water to run out of. She had two buckets hung on a shoulder yoke, and I carried them for her. If it'd been me living there, I'd have built a house on the other side of the road, and run the trough on down to it. Or better, put a pipe under the road.

While she fixed breakfast, she chattered on like someone who didn't have anyone to talk to very often. "I'm a-goin' up on the knob, when the sun comes up," she said. "I staked out a young cockerel up there last evenin'."

"Staked out a chicken?"

"Oh, that's right, yewr from up Illinois way. Yew don't know 'bout Injun Knob. It's a spirit mountain, and every full moon, the spirit comes a-hootin'."

"A-hootin'?"

"Yep. At midnight. Most folks cain't yere it, but I can, 'cause I'm a conjure woman."

"Really!"

"Yep. And it's good to give it a little somethin' now and then. I'll go up there, and the chicken'll be gone. It always is."

"Mightn't a fox have taken it?" I asked. "Or some other animal?" I'd read they still had wolves in the Ozarks.

"Not up there. Ain't no critters go up there on the night of the full moon. Fact is, up on top they ain't no critters anytime, not even birds. They know better. A couple times been young fellas went up there on a dare, the evenin' of a full moon, and they ain't none of 'em ever come back down. Then, eight, ten years ago, a perfessor come yere from the university with another feller, both of 'em wearing big ol' pistols on their side, and they never come back, neither." She cackled again. "The sheriff come with a posse, a day or two later, and combed the woods, but couldn't find hide nor hair of 'em."

The hairs on my neck started to bristle, and the old woman grinned at me. "Yew wanna go up there with me?"

I nodded. Varia had said there was more than one gate.

After breakfast, we started up the mountain on a little foot-path. Most of the birds were back for the summer, and the woods was full of their singing. I saw gray squirrel and chipmunks and rabbit turds, and lots and lots of oaks and clumps of pine. It was a long steep path, with lots of stops for the old woman to rest a minute, till finally I could see the top close ahead. There was lots of bedrock showing by that time, and the trees were sparse and small. And there weren't any more birds or squirrels or chip-munks. I'm not sure what they felt that kept them away, but I was feeling something that had my neck hairs bristling again. Either that or I was imagining.

We took one last rest, the old woman breathing hard, and frowning.

"Anything the matter?" I asked her.

She didn't answer, and after a minute we went on. At the top, she knelt down by a knee-high pine seedling with a leather thong tied to it: the tether she'd tied the chicken with. But there wasn't any chicken now, nor feathers nor blood, like a possum or bobcat would have left. Just the leather thong, which was either awful short to start with, or something had shortened it.

She still wasn't talking, and the frown was still there. She stood up and closed her eyes so tight her whole face skrinched together, and she began mumbling something I couldn't make out. Cold chills ran down me from the top of my head to my feet. After a minute she started to talk.

"Some folks were up yere last night, in the dark. Two men and two women, folks o' power. And the mountain took three of 'em—not et 'em; received 'em—two witchy women, young and perty, and one of the men. I'm a-goin' back down, right now."

We went. She didn't have anything more to say all the way to her cabin. I didn't either, but my brain was going a mile a minute.

I knew just what I was going to do: get me a job around there somewhere, on a farm or in the woods. It wouldn't need to pay cash; bed and board would be plenty, and the bed could be hay in the barn. I had twenty-seven dollars in my shoe, more than enough to buy a pistol and a good rifle, and plenty of shells. And I'd be back on top of Injun Knob before dark, on the night of the next full moon.

PART 2: The Twice-Stolen Bride

Chapter 5: Xader

The top of Injun Knob appeared ordinary in the moonlight, half bald, its scrubby trees scattered. The gate hadn't opened yet, but Varia could feel it. Chuckling, Xader put his arms around her from behind, groping her through her housedress: "Might as well enjoy ourselves while we wait," he murmured, and kissed her neck. His inborn psionic talent was sufficient that, unless she took him by surprise, he could hold off whatever magic she might try with handcuffs on. So she stamped hard on his instep, and swearing, he let her go, stepping back from her.

Abruptly the three of them were swallowed into a deep bass indigo nothingness, a nothingness with a gut-wrenching, mind-numbing sense of distortion, followed by a moment of suspension while the gate examined them. Then Varia found herself running like someone who'd just jumped from a moving car. As if the gate had spit her out. Unable to windmill her manacled arms for balance, she fell headlong onto grass. A minute later, hands raised her to her feet, a small hand on one side, a larger on the other.

She stood not in midnight now, but in sun-dappled high noon, and looked about her. They were no longer on the mountaintop, but in a cathedral-like grove of large old basswood trees. The grass was lawn-like, almost without saplings, as if grazed between the monthly openings of the gate. And in fact, on this side, in the world called Yuulith, animals and humans could enter the site freely until the first distortion of the matrix, the Web of the World, when the gate began to regenerate. Then it physically repelled them.

Several rough-clad men with spears had been waiting to collect anyone or anything that came through. They held back though, recognizing these were part of the Sisterhood. Ignoring them, Idri first untied the bandanna that held Varia's mouth shut, then removed the gag from between her teeth, leaving the handcuffs on. For just a moment she watched Varia work the kinks from her jaw, then turned and slapped Xader, the sound almost like a small-caliber pistol. Idri, like Varia, was considerably stronger than she looked.

"She's still a Sister, Xader," she snapped, "and don't forget it. Keep your hands to yourself, and remember who you are."

Remember what *you* are, Varia corrected silently. *A cull.* Occasionally a guardsman clone was flawed in some unacceptable way, and the whole batch was either kept for labor or quietly disposed of. It occurred to Varia that the Ferny Cove disaster might have left so few guardsmen alive, culls were used more widely now.

Xader had flushed with resentment. But it wasn't the slap that had stung him, Varia knew. He'd harassed her before, in the Packard, with the curtains drawn and Armik driving. And Idri had allowed it, to a point. Perhaps she rationalized it as punishment for Varia's deserting the Sisterhood, but basically she had a sadistic streak. Sitting in front, she'd ignored Varia's muffled complaints, grunted through her gag, but when Xader's hand went into his victim's pants, as it invariably had, Idri had turned as if she had eyes in the back of her head, slapped him, and chewed him out. He'd laughed and stopped—in his brutal, offensive way he was good-natured—but in an hour or two resumed his harassment.

No, what stung him now, Varia told herself, were the witnesses, the tribesmen who'd seen it. And no doubt he considered himself entrapped, for this time he'd been slapped without even putting his hand up her dress.

Varia wondered if this meant the end of his abuse. With her

gag out, she could complain in words, and Idri could hardly ignore her.

* * *

The tribesmen at the gate had been respectful enough. At Idri's order, one had led them to the village headman, who'd loaned them horses and an escort. There Idri had removed Varia's handcuffs, and both had dressed themselves in tribesmen's breeches, for riding. Then they'd ridden to Oztown and the chief's compound, arriving at dusk. Idri wasted no time; made arrangements that same evening for a squad of warriors as an escort. They left the next morning at sunup, riding eastward through mildly rolling wooded hills, and occasional large openings with farms and villages.

Xader left Varia carefully alone, though from time to time she felt his eyes.

They traveled till dusk before camping. The new escort were swaggerers, warriors of the chief's own elite. Undoubtedly they'd heard of the rape at Ferny Cove, for they eyed the Sisters appraisingly, without the respect they might once have shown. But they'd said or done nothing more offensive than look. Then Idri started the supper fires with simple hand gestures, reminding them of the Sisters' reputation for dangerous sorceries.

The escort ate separately from its charges, except Idri invited their sergeant to sit beside her. When they'd eaten, the escort and Xader had laid down their beds a little distance from the Sisters, screened by undergrowth. The men, including Xader, had warm sleeping robes against the night chill. The Sisters, with their powers, used only a pallet and a single light blanket.

* * *

Varia was awakened by a powerful hand clutching her throat, cutting off her air. The voice that murmured to her was Xader's, and she smelled whiskey on his breath. "There's a knife in my other hand," he said. "One sound and you're dead." He let go her throat then, threw the blanket aside, fumbled with the drawstring on her breeches and began tugging them down. She could sense the knife an inch from her throat; it moved to her belly as he got her breeches off her buttocks.

"Idri will crucify you for this," she whispered.

Xader chuckled, seemingly without rancor. "Idri's over by the creek bank, bobbing up and down on that sergeant's pole. And when she's done with him, she'll sleep like a sow—like the sow she is." Again he chuckled. "I know."

Her breeches were down to her knees now, down to her ankles. She struggled, twisting from side to side, intensely conscious of the knife. *Idri pushed you too far yesterday,* she thought panting. *When she wakes up, I'll be dead and you'll be gone. Sarkia will chain her in a Tiger barracks for that, but it won't do me any good.* He pricked her waist with the knife tip then, numbing her will, and using a bare foot, freed her of her breeches. Then, bare from the waist down, he forced himself between her knees. *The Sisterhood must be in bad shape,* she thought, *or you wouldn't dare do this. Sarkia would set Tomm himself on your trail.*

Once more he chuckled. "Put it in for me," he said. His face smirked in hers, his breath reeking. "I'll show you what a good man's like."

She might have cooperated—it seemed her best chance for survival—but his boast was an affront to Curtis. Reaching down as if to comply, she found his testicles, and willed a powerful jolt of electricity through them. The knife which had jabbed her waist, she fully expected to plunge into her guts, but in his agony, he lost it. As he screamed, she squeezed, with hands that had milked cows for years.

With all her strength, she rolled him off, still clutching, willed another jolt, then tore his scrotum half off, cords stretching and giving. His body doubled with spasm, then went slack. She didn't entirely trust his unconsciousness, and held on grimly while scanning with her cat vision for the knife. Someone, a sentry, had grabbed a torch and hurried over, stopping a few yards off to stare. Glancing back over her shoulder, Varia's large green eyes caught the man's and held them, dominating him even as she crouched over Xader with her buttocks bared. "Never try to rape a Sister," she hissed at him, "or you'll end up like this one."

Round-eyed, the sentry said nothing. The whole camp had wakened at Xader's scream, but they kept back. Except for Idri, who arrived only partly covered by the sergeant's long, unbuttoned tunic, his saber in her hand. Xader's eyes were open again, wide and glazed with shock, and sweat greased his forehead, though the night was chill. Varia sent another jolt through him, not as strong, bringing a thin whinny of pain.

Idri cursed. "Let him go!" she ordered.

Varia did, snatching her breeches from the ground. "Go ahead, Xader," she said. "Here's your chance to tell her what you told me: that she's a sow in heat."

Psychically Varia felt the crackle of Idri's rage, but it wasn't aimed at her. The Sister stepped and thrust, the saber striking Xader beneath the ribs and riding in. He squawked like air released from a bladder, then went slack again, and blood stained his twill shirt, purchased at J.C. Penney's in Evansville, Indiana, in another universe. Idri wiped her blade first on his bare thigh, then on his sleeve. "Leave him here," she told the wide-eyed sentry. "Let the vermin clean his bones." She turned her gaze to Varia. "Put your breeches on. You have my apologies, for what they're worth. I should have known he'd try something like this."

Their gazes met and briefly locked, and it was Idri's that turned away. *Yes,* Varia thought as she pulled her breeches on, *you knew what he was like. Probably he'd been in trouble for bothering local women at Ferny Cove, and you saved his skin. You'd love having power over an oversexed fool like that.*

But she said none of it. They had hundreds of miles to go, and she was Idri's prisoner.

Chapter 6: Welcome Home!

On the third day after crossing the Great Muddy River, they rode down out of wooded hills into the broad east-west valley of the Green River, an extensively cleared plain. At the edge of vision to the north they could see high hills dark with forest. The country they traveled through was new to Varia, though not to Idri, who whenever they crossed into a new kingdom, arranged for local escorts.

Unlike the west side of the Great Muddy, the people here lived under kings. The highway the Sisters rode was dirt—mud after rains—and along it, the farmers lived in tiny hamlets at intervals of a mile or less, half a dozen to a dozen cottages in each, plus outbuildings. Every few miles stood a village, and about once a day they came to a real town, with a reeve's palisaded fort. On a few occasions the party slept in inns, but more commonly, Idri obtained space for them at some manor house.

Clearly the Sisterhood retained some part of its old reputation and respect here, for nowhere were they refused an escort, or food or lodging. Though the obsequiousness common before the disaster at Ferny Cove was reduced now mostly to courteous or sometimes grudging compliance.

As they rode, Varia had abundant time to think. She and Idri had little to say to each other; their antagonism dated from long before Varia had arrived at Evansville with Curtis Macurdy. As girls, they'd vied for a coveted executive apprenticeship in the Dynast's office, and Varia had been chosen on the basis of a higher responsibility score, superior performance on decision-making tests, and greater talents in magic. Her only weakness had been an undistinguished aggressiveness quotient. But after a year on the job—a successful year she'd been assured—Varia had been sent to Farside, with the explanation that she provided the best blood line for breeding with the newly located Will Macurdy. That and better adaptability than any other of her clone.

Nonetheless, fifteen years later, when Idri replaced Liiset at Evansville, it had been quickly apparent her resentment was alive and well. And now—Now her look, her bearing, her aura, and an occasional oblique comment said to Varia, *I'm better than you. You think only of yourself; I think first of the Sisterhood.* But when they stopped at an inn, she took a room for herself, and took the sergeant of their escort to bed with her. Behavior entirely at odds with the Sisterhood's hard-earned image of aloof superiority. Behavior each escort would talk about and exaggerate at home, cheapening the Sisterhood.

Yet surely Sarkia knew of Idri's weakness, and tolerated it. *What will she think of* my *weakness?* Varia asked herself. *Will she look at it as a foible? Or as treason? A misdemeanor,* she decided. *There's probably not one other Sister who's provided as many children as I have.*

* * *

East of the Great Muddy they crossed three kingdoms. Then the broad valley narrowed, the country became semi-mountainous, the farmland discontinuous, the clearings ever smaller and more scattered. The men walked tall, looking self-reliant, not subservient like the peasants Varia had been seeing. These were tribesmen ruled by elected councils and chiefs. They raised crops, but herding was their principal livelihood.

Yet the road was better, and the mountain streams were bridged with stone. Dwarf work, according to the sergeant of their latest escort. Varia saw her first dwarves ever, a party of three. Not dwarves in the Farside sense; the dwarves of Yuulith were a unique phenomenon, the similarities limited. They were thick bodied and their legs were short, but not their arms, for their gnarly hands hung almost to the ground. They stood about four and a half feet tall. Packs and crossbows rode on their broad backs, swords at their hips, and they passed without a nod. Their mission must be friendly, the sergeant said when they'd gone by. Otherwise they'd have carried poleaxes as well, with shields slung on their packs.

Now, when the view allowed, they could see true mountains ahead, the Great Eastern Mountains, with jagged crests against the sky, snow fields and glaciers glinting on the upper slopes. Once their lead man called back that a great cat, a jaguar, had crossed the road just ahead, pausing to glower at him before disappearing into the forest. And on the mud along a stream bank, they saw the tracks of a night-prowling troll.

At last they entered a kingdom of the dwarves, the Dwarves in Silver Mountain. By their leave, men dwelt within its edges, living much as they did just westward, but paying land fees. For dwarves were not greatly interested in the surface, and at any rate considered these no more than foothills to the greater mountains just eastward.

In a north-south valley was the new Cloister of the Sisters, a sizeable area protected by spells and a stockade. Inside were buildings of new lumber, and areas of tents. Crews of men, no doubt hired from some king, were busy at construction. In the south end, gardens had already been set out, and new grass grew emerald between paths. In the center, Varia could see what could only be the Dynast's "palace," a large canvas pavilion. Stacks of white marble blocks stood nearby, promising a real palace like the one destroyed at Ferny Cove. She wondered where the wealth had come from to have all this built so quickly. Or indeed how the King in Silver Mountain had come to approve their settling there, for in general, dwarves avoided commitments with outsiders, except for business.

Despite her uncertain but surely not favorable status, Varia was excited to see it. Clearly many more of the Sisterhood had escaped Ferny Cove than Idri had indicated, no doubt dispersed and traveling under cover of spells cast by the more talented. Taking with them more wealth, probably in jewels, than Varia had supposed.

And in this kingdom, the community would have the protection of the dwarves, whom even the ylver relied on and were careful of. For it was dwarves who dug the ores and smelted much of the metal used by men and ylver between the oceans; dwarves who crafted the better tools and weapons. Dwarves were quick to take offense, and very slow to forgive. Further, to seriously offend any dwarvish kingdom was to offend all of them, despite their differences, rivalries, and occasional feuds. And tradition told that when they made war, they were relentless and grim, while no one knew how many thousands could come pouring from the bowels of the mountains.

This, she told herself, was a good place for the Sisterhood to recover and grow, and build its strength.

* * *

A page, a preadolescent Sister, showed them to separate quarters. Varia was taken to a low, temporary barracks, where she would share a room with clone mates. There were feather beds, and a large copper tub. Water, the page told her, was piped from a hot spring.

Her clone mates were at their duties, and though she was eager to see them, it felt good to be alone. She soaked and soaped, scrubbed her skin with a brush and toweled herself dry, then donned a clean robe and luxuriated on her feather bed.

And examined her situation. There seemed essentially no chance of getting back to Farside and Curtis—not in the near future. But life could be good here; she could adjust. There'd be lots of work, and time would bring opportunities.

That evening she ate in a women's dining hall with perhaps a hundred Sisters. Three of her clones were there; she recognized them like she recognized her face in the mirror, and shared an embrace and happy tears with Liiset. After supper, the two of them walked around the extensive grounds—a large village, essentially. They talked, Varia saying little about the Macurdies and nothing at all about her capture. As if Idri had simply requested her to come; as if she'd returned willingly. While Liiset ignored Ferny Cove, speaking of construction projects and planting, new developments in ceramics, and promising new magicks for manipulating physical traits during embryogenesis.

Finally a cold evening breeze from the mountains sent them

indoors. It had been an affectionate reunion. Liiset was more serious than in years past; hadn't shown her whimsical humor, but that was hardly surprising after the events at Ferny Cove.

Meanwhile it seemed to Varia she was *home* now, in the sense of childhood home, even if it wasn't the same location she'd left more than twenty years before. A ruder, relocated version of home.

For the first time since she'd been kidnapped, she lay down relaxed. And as she waited for sleep, it struck her Sarkia would still be interested in Curtis; she'd gone to a lot of trouble to get children from the Macurdy line. *Surely she'll let me go back for him,* Varia thought. *Or more likely have me taken back.*

She didn't doubt he'd come if she asked him. She'd put a condition on the asking though: She'd share him with the others, but Sarkia would have to let the two of them live together as man and wife.

The prospect brought warmth. It would work, she had no doubt. She could make it go right.

Chapter 7: Tigers!

She slept through breakfast and most of the morning, wakening slowly, aware finally she'd slept the clock around. *Up!* she told herself. *Up and face the day!* Then burrowed deeper into the security and comfort of the thick feather mattress.

But when she peeked again, the clock (which bore the name *Westclox* on its face and had been made in Norcross, Georgia, in another universe) said 11:32, and she discovered she was hungry. So dragging herself from bed, she washed and dressed, and by noon had joined a growing crowd of attractive women, ages twelve to perhaps ninety, in the dining room. She was among the earlier arrivals, and there was room beside her, but somehow Liiset, when she came in, took a seat at the other end of the room. Without acknowledging her wave or meeting her eyes.

A guardsman intercepted her as she left. (Recognizing identities among look-alikes was a talent that turned on early in the Sisterhood, with both girls and boys, even among those like Idri who did not see auras.) His face told her nothing, and his aura scarcely more, for this errand meant little to him, but she followed with an empty feeling. To the Dynast's office.

When she entered, she knew at once that here was trouble, the trouble she'd avoided thinking about. Two persons awaited her. One was Idri, with a look of hard-eyed satisfaction. The other was the Dynast, older than any other Sister, ever, by at least a century. A Sister of awesomely long life and memory. She'd been Dynast when Curtis's great-great-grandfather had run away. Yet she could pass easily for twenty-five, if you ignored her eyes and aura.

"Welcome home, Sister Varia," Sarkia said amiably. "I see you're pregnant."

It didn't show physically yet, but any Sister who could see auras could tell.

"You realize why you're here, of course."

Varia nodded. This would be her hearing for refusing an order, and perhaps for desertion. "Yes, Sister Sarkia."

"Very well." The Dynast recited the charges in an almost kindly tone. "Do you deny either of them, in kind or in spirit?"

"No, Sister Sarkia."

"Can you cite extenuating circumstances?"

"Only that the events at Ferny Cove were described to me as much more drastic than they actually were. It seemed to me the Sisterhood had been destroyed."

The Dynast's eyes and aura showed no agitation. "But obviously it was not," she said. "You lacked faith, no doubt because of your long separation from us. Well. We must get you back into the spirit of service and discipline. Yours is our most fertile clone, and you and Will Macurdy our most fertile pairing. You should have brought his nephew through, as ordered." She paused, seeming to consider. "I'm assigning you to duties in the crèche; this will go well with your pregnancy. Meanwhile you'll maintain your physical health by participating in the morning drills."

She stopped there and sat wordless for a minute, her eyes holding Varia like a bug on a pin. "Then, after a suitable postpartum recovery, you will be assigned to a Tiger barracks for reimpregnation."

A sudden stone sat heavily in Varia's bowels. The Tiger clones had been bred and culled for a hardness of spirit, and they were notoriously infertile. And there was more, she realized; the Dynast was not done.

"During your assignment in the crèche, you will be supervised by Sister Maliv. During your assignment in the Tiger barracks, Sister Idri will see to your welfare, and make sure you are properly chastened and corrected."

Varia had never seen Idri smile before.

* * *

While living and working at the crèche, Varia managed mostly not to dwell on her sentence. Only occasionally did she think of it, sometimes at the sight of a Tiger striding lithe and hard down some path. And sometimes when she wiped and washed some boy infant, or awakened from nightmare. Gestation seemed scarcely to take weeks, though she'd been in the Cloister more than four months when she was taken to the lying-in ward. To her surprise and dismay, Sarkia was there, and Idri.

She was delivered of two boys, about two and a half pounds each, but vigorous. When infants and mother had been cleaned up, and the babes taken to be fed (they were too small to nurse), Varia's eyes went to the Dynast, and stuck on her gaze. Sarkia's lips had thinned and twisted.

Because she'd borne only the two, Varia realized. Had only willed two, those first hours after fertilization, when in her self-induced trance, she might have willed half a dozen. Like their ylvin progenitors, most Sisters were relatively infertile. Which meant spending several nights in a breeding room each month, with selected partners. Usually the experience was enjoyable, for typically their partners were skilled and pleasant, and it was how things were done in the Sisterhood. And when a Sister became pregnant, she was expected to produce as large a litter as was safe. Five was usual.

But conception with Curtis had taken place in a different world, and the future she'd had in mind had been a different future.

Sarkia turned to Idri and muttered: "Do what you will with her."

For the second time, Varia saw Idri smile.

* * *

Over the following two months she continued in the crèche, nursing infants of mothers who had other duties, and after a bit, her own. After the first six weeks her nursing duties were gradually reduced till in the third month she went dry. And knew her sentence would soon begin.

Even so it began with a shock. Two grinning Tigers banged into her room one evening, running her roommates out. While one held her arms painfully behind her back, the other chopped her hair off with scissors, then shaved her head, leaving numerous nicks behind. When he was done, they stripped her roughly, put a coarse woolen shift on her, and hustled her from the building, arms behind her back again. That sack-like shift, which fell short of her knees, was all the clothing left to her.

Tiger barracks were different from Sister barracks—temporary squad huts with bath and latrine. Normally two half-sibling clones made a squad, and eight grinning Tigers were waiting when Varia was propelled into their breeding room. For a minute she was pushed-thrown back and forth among them like a beach ball, staggering, reeling around the small ring of naked Tigers, never allowed to fall. Then the shift was pulled from her, and the sergeant, exerting his prerogative, threw her on the bed and took her roughly.

The first round was quick. The sergeant took perhaps a minute, while the others, having watched, were mostly quicker, and she'd begun to feel hopeful this wouldn't be as bad as she'd feared. But though their fertility was low, they had the sexual energy of youth. Thus those who'd finished, restimulated by watching the others, had a second round which took much longer, and in some cases sadistic forms. Long before that round was done, Varia was weeping silently in blind desolation. She wasn't really aware when the still longer, much rougher third round began, and was unconscious well before it was over.

* * *

She awoke in the empty bath. Awoke when the Tiger sentry threw a bucket of cold water on her, then threw her shift at her, and watched grinning while she pulled it on. A sober-faced guardsman waited outside, and led her to the kitchen, barefoot and in only her wet shift, through twenty degree cold and two inches of snow. She was hardly aware of it, though she shivered violently. Most of the Sisterhood had the power to produce additional body heat by mentally controlling cellular respiration levels and circulation. In Varia's state of shock, only shivering was available to her.

At the kitchen, a younger Sister waited; an adolescent. Big-eyed at what she saw, the girl showed Varia her duties, demonstrating and helping, while Varia emerged somewhat from shock, becoming more aware, watching and duplicating: Fires were laid, then lit, in the dining room stove, the stack of ovens, and the great ceramic cook stove, and replenished in the large ceramic water heater, for the hot springs weren't hot enough for kitchen needs.

It was now Varia, hobbling and unable to stand straight, realized fully how sore she was. When the instructions were finished, and Varia, outside in the cold, had begun splitting the day's firewood, the girl vanished. Meanwhile, with the exertion and the partial return of her mental faculties, Varia had stopped shivering.

Fifteen minutes later the chief cook arrived, the Sister in charge of the kitchen, a large, strong-looking woman, handsome instead of pretty. Arrived well ahead of her usual hours, and came out to the woodpile to peer at Varia in the darkness. The woman's lips were as thin and twisted as Sarkia's had been at Varia's delivery.

Her voice was rough. "What's wrong with you?" she demanded.

Voice dead, face wooden, Varia told her, and began shivering again, violently. The woman took her arm and steered her brusquely into the kitchen where there was light, squinted at the black eye, the split and swollen lips. "Take off your shift," she ordered.

Varia did, without emotion.

"Good God!" The cook looked at the myriad black bruises and bloody spots on thighs and buttocks, arms and breasts, for when Varia had gone into shock, the Tigers had pinched and struck her, even jabbed her with knife tips, trying to elicit movement. "Here, girl," the woman said, and helped her onto a table. There, by the light of an oil lamp, she examined her as a gynecologist might have. Varia was literally raw, fore and aft, despite being slimed with semen, and undoubtedly had vaginal and rectal lesions that could become infected. Swearing, the woman turned to the now-shivering girl who'd fetched her.

"Go outside and bring me the guard."

The girl ran, and the guard came in, looking worried.

"Where did you get her?" the cook demanded.

He told her.

"*That* clone! Go back there and wake up the sergeant." The guard blanched; he was scarcely out of adolescence himself. "Tell that pile of shit his mother wants him in this kitchen within ten minutes, or I'll see his balls on my butcher block."

She hadn't raised her voice, but the intensity behind it allowed no noncompliance. As the guard reached the door, she shouted after him, "Make sure you tell him exactly what I said."

Then she sent Varia with the adolescent girl, hobbling off barefoot to the infirmary.

* * *

She was in the infirmary for three days. On the second, the chief cook came to see her. "I talked to the sergeant," the woman said. "He's one of my sons. He said Idri told him they should do whatever they wanted with you, the rougher the better. So when Idri came in to breakfast, I was waiting for her. I took her to the woodpile and shook hell out of her. She took it, too." The woman's smile was grim. "I was bred to produce Tigers. I could twist her head off if I wanted, and she knew I was on the edge. All she could say was that she was going to report me to the Dynast."

The cook laughed, a dry bark. "I'm eighty-eight years old, girl. At my age you don't have many years left before decline, and you think a bit, some of us, most of us, of how your points will balance after death; what penalties and penances might await you. Makes it easier to take the bull by the horns. In midmorning the Dynast called me to her. I told her what you'd looked like, and what my son had said.

"She didn't say a thing, but I saw her jaw tighten. Later her secretary stopped to tell me not to worry about anything Idri might want to do." Again she snorted. "As if I would. Sarkia told her she'd wanted you punished, not killed. And ordered her to latrine detail for a week; she'll love that, high and mighty as she sees herself.

"Then she had your sergeant in. Not that she raked him over the coals like I did; he's just a Tiger, the way she designed him. But she set him straight. You'll find things better when you go back."

The cook left then. And of all she'd said, the words that stuck in Varia's mind were four: "When you go back." She'd have to go back to that place.

Chapter 8: A Plan Enacted

When Varia left the infirmary at the end of the third day, she was in better condition physically than she'd expected to be. She'd been enough years on Farside she'd come to judge healing by the standards there. In the Cloister, what they lacked in science, they more than made up for with healing touches, and formulas spoken instead of manufactured.

She left wearing more than her shift, too. The healer had found a pair of work breeches for her, and mittens, and ill-fitting boots, all shabby enough to fit her punishment status, but far better than only the shift, which now became her shirt.

At the barracks, the sergeant had already given orders orally, rules of conduct toward their woman. The first was short term: she was not to be bothered that night. The second was, she was not to be struck or pinched or otherwise hurt. The third, she was not to be sodomized again, or anything done to her that could not result in pregnancy. Further, no man was to take her more than once every other night; a schedule would be posted. *That still means four each evening,* she told herself, and felt desolation wash through her again. The best she could do was remind herself it wouldn't start for another twenty-four hours.

That was the first night she thought of escape. She didn't let her mind dwell on it though; the difficulties would seem insuperable. Something she did look at was the season. She'd have no chance at all, fleeing through the wilderness, before spring came. Late spring. The mental power to warm herself was limited by her level of biological energy. On a winter night it would protect her for only a few hours, leaving her famished. It worked best when the temperature stress was moderate.

Till then she'd survive, she told herself, grow strong, and hopefully come through this without getting pregnant. Given the Tigers' low fertility, she could be optimistic.

* * *

The next morning she built and lit the kitchen fires, split a pile of wood, then during breakfast helped the adolescent scullery girls who washed the breakfast dishes, scrubbed pots and pans, and cleaned the kitchen. Before noon she ate lunch, again with the scullery girls, and went "home" for the rest of the day, sleeping most of it. Home to a room kept for breeding, its windows barred against the rare maverick like herself who might think of escape.

Supper too she ate in the scullery; ate lightly. Then, half brave, half terrified, returned to the Tiger barracks and what awaited her there.

At seven that evening, the first on the day's breeding roster entered her room, finished and left in brief minutes. Then she washed herself and sat mentally frozen, waiting on her chair. The next appeared at seven-thirty, and the next at eight. None of the three spoke. Two of them, though not blatantly abusive, were surly and rough. As if she'd wronged them, she thought bitterly; as if they blamed her for the schedule. As if it were their right to enjoy a violent hours-long orgy every night, with her the sole victim.

At eight-thirty the sergeant walked in, closed the door behind him and paused. His angle of erection was about 135 degrees. "I'm sorry about that other night," he said.

She stared. *Sorry? That helps some, I guess. After the last two it does.* "Thank you for telling me," she said quietly. "I—I appreciate that."

He came to her then and stood over her. "I don't know your name," she said.

"Skortov."

But when he mounted her, he was nothing more than a machine, driving hard, finishing, and leaving without another word.

* * *

A few days later, another woman was assigned to the squad. Each evening two of the Tigers went to a breeding room in a women's barracks. This too was a punishment action, less severe than her own but still punishment, for the Sister would be receptive to impregnation only briefly each month, yet she'd be used each night, and now only two men an evening visited Varia. But the reduction in her breeding schedule was brief. With rare quickness the other Sister became pregnant, and again Varia took on four of them each evening. When they'd finished, a tide of desolation would sweep over her. To keep from weeping, she'd daydream herself to sleep, daydream of escape, and reunion with Curtis.

Only one of the Tigers, named Corgan, treated her with blatant cruelty, masturbating before his turn, then humping her long and violently, painfully. And when his stint as sentry coincided with her time to leave for the kitchen, just before 3 A.M., he'd stop her on the doorstep, groping and kissing her roughly before he'd let her pass. She didn't report it to Skortov; didn't want to cause dangerous resentments within the squad, resentments that inevitably would worsen things for her.

Once she'd asked Skortov why sentries were posted outside the barracks door. It was standard for Tiger barracks, he said. To Varia it was apparent he'd never before wondered, and it seemed to her something was lacking in the Tigers—this clone at least—lacking in either their genes or their training or both. They ought to wonder about anything as pointless as that.

Winter's occasional snows and ice storms ended, and spring flowers bloomed. In the nearby human community, oxen pulled plows through wet soil, followed by the plowmen, and by crows that feasted on the worms and grubs exposed. On the shrubs, buds swelled and broke. Her head was shaved again. Trees began to green, lilacs bloomed, and Varia began to plan how she'd equip herself and get over the palisade. Once outside she'd have to improvise, steal a horse or maybe just walk. Afoot she'd leave a harder trail to follow.

She didn't deceive herself that her prospects were good.

Guards would be sent after her, perhaps even Tigers, and if she were caught…Thinking of that, she almost changed her mind. If she stayed, she told herself, surely she'd get pregnant before too much longer. Then she'd will sixlings, be moved out of the Tiger barracks and in with her clone. Sarkia would be pleased with her, perhaps let her work in the crèche, or the ceramics shop.

It was that thought that renewed her resolve. She realized she didn't want to live with Liiset, who'd abandoned her. And especially she didn't want to please Sarkia. It was Sarkia who'd told Idri, "Do what you will with her." In effect, who'd caused that terrible night. She should have known.

Or had she? Did she use Idri to do her evil, the evil Idri was so attracted to, then step forward to rescue the abused? Gaining the victim's gratitude and devotion, even adoration? The thought was like a blow to the stomach.

No, she'd definitely go, at an hour that would give her a long start. About midnight, for like all her clones, she could see in the dark like a cat. A night of hard rain would be best; it would wash out her trail. Then she'd have to keep ahead of any tracker sent after her. It was Tomm who frightened her most, Sarkia's best tracker. She'd heard he could follow a psychic trace as readily as tracks; she'd have to cast a web of confusion whenever she changed direction or paused to rest.

And move fast; that was important. Stay off established trails, head north and west, make her way to Ferny Cove, and go through the gate to Curtis. They'd go somewhere far from Evansville. To Oregon, a land of fertile valleys. They'd talked about Oregon before.

But she'd have to avoid recapture, or God only knew what Sarkia might have done to her. She wondered if she could survive a week like that first night.

* * *

Over the next weeks she varied the time she left for her morning duties. Normally she started for the kitchen just before the twelve to three sentry got off, but now she sometimes left just afterward, when the three to six sentry was on duty. That way if she didn't show, each would assume she'd leave, or had left, on the other's watch, and she wouldn't be missed until the cook and her assistant arrived at the kitchen about five-thirty. Cook would no doubt be furious, assume she'd overslept, and send the guard running to have her wakened. There'd be confusion then, and a search would hardly be started much before seven.

* * *

The last half of May was unusual, rainless. Finally, on the first of June, late evening brought thunder and wind. Near midnight the rain began beating on the roof.

And suddenly fear stuck the breath in Varia's throat, for this was the time, if it was to be. For several long minutes she listened to the drumming. At last, pushing out of her paralysis, she put her boots and breeches on, and the leather belt she'd asked Skortov for. Then, from beneath her mattress, she took a stolen meat knife sheathed in a tough oven mitt she'd taken. Fumbling, hands trembling, she strung it on the belt through the slits she'd cut. Finally she put her shift on over it, hiding it.

She snuffed out her oil lamp, then opened her door a few inches to peer into the men's sleeping room. For a long minute she watched and listened, gathering her nerve. Then the latrine door opened, and she was looking at the bright yellow flame of the latrine's oil lamp. She froze. Her eyes, adjusted to the dark, were briefly dazzled by the lamp, and she didn't recognize the man who stepped out.

It seemed to her he must have seen her, seen her eye peering past the doorpost, but somehow he hadn't. Turning away, he started for the front of the barracks, fully clothed, and she realized what was happening. It was midnight; he was relieving the watch. *Good God!* she thought. *How could I have overlooked that?* Her stomach churned. Was this an omen? If she'd been challenged crossing their sleeping room, she'd have been in serious trouble. Her lie wouldn't convince them all.

Through the barracks door, she saw the two Tigers' backs as they exchanged murmurs on the front stoop. Then the man off watch came in and went straight to the latrine. As soon as its door closed behind him, she swallowed her fear and slipped out, moving quietly, trying to seem legitimate. Opening the barracks door, she stepped onto the stoop—and it was Corgan who stood on guard with his spear at port arms. Her heart nearly stopped as he turned and scowled, but she had enough presence of mind to close the door behind her. The rain still fell, cascading noisily from both sides of the small roof sheltering the stoop.

"What're you doing out here?" he growled. "It's not three o'clock."

My God! If he gropes me, he'll find my belt and knife! "I've got a boyfriend."

"A boyfriend? You?"

"What's the matter? Don't you think I can have a boyfriend? All you Tigers do is hump me. I need loving from time to time." She stepped off the stoop into the rain, pausing to peer back at him. He stood puzzled, confused: The concept was beyond him. "Tell you what," she said. "When it's your turn tomorrow, if you'll take the time to stroke me a little, and kiss me nicely enough, I'll give you a special treat."

She turned then and trotted off through the downpour toward the kitchen, giggling on the edge of hysteria. When she got there, she refastened her belt on the outside of her shift. Cook had set aside two large loaves of yesterday's bread to make dressing with, and she tucked them inside her shift. The belt would keep them in. She followed them with a large slab cut from a cheese. It occurred to her then that the bread, if it got too wet, might come apart inside her shift, and looked around for something to repel the rain. *The oil-cloth in the vegetable room!* she thought. *I can wear it back-side out so the white won't show.* She took it from its table, but the rough back side was a pale beige, still too visible in the dark. With one of the knives hanging there, she cut a hole in it for her head, then smeared lard on the rough side, the beige side. That done, she opened the soot door behind the stack of ovens, and smeared soot into the lard until the oil cloth was black. *Now if the rain doesn't wash it off...*

She slipped it on black side out, then washed her hands. The lye soap didn't lather much, but it removed the sooty lard. She gave one last look around, thinking of the problems she was leaving for the cook—the nearest she had to a friend; Liiset had avoided her since their reunion. Clenching her teeth, Varia laid and lit fires beneath the oven stack and in the stoves, and replenished the fire in the water heater. It took a few minutes, but she would not wrong the cook by leaving them cold.

Then she went into the rain again. It had eased considerably, and that worried her. If it stopped, instead of her tracks being washed out, they'd be conspicuous in the rain-softened ground. For a moment she considered cancelling the attempt. She could hide the oil-cloth under the floor, for the kitchen was built on blocks, then sleep in the kitchen for two hours, and do her job as if nothing was wrong.

Swearing, she shook the thought off and trotted toward the palisade. Who knew when a better time would come? Besides, tomorrow evening that damned Corgan might be pawing and kissing her, expecting his special treat.

The next question was; did any of the sentries on the east side of the palisade catwalk have night vision. Most clones didn't. The Tiger clones did, all of them she thought, but her impression was they didn't pull sentry duty except in their own barracks. The sentries' attention should be outward, but in a time and territory of little threat, who knew where one of them might look. And surprised at seeing someone out in such weather might track her with their eyes.

When she got near enough to see, all of them were huddled in the widely spaced watch shelters, out of the rain. Temporary log buildings had been built backed up against the inside of the palisade, some with ladders leaning against them. Choosing one well removed from any watch shelter, she climbed to its roof, which put the archers' catwalk within reach. In another moment she was crouched on it. The rain had intensified again, reducing visibility. Without hesitating she tossed her knife over the side, then clambered gingerly over the sharp-ended palisade logs, let herself down to arm's length and let go. The impact buckled her knees, and she sprawled heavily in weeds and mud. It took only seconds to find her knife. Threading it on her belt again, she trotted off northward, staying close to the stockade so she wouldn't be seen from above.

And despite the danger, and the cold rain that gradually drained her energy, found herself suddenly exhilarated. She could do this! She really could! She could make it work, make her way to Ferny Cove, and to Macon County, or wherever Curtis was! Her dreams could come true despite everything.

Chapter 9: The Lion Arrives in Oz

Curtis Macurdy hiked up the slope through deepening dusk. He'd lost the conjure woman's footpath, but it wasn't that which worried him. On a hill like Injun Knob, you couldn't miss the top. If you kept going uphill, you got there.

He wore a sheepskin jacket tied round his waist by the sleeves; he'd want it later to keep warm with, sitting or lying on the ground waiting for midnight. Just now, though, sweat slicked his forehead and he breathed deeply, not entirely from climbing. For there was fear, not of the gate, but that there would be no gate. That Varia was gone beyond finding, beyond recovery. It had been a month already. What might have happened to her in that month; given how Idri hated her?

The fear had been kindled the night before, when he'd hiked that same slope, and spent the night on top in mists and drizzles, sitting, standing, dozing on the wet ground. And shivering despite the heavy jacket he'd paid two dollars for secondhand. When dawn had come with no gate, he'd hiked back down and asked the old conjure woman what had gone wrong. She'd cackled her brittle laugh and said he'd come the wrong night; come again the next.

The calendar in the sawmill had been for 1929, useless for 1930, so he'd judged by how the moon looked the night before: nearly full. When she'd told him it was the next night, he'd asked to see her calendar. She'd laughed at that, too. "Ain't got no calendar," she'd said. "Know in my bones when the moon is full."

In Washington County, every kitchen had a calendar, and

every calendar the phases of the moon. Lots of people planted, castrated pigs, and dehorned calves by the phases of the moon.

When he reached the top of Injun Knob this second try, it was dusk, the sky clear and the moon already up, its round full-ness reassuring. After a night as wakeful as the one before, he expected to fall asleep nearly as soon as he sat down. But he sat anyway, almost exactly on the top, leaning against the largest tree available, a scrubby shortleaf pine. After a few minutes, he got up and put on his jacket, then sat back down. He felt ready for whatever happened—anything except nothing at all. A Smith & Wesson .44 hung on his belt, and a Winchester .45-70 buffalo gun lay across his lap, its thick octagonal barrel feeling as heavy as a ModelT axle. Spare shells for both guns were buttoned in his jacket pockets.

The moonlight played tricks with his vision. Things moved in the shadows, images formed and shifted. And when his eye-lids slid shut, Varia met him in a garden, a garden surrounded by a palisade like the pioneer forts in his history book. They walked into a house with a windmill by the back porch—it was Will's—and inside were three other Varias. "We're your wives," one of them said, and they pushed him down on a bed and undressed him. He was compliant, but when they pulled his underwear off, there was another set beneath them, and a set beneath them... Then he was on his feet. "Varia, he said, "this isn't going to work. It's got to be just you and me. I like your sisters all right, but..."

"I'm not Varia, I'm Liiset."

He looked around at the others, then back to the first. "No," he said, "you're Varia. Why are you trying to fool me like that?"

She started to cry, and they sat down on a fallen tree by the Sycamore Bend, he with his arms around her. "Honey," he said, "it's not going to work with all four of you. It's not. You're the only one I want." Still weeping, she started to fade out of his arms, less substantial than the transparent Varia back on the farm. "Don't go away!" he cried. "I came all this way to get you back!"

He awoke shouting, lunging to his feet, the heavy buffalo

gun clopping against bare bedrock. He didn't notice, his mind still caught up in the dream. *Oh God!* he thought, *don't let it be like that!* Then blinking, looked around, breathing hard. It was quiet and peaceful, the full moon shining down between sparse trees. This was still Missouri in the U.S. of A., he was sure of it. Had midnight come and gone? The only directions he knew for certain were up and down. The moon could still be east of south, or…He found the dipper and the pointers, then the Pole Star faint in the moonlight. Not midnight yet; not for a while. He bent, picked up his rifle and sighted on the moon. The sights were undamaged, hadn't struck the rock. With a sigh he turned up his collar, sat back down against the pine, and letting his eyes close again, slept.

* * *

With a deep thrumming resonance, the gate spit him out of nightmare, rolling across the ground in bright sunlight. He woke like a frightened tomcat, hair on end, and scrambled staggering to his feet, grabbing for a rifle that wasn't there. So he snatched at his holster, drew the .44, and looked around wild-eyed. Four men stood a little way off, watching him and laughing, talking some foreign lingo he might have heard once before, when Varia and Idri had lashed each other that day in Evansville.

The men started toward him, and bracing his legs against residual dizziness, Macurdy drew his revolver. His wits began to adjust, and he was aware they carried short spears pointed his way. He pointed the revolver back at them, and when they kept coming, jabbed it in their direction. They stopped eight or ten feet away, spears at the ready. A stride forward and thrust, by any of them, and he'd be meat. One, the leader, said something to him, he had no idea what.

"Stay back," he answered. "I don't want to hurt no one."

The man spoke more sharply, and jabbed the spear at him, its point almost reaching him. Macurdy jumped backward and pulled the trigger—and nothing happened. He felt the hammer release and strike, heard it click, but no shot fired. He pulled again, and again nothing. He knew he'd loaded all six chambers. Staring around, he spied the rifle lying in the grass too far away.

The man had been saying something more. Now the others moved behind Macurdy, who looked at the revolver and swung the cylinder out. From each chamber, a center-fire cartridge peered back at him, two of them indented by the firing pin. The spearmen watched curiously. Reseating the cylinder, he tried again, and once more it clicked, so he slid the weapon back into its holster. Then a spear jabbed his left buttock, and with a yell, Macurdy jumped forward. Once more the leader spoke, beckoning, and Macurdy followed him.

On this side, the gate was in a grassy grove of large old basswood trees. The place looked nothing like Injun Knob; there wasn't even a knoll, a hump. Within a couple of minutes they were out of the woods, crossing open pasture. Several times more the spear jabbed one buttock or the other. Limping now, Macurdy felt blood trickling down the back of both legs. At each jab he jumped, and someone laughed. Glancing over his shoulder, he identified his tormentor, then the leader snapped another order and the jabbing ceased.

The pasture ended at a wide potato field. Macurdy could see a crew of men hoeing some distance away. He trudged between the potato hills, three spearmen spread behind him while their leader walked ahead. Across the field was a considerable village of log buildings.

His captors took him to a small hut, one of numerous surrounded by a twelve-foot palisade. The leader opened the door, and—Macurdy turned abruptly, grabbed the shaft of the spear that had jabbed him, wrenched it free, and doing a horizontal haft stroke, struck his tormentor on the side of the head with the hard hickory shaft. The man staggered sideways and Macurdy was on him, grabbed him by his waistband and his wadmal shirt and slammed him head first against the log wall. Then let him fall, and stood with his hands raised above his own head in submission.

The leader barked rapid words, then strode over to the fallen man, and bending, spoke to him. When the man didn't move, he kicked him, and made some rough comment. Briefly he looked Macurdy in the eye, then grunted an order to the remaining two spearsmen. One jabbed their captive hard in the belly with a spear butt, and Macurdy doubled over. The other struck him above an ear, and he fell to his knees. Moccasin-like boots began kicking him, and he dropped the rest of the way, curling up in a ball. Someone rolled him onto his back astraddle of him, fists striking at his face. Except to shield himself with his forearms, Macurdy made no resistance, and after half a minute, the leader barked another order. Reluctantly, Macurdy's pummeler got to his feet.

Macurdy got slowly to his own. Hands grasped him, frog-marched him to the door of the hut and propelled him inside, where he fell sprawling on the floor. A moment later his sheep-skin jacket was thrown in after him.

The floor he lay on was dirt. The only light came through the door, and through foot-square windows, one each in three of the walls. Beneath one of them was a trestle table with a bench on one side and a water bucket. The place smelled of wood smoke and damp ground.

An old man stood in a corner, and after a moment spoke to him—in American! "You're wearing Farside clothes!"

Macurdy got to hands and knees, then stood up, fingers exploring his face gingerly. "My name's Curtis Macurdy," he said. "From Washington County, Indiana originally, but I've been working at Neeley's Corners, in Missouri." He examined the old man, perhaps six feet tall once, now gaunt and somewhat bent, with one shoulder carried lower than the other. And bearded. Macurdy wasn't used to beards, hadn't seen half a dozen beards in his life.

The old man sat down as if weighted by Macurdy's gaze. "Did you just now"—he waved vaguely—"arrive through the, ah, aperture between universes?"

"I came through the gate on Injun Knob."

"How do you feel?"

Macurdy reached back, feeling his behind. "Not too good. That sonofabitch I slammed against the wall had been jabbing my rear end with his spear all the way from the woods." He stepped to the door and peered out. The unconscious man had been taken away, but one of the others had been left on guard. The man scowled at Macurdy, and gestured threateningly with his spear.

"Okay," Macurdy said placatingly in his direction. "Okay. I'm not looking for trouble. I don't doubt you're good to your wife and mother, and all I want to do is get along."

He backed away from the door, bent painfully and picked up his jacket, then straightened and looked the cabin over. It was about twelve by twelve feet, and low roofed. On one wall hung two sleeping pads, long sacks of straw. A pair of split-plank shelves had been built on another. At the windowless end was a mud and stick fireplace; a copper kettle and ladle hanging beside it. Embers glowed beneath a blanket of wood ash.

"And you just arrived?" the man asked. "Just now?"

"Yep."

"You don't feel ill?"

"Nope."

"Remarkable. When my companion and I came through, eight years ago, we arrived desperately ill. I had a fever, cramps, and severe diarrhea for two days. My companion was so ill, I feared for his life. I've been told that two young men died after coming through, some years before we did."

"How about two women and one man, a month ago?"

"What did they look like?"

"The women looked young, like maybe twenty years, one of them pretty, the other one twice as pretty. The prettiest one had red hair, the other reddish brown."

"And green eyes?"

"Green and tilty. What happened to them?"

"I understand they were provided with horses and an escort, and left. I didn't actually see them. They're said to belong to a powerful, um—it translates to Sisterhood, but actually it seems to be some sort of politically influential power group." He paused, curious. "What do you know of them?"

"I'm married to the red-headed one. Her name is Varia. She's a sort of witch, but nothing bad. No deals with the devil or anything."

"I've heard," the man said, "that one arrived manacled."

"That's her. That's my wife. They came and took her away while I was in town. I followed them to get her back, but didn't catch up with them, so I got me a rifle and pistol, and waited till the gate opened again." He drew the .44. "Lost the rifle when I came through, and this didn't work when I tried to use it."

"Ah. Ours didn't either. We'd thought perhaps it was the ammunition, but if yours didn't..."

"Maybe guns don't work in this world."

The old man shook his head. "Our human biochemistry functions properly here. I can't imagine why nitrocellulose wouldn't explode." He sighed, got up carefully and held out a hand. "Excuse my lack of manners. I am, or was, Doctor Edward Talbott, a professor of psychology at the University of Missouri. Just now my profession is slave, and normally at this time of day, I'd be working at some sort of hard labor. Yesterday, however, I was quite ill, with a fever, so I've been given a day to recover. My health has been surprisingly good here, so far as infections are concerned. My problems have been structural: arthritis, actually."

"Mine is that sonofabitch's spear. I don't suppose you'd look at my rear end and see how bad he stabbed me?"

"I can look, but I'm afraid I have nothing for bandages. Just a moment." A fat stub of candle squatted on the table. He took it to the fireplace and lit it at an ember, then came back. Macurdy pulled down his overalls and trousers and bent over a bit. "They don't seem severe," Talbott said. "The bleeding has stopped, though obviously there was quite a bit of it earlier."

Macurdy pulled his trousers up and sat down on the bench, hissing with pain as he did. Then they talked. Macurdy didn't have to pump Talbott; the professor was starved to talk with someone newly from the other side. Mostly he talked about this side; things the newcomer needed to know. He also speculated the sergeant who'd brought Macurdy in might suspect him of connections with the Sisterhood. "That would account for your arriving functional," he added, "and for his treating you with restraint, despite what you did to one of his men."

He changed the subject. "You referred to your wife as a witch. What does she do that seems 'witchy'? I'm very interested in the paranormal; it's what drew me to Injun Knob."

"What she does ain't any kind of normal," Macurdy answered. "For one thing, when I was five years old, she could pass for twenty. And when I was twenty-five, she could still pass for twenty, just as easy. And she can lay a spell on you, at least if you're willing.

"She says I've got the blood line for magic, too—that my great-great-grampa ran away from the Sisterhood. For a couple of weeks she spelled me about every evening and had me doing drills. To 'open up my powers,' she said. Which might be why I didn't get sick, crossing over. But I never showed much sign of magic powers."

Macurdy got off the bench, wincing again. Going to the candle, he took a cartridge from his pistol and pried the bullet out with his jackknife, planning to toss the powder onto the embers, to see if it flared up. But when he shook the cartridge case over his palm, nothing came out. He peered inside it. Empty! They'd worked when he'd taken target practice. He tried another, then went to his jacket, and from a pocket took one of the large cartridges for the .45-70; it was empty too.

Grunting, he turned to Professor Talbott. "No powder. They were fine, three, four days ago."

Talbott said nothing, just sat staring at his hands, which lay folded on his knees. For a moment Macurdy stood thoughtful, then tossed the brass case into the ashes and sat down again. "You know what you never told me?" he said. "What they call this place. Not Missouri, I don't suppose."

"Oz." Talbott pronounced it *Ohz*. "Imagine it being spelled as in *The Wonderful Wizard of Oz*, but pronounced with a broad *O*."

"I remember that book. We had it in school." Macurdy grinned. "I didn't know you could get to Oz from Missouri. Thought you had to start from Kansas.

"Hmm. O-Z, but pronounced like in Ozark. I expected there'd be Ozarks on this side, too; expected to come out on something like Injun Knob."

"There are mountains not very far west of here," Talbott answered, "considerably higher than the Ozarks. You can see them in the daytime. They may be why the forests are so thick. We seem to have an orographically-enhanced summer monsoon here, off what they call the Southern Sea, which I suspect is less landlocked than the Gulf of Mexico. And the winters are wet, with frontal storms out of the west. Though the moisture for them might be from the Southern Sea, too, brought in by cyclonic circulation around the storm front."

Macurdy only half-listened, not comprehending at all. And at any rate seeing something more interesting to him. Talbott was a gaunt, bent, oldish man, his hair and beard mostly white but with black streaks. The lines in his leathery face reflected weather and hardship. His rough wadmal breeches were in-grained with dirt; his homespun shirt had been snagged and darned. His callused hands hadn't known soap for years, and their nails were black and broken.

But as Macurdy looked, the scarecrow figure became a tall-ish, lanky man in brown tweed and a green bow tie, clean-shaven and with his hair parted neatly in the middle. Dirt and calluses had no part of the image. He saw it plain as day, and it occurred to him this kind of seeing was a magic power. Maybe, he told himself, going through the gate had jarred it loose for him.

They continued talking until Macurdy, who'd gone abruptly from midnight to noon, got sleepy. Talbott took down one of the straw-filled sleeping pads. Macurdy lay down on it and went to sleep.

* * *

To waken wide-eyed from some bad dream. Talbott had snuffed the candle, and the fire had burned down to embers again. Macurdy got up painfully and felt his way to the door, to stand outside gazing up at the sky. There was the Big Dipper, there the pointer stars. And there the North Star; in school, Mr. Anderson had called it the Pole Star, Polaris. Same stars, it seemed like, but a different world beneath them.

It struck him then that there was no longer a guard at the

door. But there remained the palisade, and according to Talbott, a spearman who patrolled the night with a large dog on a leash. Escaping now made no sense anyway, Macurdy told himself. He needed to learn the language here, and something of the people, or he'd have no chance in hell of finding Varia.

Chapter 10: The Shaman's Apprentice

When the slaves were mustered for the day's labor details, Macurdy and Talbott were put to work digging a large pit in stiff clay, the worst kind of pick and shovel labor. Brought up to work hard and fast, Macurdy impressed the overseer, and on the second day his ration was increased that evening.

Macurdy tried to share with Talbott, who would not accept it. "You need it. You're a much larger man," Talbott said, "and you work harder. But I appreciate your generosity. In a place like this, it's good to have a friend." On the other hand, Talbott insisted Macurdy share the herb tea he made, with water heated in the small kettle.

Talbott had shared the hut for several years, but recently the other man had become unable to work, and died. Talbott wouldn't say of what. Macurdy guessed he'd been taken out and put down, like a crippled horse.

A man always worked with the man he lived with, Talbott went on. When larger crews worked together, only those who lived together were allowed to talk to each other. He assumed it was to prevent escapes or uprisings being planned. That fitted with the spearman and dog who circulated at night, looking into slave huts. No one was allowed in any but their own. And the guard at the single large slave latrine, who allowed no talking.

For his first months in Oz, Talbott had shared the hut with the young man he'd arrived with. Charles Hauser had been a doctoral candidate in physics, an exfarmboy from up north in Marion County. Charles had learned the language here quite quickly, and that, along with his energy on the job, had impressed the Oz tribesmen. He learned fast and worked fast, and his practicality had resulted in job improvements. The Ozmen weren't generally open to suggestions from slaves, but they'd become receptive to Hauser's.

"Then," Talbott said, "he somehow became assigned to the local—uh—call him a shaman. Who . . ."

"What's a shaman?"

"He's a medicine man and magician, influential in local politics. Charles collects herbs for him and does routine chores. He also blows glass for him, not only bottles but crude lenses; he even made him a crude, low-powered microscope. And a simple, treadle-powered lathe, drill, grinder and tool sharpener, all in one, with hand-carved pulleys.

"They moved him in with the shaman. He sleeps in the workshop he built, and is allowed to do errands around the village. Charles comes to see me rather often. Usually he brings meat, especially fat pork in winter to help me through the cold weather. And the herbs I dutifully use to retain my health. He even got the shaman to see me one evening; the man actually helped me. Markedly. My arthritis had been severe enough then, that I felt in imminent danger of being done away with as useless."

He gestured at the kettle and its accessories. "Charles gave me those, to make the herb tea with. He also tried to get me easier work, but my particular talents aren't valuable here. And Charles is still a slave himself. He has no influence except through the shaman."

* * *

That night, Macurdy lay thinking he needed to get a special assignment like Hauser's. Not that he disliked physical labor; he enjoyed exerting his strength. But it seemed to him that working and living with Talbott, he'd learn little more than the language.

* * *

A few evenings later, Hauser came to visit, bringing a new supply of herbs. He was able to stay only minutes, and Macurdy, who'd gone to the latrine, missed him. Three days later at muster, instead of being sent to work with Talbott, he was turned over to a spearman who'd come to take him somewhere. They arrived at a long low house stuccoed with some sort of clay, and whitewashed. Moss and grass grew on its steep roof, and there were rather numerous windows, their shutters closed against the early morning chill, for they had no panes. Four chimneys marked four fireplaces, suggesting at least four rooms. It was one of the two or three most imposing structures in the village of Wolf Springs. The spearman knocked firmly but politely with his shaft.

The door opened almost at once, and Charles Hauser looked out. The spearman left Macurdy with him, and Hauser shook Macurdy's hand, then led him into an end room. The shaman looked up from his work table to gaze long and intently at his visitor before speaking at some length to Hauser. Hauser, in turn, spoke to Macurdy.

"Professor Talbott tells me you're descended from a Sisterhood breeding on one side."

"On my Dad's side, according to what my wife told me. And I guess on my Ma's, too, because her dad was a cousin of my dad's dad."

"He also told me your wife is one of the Sisters, and considered you to have a latent talent for magic. A talent that hadn't shown itself to you."

"Actually I guess it had. Only I hadn't recognized what it was—what was going on with me."

Hauser regarded him for a moment, then turned and gave the shaman a résumé before asking Macurdy what, specifically, those experiences had been. Macurdy told him of seeing Liiset in the corner of the ceiling, and finding the pictures in the attic. And finally of looking at Talbott and seeing a younger version in brown tweed wearing a green bow tie.

Hauser nodded thoughtfully. "Green leather. It was probably the only tie he owned."

He and the shaman talked for two or three minutes then, Macurdy watching with no emotion stronger than interest. Finally Hauser turned to him again. "How did it happen this Sister went to Farside and married into your family?"

Macurdy told him that, too, Hauser translating it for the shaman. When he was done, the shaman gave what seemed to be instructions again. Finally Hauser turned back to Macurdy. "You're to go to Professor Talbott's hut now, get whatever you have there, and come back. A guard will go with you. You'll live here for now, but work for the village, as you've been doing. Only you'll get off early, and I'll teach you the language, and other things you need to know.

"My master's name is Arbel. From time to time he'll test you. And if things go well, especially if you learn to speak Yuultal well enough, he'll teach you things a shaman needs to know. No one else in the village has shown talent enough for him; he has high standards. And there are precedents for slaves being trained as shamans."

Hauser paused, still gazing at Macurdy, who said nothing. "He says he can see why your wife chose you. He says your aura…"

"What's an aura?"

Hauser grunted. "It's apparently like a halo, but around the body as well as the head. Maybe stronger around the head, though." He shrugged. "I've never seen one myself. Anyway, each person's is different, and Arbel can tell a lot about you by examining it.

"Better get moving. He's a good boss, but he doesn't put up with standing around when he's given you something to do."

Macurdy returned to Talbott's hut, got his sheepskin jacket and holstered pistol. Talbott was there; his back had gotten worse, and he hadn't been sent out that day. As he rose painfully from the bench, his expression reflected both pleasure and regret. "I knew Charles would tell the shaman about you," he said.

Macurdy shook hands with him. "If I can get permission," he told the old man, "I'll come visit you." But as he said it, it seemed to him this was the last time he'd see Talbott.

"Please do," Talbott said. "It's meant a lot to me to have you here this little while."

* * *

Macurdy was given a clean straw-filled bed sack, and slept in the workshop with Hauser. The next morning, Hauser, as interpreter, accompanied him to muster at the slave compound. There Macurdy was given an ax, taken to work by himself in the forest, and put to cutting wood: fence rails, fuel wood, and logs from which planks and roof boards could be split. Whatever was assigned. Hauser told him the local words for the different products, and had him repeat them several times. The overseer or his assistant would stop by to tell him when to return home to the shaman's, and to inspect his work for the day. If his production was inadequate in quantity or quality, he'd be beaten. Meanwhile he would not eat lunch with the other slaves—that would take him away from his own work—but would carry one from the shaman's.

The overseer looked Macurdy over for a minute, then gave him a warning through Hauser. "Don't take liberties with me. It will go ill with you. And if you try to run away, your death will be slow and painful."

From then on, each morning, rain or shine, Macurdy went to the woods with his ax. The overseer or his assistant arrived at two or three o'clock, until, after a few days, he was told to leave on his own when he'd made his day's quota. They'd inspect his work at a time convenient to them. Each afternoon, often while doing another task or project, Hauser drilled him on Yuultal. And also much of the evening, except when Arbel had some test for him, Hauser acting as interpreter.

Two weeks passed before Hauser had a chance to visit Talbott again. He was back sooner than expected, and Macurdy knew why, for Hauser looked distressed.

He asked anyway. "What's the matter?"

"He's not there. The gate guard says he was taken away two weeks ago."

Put down like a wind-broken horse, Macurdy guessed. "It was his back," he said. "I think he was expecting it. He didn't say anything because he didn't want to grieve us."

"I suppose so."

"You meant a lot to him," Macurdy added. "He was proud

of you, of what you've done."

He dropped the subject then, to let Hauser deal with his grief himself.

* * *

Each Six-Day evening a slave girl was brought to the house to spend the night with Arbel. It wasn't always the same one, but she was always good-looking. And whether her demeanor was demure or playful or bold, she never seemed unhappy to find herself there. According to Hauser, Arbel had told him that working with the spirit as he did, a lissome slave girl in his bed once a week kept his body properly grounded in the physical world—a necessity for a healthy shaman. On the other hand, twice a week would be to submit to the physical world; he'd limited himself even as a young man.

"How about you?" Macurdy asked. "Do you ever get any?"

Hauser smiled ruefully. "Four times a year—at each equinox and each solstice. As a reward; work keeps me physically grounded." Again Hauser smiled. "Sometimes I find myself counting the weeks."

Macurdy tried to picture Reverend Fleming, a widower, having a slave girl brought to the parsonage once a week. It was hard to imagine. Folks would be horrified.

Occasionally Macurdy was afflicted with unease at being here while Varia was—wherever she was. But he needed to learn, learn the language well, and enough about the country and the people to travel around without ending up a slave somewhere else, or dead.

Busy as he was, and as tired at bedtime, it was relatively easy not to dwell on the problems. His thoughts of Varia were mainly sweet fantasies.

* * *

Spring became summer, then late summer. Meanwhile Macurdy discovered a non-magical talent he hadn't known he had. He already knew he had an excellent memory and learned quickly, but now discovered an unexpected skill at duplicating sounds. With such intensive instruction, not only was he rapidly learning the local language; he was already pronouncing the words nearly as well as Hauser, and Hauser spoke them almost like a local. Now Arbel began to examine Macurdy more deeply, asking most of his questions directly, guiding as much on the responses of the big slave's aura as on his verbal answers.

Arbel's "instruction" lay only partly in teaching. Even more, it involved questions, the answering of which exposed and peeled off layers of opinions, beliefs, attitudes…like peeling an onion, freeing what lay beneath. And gradually, as Arbel worked on him, Macurdy became aware of changes in himself. He'd always tended to be confident. Now he felt stronger, bolder, more self-assured. And his natural charisma was more apparent. Even as a slave, his intrinsic dominance showed, expressed as competence, a comfortable readiness to act, a dominance more over situations than over people.

Gradually he became aware others were treating him differently. Thus in dealing with Macurdy, even the overseer's assistant was—not actually courteous, but his brusqueness had lost its truculence and threat. Then one morning, Macurdy glanced at Hauser pulling on his breeches, and saw around him a sheath of warm light, mostly blue, but with elusive patterns of other colors. It glowed around him from the hips upward, flaring more widely around his head. Hauser's aura, he realized.

Before going to the woods, he looked in on Arbel, seated at his workbench. The shaman's aura was primarily shamrock green, and started about at his knees. As if he felt Macurdy's gaze, Arbel turned and looked at him with raised eyebrows. And grinned, almost the first smile Macurdy had seen on him; it lasted perhaps three seconds. Then without comment the shaman nodded and turned back to his work.

The rest of the day until quitting time, Macurdy was seeing auras of one sort or another around every living thing, mostly thin and simple, requiring conscious intention to notice. *Varia was right about me,* he told himself. *I'll never doubt her again.*

Chapter 11: Blue Wing and Maikel

Well before adolescence, Macurdy had learned to use the ax. But in Washington County, the crosscut saw was the main tool for logging, while for cutting fuel wood, the homemade bucksaw was mostly used. The ax was simply used for swamping, notching, limbing, and of course splitting.

Now, working exclusively with it, he found his skills had improved; a given task took less time. Meanwhile, Arbel had peeled away layers of imposed and assumed considerations, and Macurdy no longer felt the need to prove himself, to show how much work he could do in a unit of time.

Thus, as his axman's skills improved, instead of turning out more wood, he commonly took a nap in late morning, allowing his mental clock and hungry stomach to waken him for lunch and to finish his day's work.

One noon, with the leaves showing the first tinges of fall color, he awoke aware of being watched. Getting to his feet, he looked around, and saw no one.

"Up here!" called a voice. "In this tree."

He looked up. At first he thought it was a vulture, but its head was feathered. Its crown was scarlet above the eyes, as if it had tried to become an eagle and gotten the colors wrong, while its strong beak was longish and nearly straight.

"There," it said to him. "You've found me."

Macurdy gawped. "You can talk!" he said.

"Of course I can talk."

Macurdy pondered briefly, wondering if this was another expression of his talent. "Could anyone hear you?"

"Assuming they're not deaf, yes."

Macurdy frowned thoughtfully at his hands, as if looking to them for enlightenment. "Back home," he said, "if I told folks I'd been visiting with a giant crow wearing a red..." He stopped, lacking the Yuultal word for "pompadour," and became aware of tittering.

"That was not funny!" the bird snapped. Not it seemed at Macurdy, but at someone else nearby. With the bird's irritated response, the tittering became laughter, and Macurdy looked around for the source. It seemed to come from the base of a walnut tree, but he could see nothing there. Then his hair stood on end. There *was* something there; he could almost see it. *Relax,* Varia had told him. *Relaxing helps turn it on.* And Arbel had said *don't try too hard. Let things come.*

And there it was, looking like a small, tight-furred man, a fuzzy creature naked except for a belt, and slender, wiry. Almost at once the halfling realized his invisibility spell had been seen through, and without an instant's hesitation, sprinted with startling speed to a slender ash sapling, scrambling into its top till his weight bent it, and he could transfer to the lower branch of an oak. There he sat; Macurdy could almost see his body tremble. When he'd climbed, a small knife and bag had been visible on his belt in back.

"So much for magic," the bird called after him. "I'll take wings any time."

The halfling said nothing, simply sat with his face working, somewhat as if palsied, somewhat as if chewing, his eyes glistening black as obsidian. Faster on the ground than a squirrel, Macurdy thought, and not too much slower up the tree.

"Though I'll admit I couldn't see you," the bird added. "I'm surprised this human could."

Macurdy's attention returned to the bird. About as big as a turkey vulture, he decided; far larger than even the biggest crow. It showed an aura much like a human's, when he thought to look. "What sort of bird are you?" he asked. "What breed?"

The bird looked down his beak at Macurdy. "Not a crow, I promise you that."

"Then what?"

"Men and tomttu call us the great ravens. And while the term reflects an inadequacy of concept, for our purposes here it suffices. Keeping in mind that intellectually we are far superior to ravens, which in turn are considerably superior to crows, which are—et cetera."

"Where did you learn to talk so well? You used some big words. I'm not even sure what all of them mean."

"Um. My species tends to be more intelligent; more, let us say, scholarly. Certainly much better informed."

Macurdy stared bemused. "How did you get so smart?"

"He's got a hive mind!" the halfling called; his nerves settled now. "Or more correctly, he's part of a hive mind!"

"Hive mind?"

The bird explained. "My kind has a shared mind. Each of us is an individual, but whatever one of us learns is available to us all. When we need it or care to access it."

Macurdy frowned. He thought he understood, but it was strange.

"For example. Suppose you carried a bow and shot at me. And I saw you do it. All of my people would then avoid you."

"Wouldn't that get confusing? How do you separate in your mind what's happening to you from what's happening to someone else? And somewhere else!"

"That's not difficult; there's always a sense of where and who. And at any rate, I don't even know what my nest mates are doing right now, though I could. But if you'd shot at one of us, we'd all avoid you as dangerous, and know the reason. On the other hand, the others wouldn't know I'd been talking to you unless one of them wondered what I'd done lately that was different."

"And they're all gluttons for knowledge," the halfling put in. "Afraid there's somethin' interestin' goin' on that they're missin'."

The bird nodded. Physically nodded. "True. It's why I associate with him." He gestured toward the halfling with his head. "He's a tomttu, you know. >From time to time we great ravens form relationships with individual tomttus. They're veritable mines of lore—facts, stories, and opinions."

Macurdy saw possibilities. "Is that right! I'm new in this world, and there's a lot I don't know about it that I need to. Maybe you could help me."

"Indeed? Obviously you're no hatchling—excuse me; newborn. What do you mean; you're 'new in this world'?"

"I came through a gate last spring. From Farside."

"Indeed!" This time it was the halfling, the tomttu who spoke. "I've heard of gates to a world called Farside. I've also heard they're dangerous to men and tomttus; that only those of ylvin blood can use them."

Macurdy decided not to say too much. "Well, at least one human's come through safely. Myself."

"Farside." Blue Wing cocked his head. "Interesting. I am Blue Wing, incidentally, and my friend is Maikel. What is your name?"

Macurdy didn't answer at once. What might happen if the Sisterhood learned he'd come through? And where he was. On the other hand, suppose Varia heard. "Macurdy," he said. "Do you know of anyone by that name?"

The bird's gaze seemed to lose focus, as if he scanned the hive mind. "No, no I don't. But then, I've never run into anyone from that mythical country before. What are you doing here?"

Careful now, Macurdy, don't say too much, he warned himself. "I'm a slave. The Ozmen made a slave of me when I came through. So I can't travel around. And there's a lot I'd like to know about this world."

Bird and halfling looked at one another for a long moment, and it was the tomttu who spoke. "We'll trade you knowledge for knowledge. Yuulith for Farside."

"I'll agree to that," the bird seconded. "It's infrequent that *any* of us exchanges thoughts and knowledge with a human. And when it happens, it's usually with one of your immatures, typically female. Your immature females are more—open. They tend to feel more affinity with such as we. And it's rarer yet to have a three-cornered exchange. It should be quite interesting."

"I've a question for you," the tomttu said. "How were you able to see me? The spell I cast should have kept me invisible to you."

"I didn't, at first. I heard you laugh, and looked toward the sound. And there you were."

"Ah. Of course. I shouldn't have laughed. But you likened him to a crow, and I know what he thinks of them. And rightly, in my view, though the crows would disagree. Hmh! And you saw me! Well. Individuals differ, whether man or tomttu—or even the winged folk, in spite of their hive mind. And you were able to come through a gate, after all. Assumin' you've been truthful with us."

Macurdy shrugged. "You two seem to trust each other. You just need to stretch your trust to include me."

"Ah," said Blue Wing, "but neither of us is human. And the tomttus' experience is that humans are much less reliable."

"Humans and ylver," added the tomttu, "or so the stories have it. But humans are said to be more cruel."

Well, Macurdy, Macurdy thought to himself, *they've got us pegged.*

* * *

For nearly two weeks, the three of them met each midday, Macurdy giving up his naps to talk with them. He learned a lot about the country, and about the language, for Blue Wing used big words, and both he and Maikel sometimes used long involved sentences. And both would pause to explain, when they lost his understanding.

The great ravens, Macurdy learned, were a sparse breed, gathering only in their rookeries to raise young. Their sole passion in life was knowledge. As far as Macurdy could learn, they didn't use it for anything in particular. In a sense they *were* like crows, but instead of collecting shiny things or smooth round things, they collected odd bits of knowledge, with no real interest in what use they might be to them.

The tomttu, on the other hand, were essentially farmers and gardeners, and herders of miniature sheep. From time out of mind they'd lived almost entirely in dwarvish kingdoms, where mostly they were safe from human predation. The dwarves, in turn, traded with the tomttu for some of their foodstuffs.

Some tomttu got the wanderlust. Maikel was one. It wasn't so much an urge to see new places, he said, though that was part of it. It was more a desire to be free of the strictures and formalities of Tomttu life, and learn new things. And any tomttu who'd reached puberty could pick a living in the forest from tubers and nuts, snails and slugs and tree frogs, seeds and fleshy roots. Their magic helped them find what they needed. Some such wanderers returned home in winter, this requiring a family willing to feed one who hadn't worked. Otherwise one found a good den for winter, defended it with spells, stored as much food as he could before the weather turned bad, then slept a lot. Maikel was bound for his home in the Diamond Mountains, some thirty miles west. He'd been gone three years, and was ready to settle down.

From Maikel, Macurdy learned about dwarves and tomttus; and from Blue Wing, geography, humans, ylver and the Sisterhood. The viewpoint and evaluations were considerably different than a human's would have been, but they were valuable, particularly the information the Sisterhood was now lodged far to the east, in the Kingdom of the Dwarves in Silver Mountain. How this came to be, Blue Wing had no idea; his concepts of formal treaties, politics, and even commerce were rudimentary.

Each spoke of other creatures, as well. Macurdy learned there were jaguars, catamounts, wolves and bears in the forests. And rare but savage night-stalking trolls. Rarer yet were the great boars, large as cart ponies. Sixty stone or more, Maikel guessed; probably more. (Blue Wing's notions of weight were vague and useless.) Maikel claimed to weigh about two stone, and judged Macurdy at fifteen, so Macurdy figured a stone would be roughly fifteen pounds.

According to that, a great boar would weigh half a ton They were uncannily clever, the two agreed, and had magic of their own. For men to succeed in killing one was unheard of. If one of the great boars became sufficiently offended by them, it could lay waste a farmstead, killing the livestock, destroying the fences, and rending whoever got in its way.

Or so tradition had it; neither could cite a known instance, not even Blue Wing, with his access to the hive mind, which stretched far back in time. But the potential, they insisted, was there, and must surely have been used at some time or other.

They also agreed there were no females of the species. Privately, Macurdy considered that myth; otherwise they'd be worse than rare. He'd have suspected the two of pulling his leg, but from Arbel's lessons, he was beginning to read auras as well as see them. And it appeared to him Blue Wing and Maikel both were honest with him. Blue Wing insisted a great boar had been seen to breed a razorback sow, a very large one, but Maikel was certain it couldn't happen. "What was seen was one eatin' a sow. But breed one? Even if he'd been inclined to it, he'd have squashed her flat."

Macurdy wasn't eager to meet the great cats, or wolves, and certainly not a troll or great boar. To humans, black bears on the other hand seemed benign; tomttu had more cause to fear them.

And there was information on dwarves. "If they have no grudge against you," Maikel said, "and if you're not trespassin', they're no danger to you at all. But if you wrong them, knowingly or not, they're implacable. Implacable! They do be friendly to us though, because we're small, you see, and because we're not given to human treacheries.

"Dwarves consider that they aren't, either. But I must tell you their greed sometimes gets the better of them. Then they can cheat and lie like a human. Well, not like the worst humans, but badly enough. Still, I'd trust a dwarf before a man. Not before every man—not before yourself—but judgin' the species broadly. They deal fairly with us though, the dwarves. Close but fairly. It's dealin' with men and ylver that brings out the worst in them."

Indeed, dwarves and geography were the subjects that most interested Macurdy. For if the Sisterhood had moved to the Kingdom in Silver Mountain, it seemed to him he'd have to go there.

Then one day, Maikel didn't show up. "The nights are becoming cold," Blue Wing explained, "and he woke up this morning with the decision to continue westward to his people. He asked me to give you his best wishes. As for me—the scavenging is poor around here. The people in Miskmehr keep more sheep, and sheep are rather given to dying without apparent cause."

Then the great bird and Macurdy wished each other well, and Blue Wing flew off northward.

Chapter 12: Pursued

With the solstice near at hand, the sun rose early. From an outlook, Varia could see its luminosity through thinning clouds, but it failed to warm her. The mare she'd stolen plodded stolidly on, but more and more slowly. When it paused to browse on the young leaves of maple, Varia was scarcely aware of it, she was so sunken in hypothermia from the cold, night-long rain.

At length the mare stopped, to stand quietly on a stretch of bare bedrock almost free of shade. The sun had burned the clouds off, and shone on her wet flanks. Gradually its warmth, trapped by blackened oilcloth, seeped through Varia's torpor, and she slid from the saddle, hobbling to an outcrop to lie in the sun.

She awoke cold on one side from the rock, and warmed on the other by sunshine. Looking around slowly, she saw the mare standing broadside to the warm rays, hide steaming. Wincing, Varia got to her feet, her legs and buttocks solid pain at the effort, sore not from the saddle, but from occasional uphill hiking to rest the horse.

And you're the girl who was ready to walk to Ferny Cove, Varia thought. Barely able to hobble, she went to the horse, aware now of the blisters she'd gotten, hiking in wet, ill-fitting boots. From a saddlebag she took a broken piece of loaf and the slab of cheese, sat down in the sun on a windfall and began to gnaw. Just the act seemed to warm her. The mare watched her eat—reproachfully she thought. "You and I depend on each other now," she told it. "Be patient and we'll find you some grass pretty soon."

For a quarter hour Varia sat gnawing, and soaking up sun, her thoughts slow, her eyes on the mare. *You need a name,* she decided. *You're my best friend now; I can't just call you Horse.* She gave it a minute's thought, then nodded, her chuckle sounding a bit like the Varia of Washington County. "Maude," she said aloud. "I name you Maude." And chuckled again. Maude had been the name of her father-in-law's favorite mare, named in turn for the queen of some place in Europe.

She gnawed and sunned till the mare got restless, then wincing with pain, pulled herself into the saddle and rode slowly on. The ridge dwindled, and they slanted down its north flank to a soggy glade, the grassy headwaters of a brook. There Varia took the bit from Maude's mouth, to let the creature graze more easily. Then hobbled to a sun-heated boulder, large as a roadster, crawled onto it and quickly fell asleep.

* * *

It was near noon before she awoke and looked around. Something had wakened her, apparently not a predator, for Maude still grazed placidly. Sitting up, Varia realized what it was: Miles away, someone had found her trail, some tracker, and she'd sensed it. Tomm, it seemed to her. Such psychic incidents were well known to Sisters. She could only wish they were regular, something she could rely on to keep her informed.

Then it struck her that in the cold and rain, the night before, and later in her torpor, she'd forgotten all about casting a net of confusion. She'd remembered at the stable where she'd stolen Maude, but afterward had gone into a stupor from rain, cold, and finally fatigue.

She didn't panic though, or slip into despair. She simply got painfully from the boulder, and painfully approached Maude, who paused in her grazing to look at her. After putting the bit back in the mare's mouth, Varia pulled herself, painfully again, into the saddle, and turned westward out of the gap, working her way up the next slope.

But not before casting a net of confusion over the site.

And now, after eating and napping, she'd recovered energy enough to begin healing her painful muscles.

* * *

They traveled slowly but more or less steadily the rest of the day, Varia dozing in the saddle from time to time. Steadily, but not without short breaks, when they came to glades with good grass. There she rested Maude and let her graze. The mare seemed not to have stiffened at all. Varia grazed too, on occasional patches of wild strawberries. Speed was important, but survival also depended on endurance.

Meanwhile she took her boots off, tying them to the saddle, riding barefoot to help her blisters heal. And at intervals casting a net of confusion.

The country was more broken now, and she changed direction from time to time, sometimes taking the most favorable way and sometimes not. The idea was to throw off pursuit, for even if she succeeded in confusing Tomm, he could look at the terrain and judge which way seemed best for travel. She had to outguess him, make him wrong.

Once, in the mud at the edge of a creek, she saw tracks that were clearly of jaguar or catamount. But Maude seemed unworried, though the tracks had to have been made since the rain stopped.

Eventually evening came, and again they stopped at a headwaters in a small marshy meadow. Varia left Maude to graze, depending on a bonding spell to keep her from straying, and sheltered beneath another large thick hemlock, plucking away stones and sticks enough to make a place to lie down. To sleep, and hopefully dream of Curtis.

Curtis. She cast an earnest thought: *I'm coming to you, darling! I am! It won't be long!* And wondered if thoughts ever traveled between the worlds.

* * *

A second day and a third, they traveled mostly westward. Only when the terrain required a change in direction did she turn north, from time to time casting her spell. Once she heard wolves, but at a distance, trailing other prey. And once as they traveled a game trail, the mare shied at fresh bear dung, but they passed it by and saw no further sign.

Finally they turned north on a trail too distinct, too unbroken and purposeful not to have been made by humans. It would be faster, and it couldn't hurt to follow it for a while. After a bit evening came, and a tiny patch of meadow at a seep. Again she left Maude free to graze, stowing the saddle and saddle bags beneath a nearby blowdown. The last of the bread and cheese she put in her shift, and climbed the ridge a little way, to shelter under an overhanging ledge she'd noticed. Climbed barefoot, walking carefully among the rocks and sticks.

Before long she slept, eventually to dream something came shambling upright on two legs, then stopped and peered about while the dream-Varia lay paralyzed with fear. Suddenly Maude screamed, and Varia awoke with a start, rolling to hands and knees, heart pounding in her throat. The scream repeated, and she realized it was no dream. And there was more: a muffled half growl, half roar, that froze her where she crouched. She had no doubt it came from the throat of something whose jaws were clamped on Maude's neck.

She realized she'd drawn her knife, though it would be useless against a bear. The mare didn't scream again, but there were occasional growling grunts, and sounds as of joints being broken. She stayed where she was, crouched beneath her ledge. Dawn, she discovered, had preceded the predator, faint gray light bleeding through the treetops. As it grew, the sounds of feeding stopped. Birds awoke as if in celebration, first a robin, then a wren, then a clamor from many throats. The sun's rays would soon light the higher treetops.

Something was coming up the ridge. Varia's short hair crawled with fear, then terror. A shaggy, hulking, upright form, some eight feet tall and five or six hundred pounds, strode into sight at half a trot, one great hand shielding its eyes. Its belly was grossly distended, not with pregnancy but gorging. Its other hand held a horse's hind leg over one shoulder, like a man might carry a club.

Varia almost missed seeing the small one, perhaps smaller than herself. Unlike its mother, it ran on all fours like an ape, carrying something in its teeth. Varia couldn't see what; brush was in the way. Probably something its mother had torn off for it.

Then they were gone.

She'd always heard trolls hated daylight. The belief among the Sisters was their eyes were too sensitive. Folklore had it they stayed in their dens till twilight, not even coming out on cloudy days. That daylight turned them to stone, though no reasonable person believed that. At any rate trolls were night stalkers; that much was certain.

Still she stayed where she was till the sun was well up. When she went down to the seep, it was shocking how much of the mare had been eaten. *You're going to walk to Ferny Cove after all,* she told herself. *Poor Maude.*

Three ravens had already landed on the carcass, one a different species than the others. Large though the two were, the third was much larger, its high and feathered crown scarlet against black. Pausing in its breakfast, it looked at Varia. "Yours?" it asked. Its voice could have passed for human.

She nodded.

"Sorry. I trust you don't mind excessively. One must eat, you know." And with that, the bird returned to feeding.

Varia didn't answer. She went to where she'd left the saddle. Not only the mare had been attacked; the saddle too had been mauled, gouged by sharp teeth in smaller but still powerful jaws. Her boots had been pulled loose, and one of them torn apart. The other was missing; it might have been what the troll cub carried in its jaws. She would not only walk to Ferny Cove; like it or not, she'd walk barefoot. Certainly she couldn't stay where she was; the trolls' den had to be somewhere near.

A thought occurred to her, and she looked back at the three ravens. "Excuse me," she called softly, and the red-crowned bird looked up. "I'm afraid I'm being followed. By a man."

"Really!"

"He should be a day or two behind. If you meet, he may ask if you've seen me."

"And you want me to say I haven't."

Varia nodded. "Please."

"My name is Everheart. A name given me by a tomttu; we have our own names, unpronounceable to you. And yours?"

"Varia."

"Let me see if I can guess what's happened," the bird said. "You're a Sister, a young girl who's run away from the Cloister. Right? I've heard of such. And your Dynast will have set a tracker after you."

Varia stared.

"You're speechless; obviously I'm right."

"Not entirely. I'm—somewhat more in the Dynast's attention than a young girl would be. I'm forty-three, not some sixteen-year-old to be brought back for correction and counseling. I escaped a—a punishment house, and this time they might kill me."

It seemed to Varia if the bird had had eyebrows, they'd have arched at that. His aura suggested he didn't quite believe her. She didn't herself. They'd degrade her, perhaps break her will, even her mind, but they wouldn't deliberately kill her.

"Hmh!" the bird said. "I wish you well in your escape, and I certainly won't betray you." It chuckled. "I've been told that among humans, a gentleman never tells a lady's secrets." Pausing, he cocked his head. "I do have that right, don't I? Who might your tracker be, do you suppose?"

"A man named Tomm."

"Tomm. Tomm is known to us. In fact I know him on sight. We all do I suppose; what one of us knows, the others know, or can if we care to look. It's how, over the centuries, we've learned your language. By sharing, word by word, phrase by phrase."

Varia stared.

"But I must tell you," he went on, "that my silence won't help you much. Tomm has a talent that apparently you're not aware of. No doubt his most important talent. You see, he can question any creature, large or small, about you. Mostly birds, because we see more, and our perceptions are very largely visual, as humans' seem to be. He may not gain much detail from his questions, for the minds of most species handle only simple concepts. But the question, 'have you seen this one?' accompanied by a mental image…" Everheart physically shrugged. "The eagles and greater hawks are no more susceptible to his demands than I, for their own reasons, of course, while the vultures and goshawks and falcons?—I doubt they'd hear his thought. They are totally focused on their own affairs.

"Crows, now—crows he may or may not ask. They lie, inveterately. But if he can recognize when they lie and when they do not…Some of your Sisterhood can do that, I'm told. And crows can be bribed, if he has something they might covet. Some shiny gew-gaw. Or a piece of fat; they are fond of fat. Beyond crows, there are many susceptible species too unimaginative to lie: sparrows, bluebirds, thrushes, waxwings…And jays, the tattlers of the forest! Very definitely jays!"

The great bird paused to threaten a rival. The lesser raven drew back too slowly, and there was a moment's squawking before it rose on flapping wings, to circle in rumpled dignity. Then Everheart looked at Varia again. "He won't tell either. His species is proud, like my own, and the eagles and greater hawks. And stubborn, as you've just seen.

"Meanwhile I recommend you keep to the deeper woods, where you'll be hard to see from the air. Avoid meadows and open ridges. And jays so far as possible, for they tell everything. Now if you'll excuse me."

He began to peck and tear again at the troll-mangled flesh of poor Maude's ribs. Varia watched for just a moment, then turned and hiked off into the forest, stepping carefully with her bare feet.

* * *

Hiking barefoot went better than she'd expected; in avoiding areas where the forest roof was open, she also avoided the stonier places. Now she held northward more than westward. Occasionally, unavoidably, she roused a jay, but they seemed so territorial, she decided the odds were small Tomm would run into one of these particular jays. Crows, on the other hand, flew widely, but hopefully wouldn't see her in heavy woods.

That day she ate the last of her bread and cheese, and later stepped hard on a sharp stone, earning a bruise on her right heel. She slept hungry that night beneath another hemlock. And in a dream, Curtis Macurdy found her, and held her in his arms.

* * *

In the morning she spelled a grouse to her hand, and after begging its pardon, wrung its neck. She considered eating it raw, but couldn't bring herself to. Instead she broke dead branches, lit them with a pass of her hand, and half roasted the bird. She ate most of it on the spot—there was little more to it than breast— and stashed the greasy remains in her shift. She also took time to heal her bruised foot sufficiently for swift walking. Then she hiked again.

Toward midday she became aware of magic about her, a spell of invisibility, and saw through it to the source. In the fire-hollowed base of a great-boled golden birch stood a tiny, furry man, a tomttu. She'd seen one in a cage once, when she was a girl traveling with an embassy. This one was larger, perhaps thirty inches tall. Their eyes met, and after a long moment it was the tomttu who broke the silence.

"Good mornin' to you. I didn't realize it was a Sister comin' up the trail, or I wouldn't have cast my spell. I'd but to crawl up my hollow here, and you'd never have seen me." He shook his head. "Betrayed by my own magic! Embarrassin'!" Doffing a non-existent cap, he bowed. "I'm called Elsir."

"Do you live here?"

"Here? My no! 'tis but a place to shelter on the way. I travel, you see, short though my legs are. Like more than a few of us, I've a wanderlust." He paused, cocking his head as Everheart had. "And what are you doin' out here alone, girl? With the hair on your head no more than a copper-red cap. A runaway, I don't doubt. Your people will be worried."

She looked at him and saw a chance for help. "I'm not a girl," she said. "I'm a married woman, stolen from my husband and returning to him. Do you ever cast spells to mislead?"

He laughed. "Perhaps a small one now and then. To lead the troll away when he's near, or the great cats."

"And what of men? I've heard they sometimes capture you

for sport, or steal a girl from you."

He scowled. "You're ill-advised to speak of such things to me, if it's favors you want."

"I didn't say it to offend. And as for being stolen and mis-used by men, I know more than you about that. Can you cast a spell to throw someone off my trail? Something beyond a net of confusion?"

He stared at her for an endless minute, gnawing his lip. Finally he spoke. "You're a Sister, are you not? Who is it you'd have me mislead?"

"A tracker named Tomm."

"I know of him by reputation. It wouldn't work."

"Could you cast a spell that would hide me from birds?"

Again he stared a long moment before he spoke. "Ah! The birds. Yes, I could that." Varia stood unbreathing, while Elsir squatted, thinking, frowning. "But I won't," he said at last. "I dare not meddle in affairs of the Sisters." Then, reading the depth of disappointment in her face, and the underlying desperation, he added: "We're a careful folk, bein' small as we are. And if Tomm sensed my spell, he'd know by its nature it was one of us cast it. Your Dynast would hear of it then, and she's a vengeful woman."

Varia bowed her head. "Thank you for considering it. Is there any advice you can give me?"

The small man shook his head. "Only to hurry. Travel as fast as you can. The pass north of here is called Laurel Notch; take it and you'll be in the drainage of the Tuliptree River, the East Fork, which is only a brook at first. It will lead you north into the Kingdom of Indrossa. They might hide you there, or send you on and interfere with the tracker. It's possible."

Varia began to walk on then, and he called after her. "I'm sorry, girl. But if I cannot give you a spell, I give you my best wish that you escape them. And the wishes of a tomttu are not without force."

She paused to look back at him. "Thank you," she said softly, then trotted northward on the same trail she'd been following.

Watching her trot out of sight, the tomttu shook his head.

Ah, if only my wishes did have force, he thought. *But if it's Tomm followin' you, it's little chance you have.*

* * *

She camped that night by a spring, and healed her new stone bruises. Her feet were toughening. At daybreak she awoke, and soon after sunup called a dove down, and ate it. Raw doves had become her staple food. Near midday she reached the head of the pass, a rugged cleft in the highest ridge she'd come to. There, though the stones were harsh, she climbed to a ledge to see what she could see. The ridges northward were progressively lower. Beyond them, at the edge of vision, the land looked level, and not dark enough to be forest.

As she looked, she heard cawing, saw crows flying southward, and scrambled to hide as best she could beneath a dogberry bush, enduring its sharp spines for the concealment it gave her. When the crows had passed out of hearing, she climbed down into the notch again and trotted on.

Hungering, she spelled another dove to her, and shortly heard water rattling over rocks. Not long after that she came to a brook, and followed it near enough to keep the sound in her ears.

Her way led almost continuously downhill, and often she trotted. It seemed to her that two more days would bring her to populated country again.

* * *

That night she dreamed of Curtis. She'd found him, but he refused to believe it was her. "My Varia is young," he said, "and has beautiful long red hair. Yours is short and gray."

She raised her hands to her face and felt wrinkles, then remembered. Tomm had caught her, and she'd spent five barren brutal years in the Tiger barracks before Sarkia cast her out, broken and aged. She awoke with a cry, and saw dawnlight. And on an old blowdown near her feet, a man, lean and hard.

"Good morning, Sister Varia," he said quietly. "You've been traveling hard. I thought you should finish your sleep."

She raised to an elbow, staring at him, willing that this was still the dream. After a minute he got to his feet. "You're probably hungry for something more than the doves whose bones and skins you've left along the way." Stepping over to her, he reached down for her hand. She shrank from him.

"Come Sister. I'm not a Tiger. I won't harm you."

Her answer was hardly more than a whisper. "What greater harm than to take me back? You'll return me to my death."

"No, not to your death. Sarkia has better plans for you. She told me so when she sent me. You please her, even in rebellion; she likes your strength."

"You don't know what they did to me."

"The Tigers, you mean. I know. And Idri's been sent away, months since, to other tasks elsewhere. Sarkia intends to train you in the duties Idri did for her, as her personal aide."

Idri's duties! At the sight of Tomm, Varia had given up, but to do the work Idri had done? Her will took new strength. "What has the Sisterhood ever given you?" she asked.

His expression didn't change. "Life," he said. "And the hunt."

The hunt? Yes, that would be it. "Have you ever thought of leaving? There's work anywhere for a man with your abilities. What chains does the Sisterhood have on you?"

He didn't answer at once. Then, "Without the Sisterhood, the ylver will someday conquer the Rude Lands, to command whatever tribute they want. To see the girls and women raped, and punish those who displease them."

It seemed to Varia that he recited, rather than speaking spontaneously. "And what did the Dynast have done to me? I was raped more than any Sister at Ferny Cove, my punishment for displeasing Idri and Sarkia.

"As for the ylver—the Sisterhood can't stop them. It has no great army to hold them off, nor will the tribes and kingdoms gather to Sarkia in support. Consider how helpless they were at Ferny Cove, when an ylvin army came!"

Just for a moment he showed emotion. Fervor. "That is ever in my mind. I was there; the cruelties went beyond evil. But helpless? Sarkia's magic troubled them greatly. We found our way through them by dint of her spells—hers and those she'd trained. Dense fogs arose in broad daylight, spreading over the country, and only the chosen could see through them. While ylvin warriors—even ylvin!—fell asleep on horseback, or at their posts. Else I'd be dead, as your children are."

My children! Would I even have recognized them? "On Farside," she answered, "each mother raises and cherishes her own children, and each child cherishes its mother. Have you ever wished to cherish your mother?"

He shrugged. "It is all the same to me. The Sisterhood is my mother."

"It's not the same to me! I have a husband who has sworn himself to me, and I to him. By our own choice. Idri stole me from him—Idri and a cull named Xader—and brought me back through the Oz Gate. My husband and I love each other; we were happy beyond anything you've known. And if I can, I'll return to him. Together we'll go far from any gate, have children by ones and twos, raise them ourselves, and love them."

She couldn't read the man at all; his aura hardly changed. What must Sarkia have done to him when she'd chosen to train him as a tracker! After a moment he spoke, as impassive as before. "But you can't, you see. Return to him. For I've caught you, and we are going back to the Cloister together. This time you'll like it there."

She stared quietly for a moment, then softly her mind caressed his. "Have you ever had a woman, Tomm? Held one in your arms?"

"I have never wished for one. But if I did, Sarkia would give one to me. You waste your breath, Varia."

"You've never wished for one because Sarkia spelled you as a child. Deprived you of your birthright, as she deprived you of your mother's love. Sarkia is evil, Tomm."

Again the pause before his answer. "If she does evil, it's for a greater good."

"Ah! So now evil is good! And day is night, and hunger a full belly! She's twisted your mind, Tomm, as she did the minds of us all. As the first Dynast did hers. But I lived more than twenty years on Farside, and unlearned much that I'd been taught. I wish I could take you through with me. You'd like my husband, Curtis Macurdy. He is honest and good, and you would have a friend at last. The two of you could farm together, drink coffee and talk together. Go to Decatur, eat 'ice cream' "—she said the words in English— "and see a 'movie.' You could even learn to laugh!"

Tomm stared at her silently for so long, she wondered if he'd answer at all. "You must get up now," he said at last, patiently. "It's time to start back." There was no more expression in his voice than before.

She got to her feet without help. *You won't take me back,* she vowed to herself. *You won't. Somewhere along the way you'll let your guard down, and I'll kill you. With knife or rock, or sharp stick through your eye, I'll kill you. Then I'll walk to Ferny Cove, and once I've gated through, they'll never catch me. Not again.*

Chapter 13: Cyncaidh

The trail was familiar from the day before, but much slower now. She was drained, physically and emotionally, the urgency was past, and the trail was mostly uphill. In late afternoon they were still short of Laurel Notch.

It was Tomm's responsibility to keep alert, thus she'd let her mind wander. She imagined him dead and her slipping through the gate at Ferny Cove. And finding Curtis: She visualized it happening at the farm in Indiana. He'd be overjoyed. They'd hug and cry and kiss, then run together into the house and make love, and the terrible months in the Tiger barracks would be forgotten.

For now, though, Tomm padded a few strides behind her. He hadn't tied her hands, for which she was grateful. Probably he would when they stopped to sleep. She'd been walking slowly, and so far he hadn't hurried her. He was tired too.

Tall clouds had built and a wind had risen, swooshing the trees overhead, and she considered suggesting they look for shelter. Thinking about that, she missed the sound of the arrow that struck Tomm. Then men were all around. Tomm, a feathered shaft protruding from his chest, tried to stand, and one of them raised his sword to finish him. Varia screamed, and lunged reflexively to stop it, but strong hands grabbed and held her. The blade chopped down, taking Tomm through the back, and she screamed again. Then her knees buckled, but whoever held her, kept her upright.

"You're all right," another said. "You're safe now."

She looked around to see who'd spoken. A tall man...No,

a tall ylf, his eyes tilted like hers but blue, his skin fair, his hair raven black. His eyes and coloring and magician's aura all gave him away: an ylf, though he stood before her in the fringed and greasy buckskins of a fur hunter. "We know who he was, and who you are. A tomttu told us. He was afraid for you; the tracker was so close behind."

Safe now? Did he mean it? Hope surged. "Am I free then? Free to go?"

He looked long at her without answering. "Free of him," he said at last. "Free of those you fled from."

"Not truly free then? Just new captors?"

"There are things we need to learn from you."

"I heard how you questioned my Sisters at Ferny Cove." Her words were little more than a hoarse whisper now. "When your army raped sixty of them repeatedly before you killed them. In front of the people there."

"No," he said quietly. "Not the army."

"Who then?" The question was defiant.

His expression was bleak. "The Kormehri. Men and boys of the town. Farmers of the district."

"You lie!"

He shook his head. "General Quaie ordered it. The original plan had been to capture all the Sisters and their children, or as nearly all as might be, and bring them to the Empire. Unharmed so far as possible. But your magic was more powerful than we'd supposed, and most escaped. So those we caught—" He paused, took a deep breath. "Those we caught, Quaie required the local men to rape publicly. Even the dogs that afterward destroyed the victims were war dogs of King Vertorus. They'd been useless against us, against our magic. Now Quaie made his own use of them. The story would spread, Quaie said, and no one in the Rude Lands would ever regard the Sisterhood as they had before. They'd see a Sister and remember them humiliated, raped by a line of men like themselves, their magic broken. Then torn—even eaten—by dogs.

"He didn't even bring one home to question. Said it was needless. Pointless. That the Sisterhood was finished, and the lesson of Ferny Cove was best taught his way."

The ylf's face had twisted as if the words were bitter in his mouth. He stopped, breathed, stabilized. "That was Quaie's reasoning," he went on, "and to some degree it worked as he'd said. But the business was vile, and on our return, the Emperor dismissed him, both from command and from his seat on the council." He shrugged. "And as the story spread, it has harmed us everywhere. As I warned Quaie it would when he gave the orders."

Varia stared. "You were there!"

He nodded. "I was there."

She looked around and saw six others. Except for the leader, they were men. Or no—half-ylver who could pass for men. Six that she could see; there might be others. Her voice became little more than a whisper. "What will you do with me?"

He looked down at her from his six-feet-four height, and shook his head. "Not that. Nothing like that, I promise you. But we have to take you with us. To be questioned."

"Take me where?"

"To our own country. The Empire."

Again her tears sprang silently. Truly there could be no more hope.

* * *

Tomm's cloak was taken from his pack, and put over Varia with its storm hood up to conceal her telltale Sister's face. Then bronze manacles were put on her wrists, manacles with a twelve-inch chain that allowed some use of her hands. Meanwhile the storm had begun, flashing and booming, but the rain passed in a minute, a spattering of large cold drops with wind and a smell of ozone, to blow off northeastward. Then her captors set her on one of their spare horses and started northward. They would travel by night now, albeit the nights were short in that season.

Varia scarcely noticed. Her mind was numb. On their brief stops, she neither ate nor drank. Finally, as dawn paled, they left the trail, set sentries and cooked. A military camp, for despite their clothing, these were soldiers. One of them led Varia a little distance off, gave her cloth and a pan with water, to use after relieving herself, removed her manacles and left her in privacy. After a bit he reappeared and took her to the others. She accepted food—a thick, honey-sweetened corn meal mush, and cheese—and drank from a cup that was offered. There was more in it than water or brandy—some potion—and she fell quickly asleep.

They rested through the day, ate again as the sun set, and moved on. Before dawn they'd passed the first farms. Meanwhile she'd grown more alert, and begun thinking of escape. To her it was obvious their leader had set a spell to help them ride unnoticed. Not an invisibility spell—that wasn't practical for a traveling party—but a spell that made them easy to ignore, to be paid no attention to. It would hardly cover an uproar though. Perhaps, she thought, she could make an outcry, screaming and struggling, when they passed through some town, or met some large party of travelers.

But the two villages they passed through that night were tiny and fast asleep, too small to waste what would undoubtedly be a single chance. Nor did they pass any travelers. And as if her captors knew her thoughts, the next evening she was gagged before they broke camp. Apologetically it's true, complete with explanation, and not brutally as Idri had gagged her, but still firmly gagged. She glared as the leader tied it.

In camp she was left ungagged and mostly unchained, but somewhat segregated from most of the party. One of the half-ylver had been assigned as her guard and companion. His name was Caerith, and when they camped, he talked to her. By the third day her reserve had softened, and his occasional brief monologs had become limited, intermittent conversations. This had been a reconnaissance party, she learned, sent to explore the territory where reportedly the Sisterhood had relocated. Not that there was any intention to make war, he insisted. For one thing, the new location was in a dwarf kingdom. This had been simply a matter of intelligence-gathering. What they'd do with such intelligence, Caerith didn't know.

After the third day, with the country increasingly peopled, they turned to one of the pack horses and replaced their buckskins with more civilized travel clothing. Oddly, there was even a set which more or less fitted Varia, though she continued to wear Tomm's too-large cloak for concealment.

They continued to travel only by night. Varia knew the pole star, and saw their road took them more northwestward than north. Ferny Cove was northwesterly. Each time she thought of it, she felt a pang of desperation. Thus, in camp after the fifth day, she went to the leader.

"You're Cyncaidh?" she asked.

His expression was calm but grave, his face not only handsome but aristocratic, though few aristocrats had one like it. "Yes," he said, "I'm the Cyncaidh."

"I lived for more than twenty years on Farside, and have a husband there. Then the Sisterhood stole me from him and brought me back. They kept me in detention at the Cloister, and—used me badly, but I watched for my chance, and ran away. When the tracker caught me, I'd been traveling northwest, working my way toward Ferny Cove, to the gate there. To find my husband again. We can't be many days walk from there now. I want you to let me go."

She saw and felt his gaze, and before she'd well started, a sense of pending refusal tightened her throat, raising the pitch of her voice.

"I'm sorry," he said quietly. "It's not possible. Not now. You have information more valuable to us than you realize. And beyond that, the Kormehri feel the Sisterhood abandoned them: While Quaie butchered his Kormehri prisoners of war, the Sisterhood used its magic to escape. And—the rape at Ferny Cove had an ugly effect on the Kormehri. It would be terribly dangerous for you to go there. You'd never..."

Her shrill anger cut him short. *"Dangerous? Dangerous! I escaped from a Tiger barracks at the Cloister! Got out over the wall, under the noses of sentries! Traveled the wilderness for days, alone! A troll killed my horse, and another ran off with my boots! And you talk to me about danger?"*

"My lady, I cannot release you. Jaguars and catamounts, bears and trolls, are not as terrible as men can be. And..."

She screamed and lunged, her unshackled hands raking at his face, his eyes. He caught her wrists, astonished at her violent strength, and held her arms overhead while she screamed and kicked and spat. Caerith grabbed her, wrestled her down squalling and struggling, then wide-eyed, looked up at Cyncaidh. The leader stood white-faced, lines of oozing red scoring his cheeks and forehead.

Kneeling, he opened his kit and took out two pills. "Open her mouth," he said quietly. Caerith pressed hard with his thumbs on the latches of her jaw, forcing her mouth open as he might a cat's. Then Cyncaidh dropped in the pills, far back where she couldn't spit them out, though she tried. They held her down while she strained red-faced, then gradually she went slack. Her pupils dilated further, and her eyelids slid shut.

Cyncaidh nodded, and with Caerith carried her to where she'd spread her cloak and blanket. "That," Cyncaidh said, "is a woman of character and strength. They are fools back there, as well as evil, to have dealt with her so cruelly."

And speaking of cruelty, he asked himself, *what of your own? You intended to steal a Sister if the chance arose, take her away, and wring out her mind for your own purposes, yours and the Emperor's. And then what? Not send her home again; that would never do. You hadn't thought about that, had you?*

* * *

Varia spoke to no one the rest of the way to the Big River, not even in camp. Occasionally she wept, but always silently, inconspicuously. And now not only Caerith looked after her, but from a little distance, Cyncaidh as well.

* * *

They reached the Big River and the Inderstown ferry docks in the black hour before dawn, to wait for daylight and a ferry crew. The soldiers, with their commander's permission, got down from their horses, and napped or sat talking on the shore. Cyncaidh, however, waited in the saddle. Perhaps, Varia thought, because she did. Her anger had passed, replaced by resignation, but she refused to show anything less than deep offense at her captivity. She was here against her will, a prisoner guilty of nothing—certainly not against these people—and she would not seem reconciled to her captivity.

Varia pulled her mind from her situation, focusing on the Big River. She'd never seen it before. Its Farside equivalent, the Ohio, she knew well from visits to Evansville, and it was large, but the Big River was clearly larger. A meteorologist might have told her the conformation of the east coast, combined with this world's equivalent of the Bermuda High, the size and circulation of the Southern Sea, and orographic effects of the Great Eastern Mountains, combined to produce high and fairly constant run-offs from its extensive watershed.

On its north side lay the so-called "Marches"—kingdoms not ylvin, but which paid tribute to the ylver's Western Empire, acknowledging its Emperor as their suzerain. She knew little about them, she realized. At the children's school in the Cloister, they taught the Marches had been conquered in a bloody war which ended with the ylvin boot on their necks. And the ylver planned the same fate for the Rude Lands. How much of it was true she didn't know. Some of it no doubt.

Finally, with the sun clear of the horizon, a crew arrived. From her horse's back, Varia watched the oarsmen clomp down the wharf and board the ferry, muscular men in short, open, canvas vests, gibing each other, laughing and roughing. Shortly, chains rattled as two of the ferry's crew lowered the end gate, which became a ramp for loading. Led by Caerith, she rode her mount out onto the ferry, hooves clopping on the wooden deck. Then Caerith dismounted and tied her reins to a rail. She watched oarsmen unship their oars, heard commands shouted, saw them lowered, dip, pull, and they moved away from the wharf, a dull drum beat regulating the strokes.

"It's a fine sight, the river," Caerith said.

She looked coldly at him from within her hood. She had nothing against the half-ylf. He was decent and patient with her. But four or five days' westward was Ferny Cove. She didn't doubt it held the dangers Cyncaidh had implied. But neither did she doubt that, with care and stealth, she could be within dashing distance of the gate when next it opened. Now she'd get farther from it every day.

The crossing did not take many minutes. When they were firmly docked, the gate at the shore end was lowered. Then the riders untied their mounts, and Caerith led his horse and Varia's off the craft. Again they waited on the shore, while the half-ylvin soldiers roped the pack string and remounts into an orderly file. When they were ready, Cyncaidh, instead of mounting and giving the order to move out, walked over to his captive and reached up to her.

"Let me help you down, my lady."

For a moment his offer and form of address unsettled her. Then she turned, leaning sideways a bit, and he took her under the arms, lifting her down. "Your wrists, please," he said, and when she'd extended her hands from the cloak, he removed first the manacles, then the gag.

"We're entirely safe here, my men and I. And you."

He turned and walked to his horse. Caerith stepped up to help her mount, but she shook her head. "Thank you, Caerith," she told him, "I can do for myself now," and raising a foot to the stirrup, swung into the saddle.

A moment later, Cyncaidh gave the command, and men, horses, and captive started up the road from the river bank, Varia looking ahead at him with a new unease. Dismounting had been difficult with manacles, and Caerith had usually helped her. But that had been simply a soldier helping a lady from her horse. When Cyncaidh's large hands had lifted her down, it had triggered her heart, speeded her blood. The feeling was one she hadn't wanted; not in this world.

She set her jaw, concentrating on the easy movement of the mare beneath her.

* * *

They rode no farther than a livery stable at the north edge of Parnston, for their horses were worn out from long use and no grain. The proprietor brokered a sale with a local breeder, and before noon they had new mounts. Not especially good animals, but adequate, well fed, and rested. Meanwhile, the travelers actually ate breakfast at an inn, and an early lunch. Varia had thought they might lay over a day, but Cyncaidh didn't even give his men time to fall asleep at the table before ordering them back into the saddle.

It threatened to be a long afternoon, not having slept the night before, and in the pleasant warmth, Varia dozed off and on in the saddle. Clearly Cyncaidh's method of changing from night travel to day travel was to ride all day. They were seasoned riders; no one would fall out of the saddle simply because he dozed. And when they did camp, no one would have trouble falling asleep.

The country here was as much open farmland as woods, but even where the road passed through fields, maples, oaks, or tuliptrees shaded it. It was a better road than any she'd seen in the Rude Lands, ditched through low stretches, with a bridge or white oak culvert where it crossed a stream. In the soft stretches, rock and clay had been dumped, covered with gravel and leveled, to prevent miring and rutting.

The towns had no defenses; not even a bailiff's stronghold or a reeve's stockade. Varia hardly noticed. Repeatedly her lids slid shut, her mind drifting dreamward from lack of sleep.

In mid-afternoon, Cyncaidh, who seemed an iron man, took pity on them and stopped at a large crossroads inn. A sign outside proclaimed the bedding was boiled with every change of users, and each room treated by sorcery to destroy possible vermin. An expensive place then; Cyncaidh's expedition, she decided, must be well financed.

It was early enough they had a choice of rooms. Cyncaidh's choice, not hers. Off a larger room there was a smaller, without an independent exit. The larger, Cyncaidh would share with Caerith. The smaller was hers, complete with undersized chairs and a low table, clearly intended for children. But the bed was long enough.

She looked at the door—all that would stand between her and Cyncaidh when night came. It had no bolt. She didn't like the twinge of excitement that accompanied the thought. *Don't be silly,* she told herself. *If he was going to try something like that, he'd have done it days ago.*

She looked for some thought to displace it, and escape came to mind; each day now was a day in the wrong direction. She went to the window and peered out thoughtfully. *I could use bedding as a rope, and climb down into the courtyard tonight. Or jump, as far as that's concerned! It's not as far as I dropped from the palisade, escaping the Cloister.*

The problem was, she'd still have to get out of the courtyard. And if she did, then what?

Wait, she told herself, *and see what opportunities time provides. Maybe when they're done questioning you—maybe they'll let you go. Maybe even with a horse, and money to eat with. Cyncaidh seems decent; he might do that.* It seemed to her he would.

Someone knocked—Caerith, with clean traveling clothes for her, obtained from the innkeeper, who also kept a small store for travelers. Clean clothes and word the inn provided baths—two of them, actually, one for women. They went downstairs together and crossed the courtyard. The tub she found was scarcely large enough for four or five—women travelers would be few—but she'd have it to herself, with bathing utensils, towels, a small bowl of soap and one of sweet-smelling oil, all neatly arranged along a low bench. The tub was oval, with a ledge to sit on, and its distinctive tiles were surely Cloister made, arriving through who knew what avenues of trade. She fiddled with the water gates. The flow was fast, both the hot and the cool, for this was limestone country, with great flowing springs, and abundant good oak to heat water with. She stripped while it filled, then stepped down into it.

It was the most luxurious bath she'd had since she'd left the old Cloister at Ferny Cove. Her scalp, its hair less than an inch long, she scoured thoroughly under water. The rest of her she scrubbed till her skin was pink, then soaked some more at her leisure, relaxing, watching her toes peek out at her from the water.

When she'd soaked long enough, she toweled off, and tried on the new clothes. They were a reasonable fit, and included a light tunic with a hood that would hide her scalp. She was grateful for that. She left, to find Caerith waiting, still unbathed. For the first time his aura reflected sexual thoughts; perhaps he'd fantasized sharing her bath. It was nothing like the aura of a Xader or Corgan though; more like that of Curtis in adolescence. She discovered she felt a sisterly fondness for the half-ylf.

"When do you get to bathe?" she asked.

He smiled ruefully. "As soon as I deliver you to the Cyncaidh for safekeeping."

She surprised herself by laughing for the first time in more than a year, and they sauntered together across the courtyard, toward the wing they were housed in, Caerith carrying her dirty clothes. "What if your Cyncaidh's still in the bath?" she asked.

He shook his head. "The enlisted men, perhaps. But he'll have been quick so I won't have to wait. He's a rare commander, the Cyncaidh."

She said nothing more. When they got upstairs, Cyncaidh was waiting, scrubbed and in uniform, damnably attractive. She went into her room and found a clean, soft cotton sleeping-shift on the bed. Though it was still afternoon, she changed into it, lay down, and rather quickly slept.

* * *

Caerith's knocking drew her reluctantly from sleep. "It's almost time for supper," he called. She dressed and found him uniformed, and they went downstairs together. There were several alcoves off the dining room, and the soldiers, their commander and prisoner, were shown to one of the larger. Their conversations were quiet, perhaps because their commander was seated with them. When Varia had finished, she sat quietly watching him, observing her own response to his attractiveness. *You'll have to live with it, deal with it,* she told herself. *It's physical, that's all. Not love like you feel for Curtis. Just ignore it.*

When most were done, Cyncaidh excused those who wished to leave. Varia waited till Caerith had finished his rhubarb cobbler, then left, the half-ylf a step behind.

"Can we go to the river bank and sit awhile?" she asked.

"Certainly, my lady."

My lady. He sounds like Cyncaidh, she thought. The river passed perhaps a hundred yards from the inn, forty yards wide and of uncertain depth, a thinly milky blue from dissolved limestone. Someone, presumably the town fathers, had put out split-log benches, and they sat on one, the late sun behind them off their right shoulders.

She touched the bronze lozenge on Caerith's collar. "What does this signify?" she asked.

"That I'm a sublieutenant in the imperial army."

"An officer! I'd assumed you're only half ylvin."

He nodded. "That's right, my lady."

"What's it like, being half ylvin?"

He looked at her with dark brown eyes, good-looking in his clean uniform, young in years as well as appearance, his brown hair washed and brushed now. "The Sisters are half ylvin, aren't they?" he countered.

"In our ancestry, rather more than half. But we're a people of our own. We don't live under ylvin domination."

He let that pass, turning instead to her question. "Life as a half ylf? Hmm. There's no simple answer. Too many variables— who your father is, your mother, their ranks...It's my father who's full ylvin, a baronet's son who was captain of the governor-general's guard in the Kingdom of Quabak. My mother was the human, a daughter of the regent. It was a minor political marriage, but a happy one."

"So you grew up in the Marches?"

"No. When I was four, my father was transferred to Duinarog, the imperial capital. I grew up within a mile of the imperial palace, wanting to be a soldier."

"And what was that like, growing up in"—she paused over the name, realizing she'd never heard it before, and finding that strange—"in Duinarog?"

He laughed, something he hadn't done in any conversation they'd had till now. "Ask me again when you have a day to spare. Mostly it was good."

"Was there prejudice? Because your mother wasn't ylvin?"

"Sometimes. Children can be cruel. But nothing troublesome. I had good friends."

"And your career?"

He thought about his answer. "I'm unlikely ever to attain high rank, though such things aren't unheard of. But then, few of my cadet class will, though only three of us were half ylvin. You hope for a good commander and serve diligently, and if he notices your service favorably, he'll see to your development and advancement."

"And you were assigned to serve Cyncaidh?"

"Not initially. The Cyncaidh is a general; he commands the Second Legion. I served in its Third Cohort, under Colonel Lonuaigh. Then I learned of a confidential mission I could apply for." He exposed a smooth forearm. "Except for having little body hair, I hardly look ylvin at all, and I'd had certain training." He shrugged. "Colonel Lonuaigh recommended me."

His aura suggested he'd become uncomfortable with the subject, so she changed it. "I've assumed your commander's name is Cyncaidh," she said. "Yet you refer to him as 'the Cyncaidh,' as if it's his title."

"The Cyncaidh family is one of the noblest in the Empire. They rule a large domain on the Northern Sea—a sweet water sea bigger than all the Marches combined. Cyncaidhs have been regents, ministers of state, and chief counselors. One was even a pretender to the throne, in the Time of Troubles, though I'm sure the family doesn't boast of it." Sublieutenant Caerith grinned at that, then rearranged his face. "I hope you won't tell him you know."

"Would he be angry with you?"

"He'd be disappointed in me. It would seem I gossiped."

"You still haven't said why you refer to him as 'the Cyncaidh.' "

"It's simply custom. Whoever is head of the family is referred to as 'the Cyncaidh.' "

Varia examined what he'd told her. In Farside terms, it was equivalent to learning a reconnaissance patrol, a squad, was being led not by a sergeant or lieutenant, but a general—a general who was also governor of New York! And she was his prisoner.

"Then why," she asked, and waved vaguely southward, "was he leading this patrol?"

"My lady, I don't know; truly I don't. And if I did, I couldn't talk about it. Nothing against you, you understand; I admire you as much as he does. But it wouldn't be proper."

Admire you as much as he does. The comment introverted her. After a minute Caerith spoke again. "We should go back to the inn now. This conversation has outgrown us."

I'm not sure "outgrown" is the word, she thought as they walked, *but I certainly don't know where it might take us from here.*

* * *

The next day they replaced their packhorses, and each day after that made at least twice the distance they had on any day south of the river. They traveled by daylight, no longer had to make and break camp, and the summer solstice was at hand, so the days were long. And happily cool, with skies that held only small and transient clouds. On the third such day, they arrived for a late supper at Fort Ternass, where an imperial garrison was stationed. They'd resupply there, Caerith said, and get fresh horses, ylvin horses. They had, he commented, a long way to travel yet.

* * *

Before they left the next morning, Cyncaidh brought a young woman to Varia, a girl lightly tanned and rather pretty, with honey-blond hair. "My lady," he said, "this is Hermiss. Her father is a professor, supervisor of the local commons school. I've obtained her services as your traveling companion and lady-in-waiting; it's time to give Lieutenant Caerith other duties. Hermiss has been employed as the companion of Colonel Faimler's daughter, who's at Port Arligh just now, visiting her grandmother. I trust you'll enjoy each other's company."

The move took Varia completely by surprise. She wondered if Caerith had asked his commander to be relieved. Meanwhile Hermiss crossed her hands on her chest and dipped a slight bow. Varia didn't know whether to reply in kind, then decided not to;

she was, after all, "your lady." The girl's act was probably the equivalent of the curtsies she'd read about on Farside, and seen in movies. "I'm happy to meet you, Hermiss," she said instead. And thought: *I have absolutely no idea how to relate to you, girl. We may look the same age, but I've got perhaps twenty-five years on you, and twenty times the experience. Our lives have been totally different.*

It struck her then she'd never before spoken with a woman in this world except Sisters; this girl had a whole area of experience she didn't. Her smile surprised both Hermiss and Cyncaidh. "I'm sure we'll have some interesting conversations," she added.

* * *

Fort Ternass was on another major crossroads, and instead of continuing north, they turned west. The weather turned too, from dry and pleasantly cool, to sodden and cold. At intervals they met thunderstorms, and between storms it still rained, sometimes hard. The countryside seemed abandoned. Most travelers had holed up in inns, and farmers were staying indoors. In the pastures, cattle and horses grazed humpbacked, rain streaming from them.

Cyncaidh's party was the exception; they rode despite the rain, as if they had to be somewhere by a certain time. Which might have been true; no one had confided in Varia. She'd thought of asking Cyncaidh, then decided not to; she felt too ill at ease with the attraction he held for her. She also thought of asking Caerith, but told herself no; if she wasn't willing to ask Cyncaidh, she'd do without knowing.

At least they stayed at inns.

As for the interesting conversations she'd expected with Hermiss—on the road they were too rain-beaten to talk much, and the first two evenings they'd ridden late. The third day started a bit better, with snatches of sunshine in the morning, and they did talk a bit. But after noon, sporadic showers fell, soaking their breeches where their knees peered from their rain capes, the moisture proceeding coldly upward by capillarity to their hips, chilling their spirits as well as their bodies.

As afternoon rounded into evening, a coming storm darkened the sky in the west, like early dusk. The clouds pulsed with lightning, and soon were near enough that their thunder could be heard. Wind had begun to gust and swirl when an inn came into sight at a crossroads ahead. Cyncaidh shouted an order and they began to canter, slowing at the last minute, thudding into the hoof-churned yard. Stable boys ran out through the first skirmishers of rain to help the soldiers with the animals, while Varia and Hermiss slid down and ran inside, to stand panting and red-cheeked in the potroom.

Poorly-lit and steamy with moisture, it was already mostly full of travelers, men. They were the only women, and stares, leers, and randy comments were the order of the moment. The men inside didn't know about the soldiers. A twentyish potboy came over and said loudly, "If you're here to do a little business, you'll owe the house a half share." Then guffawed, smirking around at the men seated there. There were whistles and cat yowls; mugs banged on tables.

Varia would never know why she said what she said next. Perhaps it was a reaction to the smart-mouthed potboy: If he wanted an uproar, so be it. Whatever the reason, she said it loudly: "We'll eat first. Then, if you can let us use a bed..." The cat yowls and whistles swelled, and there were shouts of "you can use ours!" followed by laughter.

They sat down at a table, and Varia quickly realized how seriously she'd erred, for several of the bolder men came leering to their table, leaning over them and making propositions. Hermiss was big-eyed with fright, and Varia, feeling responsible, stood up abruptly.

"You've got us wrong!" She said this loudly too. "We want the bed for sleeping!" That turned most of the yowling to laughter, and for the moment disarmed the more aggressive. Then someone called, "She's playing with you, Barney!" and one of the men grabbed her.

"Just a little kiss to start with," he said, and pushed his stubbly face in hers. She grabbed him rather as she had Xader, though much less strongly. The electric charge she gave him wasn't as strong, either, but he screamed, leaping backward with a force that astonished everyone but Varia, to lay curled on the floor mewling.

"Come on, Hermiss," Varia said, "let's get out of here."

No one got in their way, and outside, they stood under the entryway roof, watching rain pour down. Lightning struck nearby with a tremendous *snap! BLAM!* that shook the porch and almost knocked them down.

A minute later Cyncaidh came loping through the deluge and stopped near the two girls, grinning like a boy. "We made it just in time! I'm not sure what the possibilities are for lodging though." With his head he gestured toward the stable. "There were barely stalls enough for our saddle mounts. The remounts and pack animals are tied in a shelter without walls." He looked at the two women more closely now, examining their auras, especially Hermiss's. "What's wrong?"

"I said something stupid," Varia told him.

He peered at her a moment, then went in, leaving them outside. Two of the soldiers loped up, also drenched and grinning, nodded to the girls and followed their commander.

"What's going to happen?" Hermiss said timidly.

"Nothing." *I hope.* "Wait here."

Varia went back in, her senses turned high. The air was a mixture of resentment and caution, but gratefully she sensed no impending violence. The man she'd grabbed had made it to hands and knees, to puke out his supper and ale on the plank floor. There wasn't one whistle or cat yowl. She stood behind Cyncaidh, who was waiting to arrange for seating and beds, and murmured: "I'm afraid I caused some trouble."

"I've noticed." His tone was dry, acid.

"I didn't intend to."

"I'll take your word for it."

The innkeeper came out then, and recognizing Cyncaidh as an ylf, nodded deeply, almost a shallow bow. Food, he said, was no problem. But as for rooms...

When his troops had gathered at the table, Cyncaid told them they'd bed in the hayloft that evening. *And no doubt pay for it,* Varia thought. She wondered if she was to blame, and decided she probably wasn't; the place was simply full. Then Cyncaidh turned to her and told her a bed of hay was being made for Hermiss and herself in a box stall normally used for storage.

The meal proved barely edible, perhaps as repayment for what the innkeeper considered ylvin troublemaking. The soldiers endured it glumly. The Cyncaidh, by contrast, was grim, not glum. From his aura, Varia surmised he was irked with her for putting the ylver in a bad light.

The rain still poured thick and cold when they left the building, but as the two girls ran through it, Hermiss laughed in a sort of high glee. She'd eaten little but the bread and cheese, trimming the mold off, and had had a single mug of ale. Varia decided the girl's mood was more an aftereffect of the initial excitement than of drink.

The storm-dimmed daylight had graded through dusk into twilight. Someone, probably a stable boy, had hung a lantern inside the stable's front entrance. A clutter of old single-trees, eveners, pack saddles and the like was piled outside a box stall, cleared from it to make room for the two of them.

A soldier entered the stable carrying a stack of large coarse blankets provided by the innkeeper. He took off the piece of canvas protecting them, then came over and handed a pair to Varia. She looked at them with more than her cat vision, then began to pass her hands over them.

"What are you doing?" Hermiss asked.

"Killing the vermin."

"Really?"

"Certainly."

"What kind of vermin?"

Varia paused, concentrating. "Let's see. There are lice—and fleas. No bedbugs."

Hermiss giggled. "You're fooling."

Varia shrugged and made her final passes, then spread the blankets side by side on the thick hay. The air was pungent, but not unpleasant, with horse urine and manure blending with the smell of hay—clover and timothy. From their cubby she could hear the low easy talking of the half-ylvin soldiers, the sound somehow comforting as they climbed the ladder into the hayloft. *There are worse places than this to be,* she told herself.

Earlier a soldier had brought their oiled leather bags from a horse pack and hung them on harness pegs. She pulled dry clothes from hers and changed into them, draping her wet breeches and socks on the edge of the manger, and her tunic over a horse collar still hanging on its peg. Her wet boots she stood near the stall's entrance. Hermiss followed her example.

Then they lay down on their blankets. Varia willed the girl to be quiet and go to sleep, and lay quiet herself, her eyes closed, waiting for the drumming rain to still her mind, a mind beset by unwanted thoughts. Of Idri. Of Liiset, who'd abandoned her. Of what Tomm had said about Sarkia's plans for her. Of how far they were now from where she wanted to be. Interrupted by the sound of a man running in through the stable door—a man alone—bringing her out of herself. Cyncaidh, she decided. He'd probably been talking with the innkeeper. She closed her eyes again.

"*Were* you fooling about killing vermin?" Hermiss murmured. The question almost made Varia jump; she'd thought the girl was sleeping. Looking at her, she shook her head.

"I really wasn't. Fooling, that is."

Somehow this brought giggles from Hermiss, followed by a question in, for whatever reason, a conspiratorial tone: "What did you do to that man who tried to kiss you? Really do."

"Our term for it is shock fingers. I gave him shock fingers in his crotch."

Hermiss almost burst, trying to control the giggles bubbling out of her. When she'd calmed again, she murmured, "He had it coming."

"True. But I shouldn't have said what I did. Then *he* might not have."

"They were all whistling and saying things before you ever said anything."

"True again. But I still shouldn't have. Especially when they were whistling and yowling like that."

There was a moment's silence. Varia lay back and closed her eyes again.

"What do you think would have happened if you didn't know how to do shock fingers? And the soldiers hadn't come in?"

Varia sighed, answering without opening her eyes. "Nothing. Because I'd have turned around and gone back out as soon as the whistling started."

"Do you think they'd have raped us?"

Hermiss, you're a blockhead, Varia thought, but said nothing. Hermiss interpreted her silence, and this time her words were soft, quiet.

"Were you ever raped, Varia?"

Varia said nothing.

"I wonder what it would be like."

"It's ugly. Painful. You feel like shit." *Time after time. Night after night.*

Silence again for a moment. Then, contritely: "I'm sorry I asked, Varia. I really am."

Varia opened her eyes. Her voice was wooden, a monotone. "It's all right. You're young. Just be careful in a situation like we walked into. Turn around and walk out." *If you can.* Varia discovered her guts were tied in knots.

"Are you young?" Hermiss asked. "I'd forgotten you're like the ylver; that you can look young for a long time. I thought you might be—twenty."

Varia looked at the earnest face on the blanket beside hers, and felt a sudden pang of—something. Loss. "I have daughters about your age," she said. *Had,* she corrected herself.

The face looked troubled again, and this time Varia broke the silence. "Tell me what it's like to be a girl growing up in Ternass."

Hermiss told of school and parties. And about the colonel's daughter, who sounded a bit full of herself but pleasant enough. And especially about the young men of Ternass, and the ylvin soldiers stationed there. Of flirtations, stories of occasional love affairs and briefly broken hearts. The ylver, Hermiss said, were especially exciting because they were supposed to be better lovers, and being relatively infertile, were less likely to get a girl pregnant. But the imperial army had rules against "slipping it to" local girls, and other rules against marrying them without official sanction, which involved a lot of time and trouble.

She also told about her father. "He knows an awful lot. He's read hundreds of books, some of them ten times, I guess, and thought about them all. He knows a lot about the ylver. Some people at home don't like them very much; some don't like them at all. But my father says ylver are just people with tilty eyes and pointy ears. Some of them can't even do magic, he says. And they don't live forever; they just stay young a long time. He says we're lucky they're here. For every person in the kingdom who died during the war, he says probably three have been saved because we don't fight our neighbors anymore."

Varia didn't reply. She was thinking it would be better if there weren't wars at all.

"What was it like growing up a Sister?" Hermiss prompted.

"Different than you told about. We had duties."

"Like what?"

"Whatever work they trained you for, assigned you to. Making jewelry, all kinds of ceramics, taking care of babies, working in the dining room...I was best in the kitchen. I got to be a very good cook."

"Really?" Pause. "Did you, you know—have to make babies?" Hermiss paused, then added, "I've heard..." and trailed off.

"After I grew up, I was sent to Farside to marry a man the Sisterhood wanted me to have babies with."

"Farside!?"

"Farside."

"What happened to him?"

Varia began to cry, quietly as usual. Hermiss could hear something though, and peered intently at her in the seepage of lantern light. "Are—you crying, Varia?"

Varia nodded, fighting now to keep silent.

"Oh Varia! I'm so sorry!" Hermiss too began to cry, and put

her arms around her. "I shouldn't have asked. I shouldn't. I've been terrible to you!"

The girl tried to cry quietly, too, but began to sob and hiccup, and now it was Varia doing the comforting, hugging her, patting her shoulder. "It's all right, Hermy, it's all right. You couldn't know. You couldn't know."

Hermiss quieted and they let each other go. After a bit, Varia could see the girl's aura smoothen, softening in sleep, but she herself was wide awake now, listening to the rain drum on the roof. "God, Curtis," she whispered drily, "how I wish! How I wish!"

She became aware of movement then, as if someone had been outside the stall and was moving away. Rolling to her knees, she got up and peered out. Cyncaidh was at the hayloft ladder, a hand on a riser. Realizing he'd been seen, he stopped, stood waiting. Varia walked to whispering distance.

"It's all right," she murmured. "The trouble in the potroom got to her, that's all. And the ale. She's fine now. Sleeping."

Cyncaidh stared at her, his eyes dark in the lantern light, and she realized he hadn't just come down to investigate Hermiss's sobbing. His aura was thick with emotions: embarrassment, grief...something else.

"You were listening," she said.

He nodded.

"From the beginning."

"From when Hermiss said something about killing vermin. Then she asked what you did when the man tried to kiss you. I'd come down to hear your version of what happened in the potroom, so I stayed where I was and listened. And found out. Then—I stayed and heard the rest of it."

She stared long at Cyncaidh and his aura. "If you're to be my jailer," she said at last, "I suppose it's best you know. And I could never have told you directly."

He nodded, stood silent for a moment. "Good night Varia," he said quietly, and reaching, almost touched her face, then turned and climbed the ladder.

She watched him disappear, heard Caerith's voice question

softly and Cyncaidh's reply. Then she turned and went back to the box stall, settling onto her blanket again.

To stare blankly into the darkness above her, her mind's eye seeing Cyncaidh's aura as it had been by the ladder. *What am I going to do?* she asked herself. *What in hell am I going to do now?* For she realized what another part of Cyncaidh's emotional mix was. She should have seen it sooner, she realized. It had been there all along.

My god, she thought numbly, *he loves me! He's not just attracted to me physically, though that's part of it. And he's not attracted because I'm a pretty woman in a trap. He actually loves me!*

The rain continued to beat. She willed it to beat forever—beat until it washed the world away; that part of it at least. Then shook her head at what seemed weakness. *Just keep us here long enough for me to figure out what to do,* she corrected. *I'll settle for that.*

As if in answer, thunders rumbled, then boomed; another convection cell was moving in. "That's the way," she muttered, and closed her eyes, inviting sleep.

I'm his prisoner, she whispered in her mind, *and he loves me. He'll never help me get back to a gate. Not that he ever said he would. I'll have to get there on my own or not at all.*

Chapter 14: A Different Land

Varia awoke in the night needing to relieve herself. Rain still drummed on the roof, and she was reluctant to run sixty yards through it to the latrine; her dry clothes would get soaked. She decided instead to duck out the back door, wearing only her rain cape, and use the wide overhang of the shelter where the packhorses were. They wouldn't mind, and it was only seven or eight yards away.

By the time she got back, she had a plan.

* * *

She next awoke to Caerith knocking on the outside of the box stall. Rain still fell, but now it only muttered on the shingles, barely audible. Breakfast was far better than supper, and Varia wondered what Cyncaidh had said to the innkeeper, the night before. There was oatmeal without lumps, crisp side pork, cheese, bread and butter and buttermilk. By the time they finished eating, the rain had stopped. Outside, the sun shone through a broad gap in the clouds.

The soldiers were not energetic this morning, but Cyncaidh pushed them, and in half an hour the pack string was loaded, ready for the road again. Varia was ready before them, tight with nerves and purpose, keeping mostly out of sight, not wanting Cyncaidh to note the tension in her aura.

Her plan, such as it was, included only an overall purpose, a general strategy, and a first step. Mostly it was unknowns and assumptions. *When you're desperate enough,* she told herself, *and the alternatives are unacceptable, you grab whatever op-*

portunity you find, and hope something good happens. The odds, it seemed to her, were at least as good as she'd faced when she'd stepped out the door of the Tiger barracks a few weeks earlier, and that had worked out. More or less. To a degree.

Then Cyncaidh called to fall in and mount up. Varia and Hermiss led their horses from the stable and swung into their saddles, Varia barefoot, her still-wet boots tied to saddle rings—to get them drier, she'd told Hermiss. Cyncaidh, after looking back over the column, shouted another order, and they rode out of the inn's muddy yard.

Until they'd left Fort Ternass, Varia had always been kept in the midst of the mounted men. But since Hermiss had been added to the party, they'd been put behind the remount string, in front of the pack string, with the horse handler the only soldier behind them, back at the very end. Apparently to give them privacy if they wished to talk.

It was Varia who opened the conversation now, telling stories about Washington County and the Macurdies, recounting the funnier things she could remember. Beginning with the time seven-year-old Curtis had tried to ride a calf and gotten bucked off into a wheelbarrow full of mucky cow manure. He'd run howling and stinking into the house, tracking manure on the linoleum, which enraged his mother. With a grip developed by years of wringing laundry by hand, she'd taken him by the ear to the windmill. It was March, still given to freezing at night, and after stripping him, she'd immersed him in the icy water of the horse tank, which set him howling even louder, then scrubbed him with a gunny sack.

Hermiss' peals of laughter brought a curious glance from Cyncaidh at the head of the column.

Next she told of one of Will's "notions," which struck him during silo filling. For years a neighbor, Deacon Stuart, had pestered Will about his non-attendance at church, hinting at hellfire. Then a skunk had taken residence under Will's barn floor, to make nighttime forays on the hen house, so Will had caught it in a Victor #1 trap. And when the deacon was up in the silo tromping down, Will had thrown the dead skunk into the silo filler. Chopped skunk, along with the content of its scent gland, had shot up the pipe and rained down on the deacon. The silo had been only about five feet short of full, and the overweight deacon, almost overcome by the stink, had clambered over the side and hung by his hands, his feet dangling some twenty feet above the ground. Then, realizing there was little relief in that—the vile smell was as much on him as in the silo—he'd tried to climb back in and couldn't. He'd hung there yelling for help: using language not suited to a deacon, and Will had gone up and rescued him. For two or three years after that, the deacon refused to trade work with Will, but he also stopped badgering him.

That story hadn't worked as well for Hermiss. She knew about corn and skunks, and was familiar with a concept not greatly dissimilar to hellfire, but Varia had had to stop at intervals to explain "deacon" and "Sunday services," "silo" and "ensilage" and "silo filler."

She'd begun telling of a time when Charley, her father-in-law, had been hauling bundles to the corn shredder, when she saw a bridge ahead. Her guts tightened, but she continued the story until she was well out on the bridge planking. Then, with the reins and a mental command, she caused her horse to rear. Behind her, the horse handler shouted a "whoa" to halt his pack string, while Varia, as if fearing she'd be thrown, dismounted. Before anyone was aware of what she intended, she'd vaulted onto the bridge railing and leaped off.

The river was a large one, and swollen now from days and nights of rain. She knew nothing more about it. Not its name, what towns it flowed past, anything. Her assumptions were that it flowed southward to join the Big River; that it flowed fast enough for her purposes; and that there'd be boats tied to the bank here and there, hopefully with oars or a paddle. And that she could swim long enough to come to one of them.

As she plunged beneath the water, she was astonished at how powerful the flow was, how swift. The water of a normally forty-yard-wide river, now storm swollen, with flooding several feet deep on the flood plain, was pouring with a tremendous surge between bridge abutments no more than thirty yards apart.

She stayed under water as she'd intended, swimming with the current to put as much distance as possible between herself and the bridge. Her hope was that the soldiers would wait to see her come up before anyone else jumped. By that time, hopefully she'd be far enough away that no one would, that the odds of reaching her would seem too poor. Maybe they'd even fail to see her, and think she'd drowned.

She was neither a skilled nor a strong swimmer, nor experienced at staying under water more than briefly. She stroked as hard she could, feeling increasingly the need for air, and fighting it. Her water-soaked breeches and tunic were like weights, hampering her movements more than she'd expected, while the water was too muddy to see in. She became desperate for breath, and realizing she didn't know how deep she was, fought to the surface, gasping, gulping air.

For just a moment she glanced back. She'd left the bridge farther behind than she'd hoped—perhaps eighty yards, thanks to the tremendous bridge surge—and was almost cut off from view by a curve. Men on horseback lined its railing, but she heard no shouts. Perhaps they hadn't spotted her!

Now she gave her attention to the banks. On the Mustoka River, in Washington County, there'd be rowboats and skiffs now and again, tied or chained to trees along the bank. But this wasn't the Mustoka in any universe, and the water was eight feet above normal. If there were any boats tied there, they'd be swamped. She kept swimming, the current carrying her swiftly. Another hundred yards and she was tiring badly. Some distance ahead and to her left, she saw an oak being swept along, its trunk submerged so its top resembled a great floating thicket. If she could reach it—but it was traveling nearly as fast as she was. Some distance behind her and near the west shore, she saw a larger tree riding the current, a big silver maple floating higher in the water than the oak, and it seemed to her she could intercept it if she swam hard.

She struck out for it, raising her arms out of the water now in a clumsy crawl stroke, breathing hard. *I'm going to make it!* she thought. But when she'd almost reached it, a submerged branch struck her, snatching her under. She panicked, struggling, swallowed water, somehow pulled free and popped to the surface, strangling and splashing. And went under again, this time because she wasn't swimming anymore but simply flailing. Her natural buoyancy popped her up again, still strangling on water—and a hand grasped her tunic. Once more she went under—someone was pulling on her—and twisting, grabbed whoever it was, pulling him under, too. Then somehow, through her panic, she realized she might drown him, might drown them both, and stopped struggling, letting herself be towed. Again her head broke the surface.

Through her choking and coughing, she recognized Cyncaidh. A bank eddy carried them into the floodplain backwater, and his feet touched bottom. Woofing for air, he towed her heavily toward the high bank behind it. A few yards farther, he reached the submerged slope of a natural levee formed by the sediments and back currents of past floods. Varia felt her own feet touch then, and the two of them crawled onto its top, to kneel half out of the water.

Lungs heaving, eyes wide, they stared at each other, tunics stuck to them, Cyncaidh's hair plastered to his skull. After a minute he spoke: "God, Varia! What a terrible thing to do! What a terrible, terrible thing to do! Never do anything like that again!"

Shortly they got to their feet and waded staggering toward high ground. A few steps took them off the back of the levee, where they found she could still wade, the water to her armpits. Soon they were at the high bank, sprawling on its slope, Cyncaidh still wearing his boots. A voice reached them now. Above the highbank was a pasture, and a soldier trotted his horse along its edge, calling for his commander.

"Here!" Cyncaidh shouted hoarsely, then helped Varia to her feet and up the bank. As they stumbled out of the woods, the soldier saw them and trotted his horse over. "Thank God, General!" he said dismounting. Cyncaidh leaned on the horse for a long moment, clinging to the saddle, while Varia sank to the ground. Finally he put a foot in the stirrup and raised himself heavily onto the horse, then beckoned. "Help her," he said. The half-ylf helped Varia to her feet, then laced his fingers, making a step for her, and boosted her up behind Cyncaidh.

"I'll follow on foot, sir," he said. "It won't take me long at all."

"Thank you, Sergeant," Cyncaidh answered heavily, and nudging the horse with his heels, started for the bridge.

* * *

No one talked when they got back. Without changing into dry clothes, Cyncaidh and Varia got on their own horses, and when the soldier on foot got back, the column started west again. They didn't stop till they came to a substantial village. At the common, Cyncaidh pulled his party off into its open, park-like woods. A soldier dug his commander's gear bag from a pack, while Hermiss dug out Varia's from another. Then Caerith accompanied the two of them to the nearby chairman's house, recognizable by the pennant on its roof, and knocked at the door. Another soldier had followed, carrying the bags.

Seeing imperial uniforms, the chairman's wife let them in, got towels, and led them to rooms where they could change. When she was dressed again, Varia walked barefoot into the hall, where Cyncaidh waited alone. He put his arms around her, clasping her tightly. "Promise you won't do anything like that again," he whispered, then held her at arms length. "What have I done that you fear me so?"

"Fear you?"

"Enough to try killing yourself."

She shook her head. "I wasn't trying to kill myself."

He gawped. "What, then?"

"I was trying to get back to my husband. I thought I could find a boat. Hoped I could."

He stared, his face slack. His emotion, it seemed to her, was dismay. After a moment he shook his head. "Come," he said tiredly. "There'll be an inn here. The men need to eat."

* * *

It didn't rain for several days, and they made good time. Then they turned north again, and a few days later reached the border with the empire itself. Once again the country changed. The main roads all were graveled and ditched now and frequent mansions showed the existence of a sizeable upper class. With the mansions were compounds, whose cabins could hardly have more than three rooms plus loft, but even they had fruit trees, and small gardens where bean and pea vines climbed frames, while gourd vines climbed the walls.

At the first military post, the quartermaster fitted Varia with a pair of field uniforms. And a female soldier, an ylvin corporal, replaced Hermiss, who'd be sent back to Fort Ternass and the colonel's daughter. Physically, Corporal Keoth could be considered gifted, but personality-wise she was stiff, a stick. She wore her hair in a military bob; its typical ylvin black shone from a good diet and much brushing.

They rested there a day, replaced worn equipment and their whole complement of horses. When the column was ready to leave, Hermiss and Varia embraced. "I don't suppose you'll write to me," Hermiss said.

"Why not?"

"Because—because you're wiser than me, and I'm not ylvin or a Sister or anything."

"I'll write if I can."

"I—hope you'll be happy. You should be. I mean, you ought to be. You deserve to be."

"Everyone deserves to be," Varia answered, then wondered. *Do they, really? Does Idri? Sarkia? Corgan? What would it have taken to make Xader happy? Let him hump every good-looking woman he saw, probably, whether she wanted to or not.*

"I'll write to you, Varia, I promise. And you won't have to write back unless you feel like it."

"Thank you, Hermy. I'll feel like it, but…" Varia shrugged. "Who knows what will happen when I get where they're taking me?" She paused, feeling that was a poor note to end their goodbye on. "I'll be glad to get your letters," she finished.

They hugged again. Corporal Keoth stood waiting with a scowl of disapproval. Varia couldn't be sure whether it was for the merely human Hermiss or the evil Sister. *Both,* she decided.

She turned, went to her horse, and climbed into the saddle; Cyncaidh gave the command, and the column moved out. As they turned onto the road, Varia looked back. Hermiss still waved, and briefly Varia waved back before looking ahead.

So much for not knowing how to relate, she told herself. And wondered briefly whether she'd ever see either of her remaining children again. Curtis's children. Or know them if she did. Or whether they'd care; they'd probably scorn her for deserting the Sisterhood. Idri would make sure they knew.

Idri. Now she knew who Corporal Keoth reminded her of.

* * *

Cyncaidh stayed away from her, but she was aware he watched her now and then, as if to see how she was doing. Keoth wasn't overtly rude, but clearly she disapproved of Varia. Cyncaidh noticed too. After three days, he left the corporal off at a district seat, at the office of the imperial representative, with a written order to have her returned to her base. And again it was Caerith who rode beside Varia.

They traveled till she was tired of riding and inns and an unchanging countryside. Tired even of Caerith, for they'd run out of things they were willing to talk about. But after ten days the country began to change. Forest increased while farmland diminished. >From time to time they passed open bogs, often with a small lake in the middle. Lakes were conspicuous in the landscape, and some of the trees were unfamiliar, evergreens of several kinds, some dark and pointed. The golden-barked birches she'd come to know so well in the mountains, returned, joined by much smaller birches whose bark was white as chalk.

After some days of this, with the forest more and more evergreen, they entered a district of large hills ahead. Not mountains, but hills higher than she'd seen since Cyncaidh had brought her out of the Granite Range.

They spent three days crossing them, then came out on level land again, with forests of a pine taller and more graceful than she'd ever seen. And sometimes of other pines, much smaller and with no blue to their greenness, their stands often very dense, with slender trunks and narrow crowns. She wouldn't have thought to find such level land so beautiful. Here too they passed bogs again, moss bogs, Cyncaidh said, though she could see grasses and sedges growing thickly in them, and often knee-high bushes. Even the bogs were aesthetic in their way, though she might not have thought so if the mosquitoes and horse flies and deer flies could have penetrated the spells that she and the others cast against them.

One of the inns they stopped at faced a lovely lake, with a view framed by exceptional pines, thick-boled as old tuliptrees, and even taller. When she'd finished supper, Varia crossed the trail and sat down on a fallen tree to admire the sight. Shortly, Cyncaidh came and sat by her.

"You like this part of the world, I think," he said smiling.

"I do. It's very beautiful."

"It—suits you nicely. I'm glad I could show you to each other."

She smiled back at him. "You're a nice man, Cyncaidh. If I have to be someone's prisoner, I'm fortunate it's you."

He wanted to smile back, and suppressed it. *Guilty conscience,* she thought. It occurred to her then she might have erred, in the stable in the rain storm, erred in thinking he was taking her north simply because he wanted her. That the interrogation he'd spoken of was only an excuse, that he'd never help her to Ferny Cove after she'd been questioned. Perhaps he would. Perhaps.

Half turning, she faced him. "It's true, you know. You are nice. You've never exercised your advantage over me. You were as gentle as you could have been, back in the Rude Lands, even when I attacked you." She paused, looking back in time. "You provided me with Hermiss when I needed someone like her." Again she paused, this time to laugh. "And rid me of Corporal Keoth without my asking."

She lay her hand on his arm. "You even saved my life."

He stood up, and she stood with him. "I couldn't not have," he said, suddenly flustered. "You—are important to me. Personally. You've known since that night in the stable." He paused. "And you've never exercised your advantage over me, either.

You're not the only one who's vulnerable, you know."

Then he turned and strode away, straight-backed but embarrassed, Varia watching him go.

* * *

Four days brought them to hills again, high and rocky. The forest here was varied, but with none of the familiar, more southerly trees. The large pines were present in scattered groups, among various smaller evergreens and white-barked birches, and other pale-barked trees whose leaves fluttered prettily in the faintest breeze. As they approached a rock outcrop, she saw a jaguar lying on it, gazing fearlessly at them. As far as she could tell, Cyncaidh cast no protective spell, so she withheld her own.

The cat seemed definitely larger than the jaguars she'd once seen in a menagerie. The horses rolled their eyes and quick-stepped nervously, while their ylvin masters soothed them.

The whole column slowed, watching the animal. When they were past, Varia quickened her horse's pace, pulling up beside Cyncaidh. "It was beautiful," she said. "In the south, I doubt you'd ever see one so close."

He grinned. He'd been smiling more lately; she'd decided he must be getting close to home. "Wait till you see one in winter," he said. "Their coat gets longer, soft and thick, and turns almost white. A pale ice blue, actually, with blue-gray rosettes."

See one in winter? The words triggered anxiety. "How will I come to see one in winter?" she asked.

He hadn't noticed the change in her aura. That required attention, and his was on his thoughts. "We have a place, my family, where we—" He stopped. "You may not have the word for them in the Rude Lands. We fasten long slender boards on our feet, and run on them across the snow. Which up here covers the ground for about half the year."

"They have them on Farside," Varia said. "In my husband's language they're called *skis*."

His smiled faded. "Well, then," he said, "you know what I mean." He continued with less enthusiasm. "There are several of them there, the Great Cats, and we've developed a sort of mutual trust. We track one or another of them sometimes, to observe them, and sometimes they track us. They neither flee nor offer to attack, though ambush is their favored hunting strategy."

She couldn't tell him she'd love to see one. He might infer an interest in staying. Introverted, she said something vague and dropped back to where Caerith rode. She knew what had killed Cyncaidh's enthusiasm: she'd referred to her husband. While her wonder over the jaguar had died when he'd implied she'd still be with him in the winter. *We need to thrash this out,* she thought. But not yet. She wouldn't be able to stand it if he said she couldn't go back. Or even if he equivocated.

* * *

The next afternoon they topped a final ridge that looked across forest to the Great Northern Sea. Cyncaidh stopped, the rest of the party stopping too, and Varia rode up to sit beside him. She liked his grin; it made him look boyish. "That's it," he said pointing. "I've sailed it—including by ice sloop—and skied and skated on it. Everything but swim in it."

"You haven't swum in it?"

He shook his head. "It's too cold. You wouldn't last a minute. Well maybe a minute, but certainly not ten. Probably not five." He pointed northwestward. "My home is off there. Aaerodh Manor. We'll stay in Cyncaidh Harbor tonight, at an inn, and be home about midday tomorrow.

"I love it there. When I speak of home, that's where I mean. That was home even during my twelve years at Duinarog. Though it was about three weeks away by ship, up rivers and across both the Middle and Northern Seas."

The Middle Sea. I never even heard of it before, she thought. *Nor of Duinarog or the Northern Sea, until Caerith mentioned them.* Varia realized again how limited the teaching was at the Cloister. She knew far more about the geography of Farside than about her own world, or even her own continent.

Cyncaidh grinned down at her. "You'll love it too," he said. "It's made for you. It's beautiful."

* * *

The inn was a surprise to Varia. When Cyncaidh got down

from his horse, a stable boy, a middle-aged human, took the reins grinning. "Good to see you again, Your Excellency," he said. His voice was respectful, but not at all obsequious. Cyncaidh had the man's name ready to his tongue: "It's good to see you, Joleth," he answered. It occurred to Varia then the inn might be owned by Cyncaidh's family.

It seemed to bustle when they entered. The house staff, mostly ylvin, treated Cyncaidh like royalty. >From their auras, they were honestly pleased to see him, and Cyncaidh, in his turn, was friendly—not overly familiar but not at all aloof. The place was almost crowded; the manager told Cyncaidh a cruise ship had arrived that day.

A small dining room, reserved for special parties, was set up for him and his soldiers. At supper he seated Varia beside him, and the ylvin potboy's treatment of her went almost beyond courtesy, despite her road-worn uniform. In fact, the entire staff was friendly, and seemed to have been expecting her. It introverted her a bit.

While they ate dessert, Cyncaidh leaned toward her. "Stay near me after supper," he murmured.

Afterward the soldiers dispersed, some to sit in a common room for drinks and conversation, while others left to walk around. Apparently none had been in Cyncaidh Harbor before. After speaking briefly with the manager, Cyncaidh took Varia's arm, and together they climbed a flight of interior stairs to a hall, then down it to a large room with a fireplace and upholstered chairs. And a bed, which sent a brief twinge of unease through her.

Her glance moved to the flames dancing in the fireplace, then to the balcony. She walked past Cyncaidh and out onto it. It was flanked by what he'd told her on the trail were spruces, and seemed higher than a second story because the inn was built on a low rocky bluff. Before her lay a bay, with a rocky point on the west that extended well into the lake. *Not a lake,* she told herself. *A sea. A blue, sweet-water sea.* There were docks and a trio of schooners, one of them a long four-master, sleek and clean, painted a strong sky blue. The cruise ship, she supposed.

Cyncaidh stepped out beside her, and their arms touched. She was very conscious of his nearness and size. "Do you find it beautiful?" he asked. He wasn't smiling now, she knew without looking.

He's hung his boyish mood in the closet, she thought. It was a mood she liked, when he showed it, but in her experience it was fragile. She wondered what he'd be serious about this evening. "Very beautiful," she said.

"It seems to me you've been happy these last days."

"I have. More than any time since I was kidnapped and brought back to Yuulith."

As she said it, she remembered the day of her arrival at the new Cloister. She'd bathed, eaten with clone mates, and spent the evening walking and talking with Liiset. It had been a beautiful half day, half a day of blind and foolish optimism.

"I'm glad it pleases you," Cyncaidh said. "I love you, you know."

"I thought perhaps you did." She turned to him, to say more, to tell him she loved Curtis Macurdy, but his arms slipped around her, and his lips lowered to hers. His kiss was not forceful but gentle, lingering. She was passive, neither returning nor resisting. He stepped back, hands on her arms, his face sober, his aura showing not arousal but love.

"I've wanted to do that—and tell you that—almost since we rescued you. If rescue is the word. And told myself I mustn't; that it wouldn't be fair. Perhaps it isn't now, either, but it seemed necessary that you know."

She stared at him, her fingertips on the lips he'd kissed.

"Tomorrow we'll be at Aaerodh Manor," he went on, "and you'll learn things there. You needed to know this first, know it with certainty." He took a deep breath and half turned, offering his arm. "Let me take you to the steward. You haven't seen your room yet."

* * *

He left her with the steward, a robust ylf whose face and aura reflected an even-tempered competence. Instead of assigning a page to guide her, he took her up himself, let her in, then gave her the key and left. The room was a duplicate of the other, with its own balcony facing the lake, and its own fireplace. A fire had been set and lit for her, and her bag lay on a high bench next to the bed. A robe and nightgown hung from a rod. There was a basket on the table, with cheese and bread, and a knife for slicing. A bottle of wine stood beside it.

The sun was low, its light golden on the trees along the water's edge. She stood on the balcony watching it set, saying nothing, almost thinking nothing. Then turned back the covers on her bed, donned the nightgown, and lay down. Thoughts came to her, of being kissed by Cyncaidh, and in them he didn't step away from her, but kept kissing her, murmuring his love while they undressed each other and lay down together.

With a mental jerk, she pushed the images away and stared dismayed at the ceiling. *What are you doing?* she asked herself. And answered it was only fantasy. *Dangerous fantasy,* she replied. *This man loves you, wants you. Controls you. If you weaken, he'll have you. You'll never get away.*

"Then dream of Curtis," she murmured aloud. "Of sweet Curtis, who was so good, so—innocent." She chuckled. "And had such marvelous staying power."

But this far from Ferny Cove or Oz, to daydream of Curtis was to abrade old wounds. She drank half of the wine before she slept.

Chapter 15: Mariil

They slept in—at least Varia did—had a late breakfast and a later start. Apparently Cyncaidh did not intend to gallop home like an eager schoolboy. They rode through wild and rocky forest for more than three hours when the road—a good road for such wild country—brought them to an extensive opening with farms. Halfway across it stood a building, almost a palace, half seen through shade trees. Cyncaidh pulled aside and turned. "Aaerodh Manor," he said pointing.

His words, his gesture, were for the whole party, but it seemed to Varia he'd addressed mainly her. She was impressed with the size of it, not entirely favorably. To her, a house so large could hardly seem like home. *But it may to him,* she thought. *And I'm not going to live there.*

As they rode on, it held her attention. At least it was handsome, she told herself. Not like the square gray Tudor castles and manors she'd seen pictures of in books, nor the homes of royalty in the Rude Lands. Its designer had been an artist, with a sense of proportion and grace. The walls were white marble, while the roofs were tiled, some green, some red, others blue, their colors saturated. She wondered how often it required cleaning.

Perhaps most interesting, it had no defensive wall, though as they neared it, she could see a tall fence of ornamental black iron pales surrounding the grounds. But the gatehouse, she discovered, had no guards, and the gate was open. They entered, and a graveled lane led them across a green lawn, with flowerbeds, shrubs, and scattered groups of trees. Their approach had been seen, for a major domo met them at the broad steps, a tall, big-framed, uniformed ylf who'd reached the time of decline, his face and figure aging. Nonetheless he shared a strong embrace with the Cyncaidh.

Cyncaidh stepped back. "It's *very* good to see you again, Ahain."

"We've been waiting for the day, Your Excellency."

"How is Mariil?" Cyncaidh spoke with concern.

"Well enough to have visitors, sir. I have no doubt that seeing you"—his glance shifted to Varia then—"and you, my lady, will be better for her than anything else."

"Good," Cyncaidh said. "I'd been afraid. Is she available now?"

"Yes sir. Your messenger arrived last evening before she slept, and her ladyship's been up for some time. She's breakfasted, and waiting for you in her suite I believe."

His mother, Varia thought, *and in her decline, obviously. Why would she be pleased to see me?*

Cyncaidh turned to her. "Varia," he said, "come with me. I want you to meet my wife."

* * *

Bewildered, Varia followed him up stairs she was scarcely aware of, and down a hall she hardly saw. He knocked at a door, which opened almost at once. An ylvin nurse let them in, and they followed her onto a deck where a woman sat in the sun, withered and frail on a lounge seat, wrapped in a robe against a breeze that felt balmy to Varia. It seemed to her Mariil must have been lovely, a decade earlier.

But if her old body was frail, Mariil's spirit showed strong and clear in her aura, which was not depressed by her physical decline. And her ylvin eyes were unclouded; Varia felt thoroughly evaluated by them. "Welcome to Aaerodh Manor," the old woman said. "I'm glad to have you here."

"Thank you. Why?"

The old woman chuckled drily. "Why indeed? I saw strength and endurance in you before you spoke. And the ability to learn, and grow in wisdom. They aren't the same thing, those last two, you know. And I see decency, and an honesty that includes self-honesty. Is that enough for you?"

"Do you see information too? Your husband says he's interested in knowledge he thinks I have. He may overestimate me. I spent more than twenty years on Farside, and I've only been back about sixteen months, most of it as his prisoner or the Dynast's. It may not take long to learn all I know of the Sisterhood, beyond what I suppose you know already."

"Indeed. That's the least of my interest." She turned to Cyncaidh. "Raien, I have questions to ask you. Before we talk to A'duaill. You'll want lunch first, though, I suppose."

"That's right. I'll come again afterward."

Kissing Mariil's dry lips then, he left with Varia, neither of them saying anything, and took her to a study, where he rang a bell. A half-ylf answered, the second steward, and Cyncaidh told him to guide his guest through the book shelves which covered one wall. "I'll be back for you when lunch is ready," he told her. "I need to be sure my men are properly settled."

Varia watched him leave. *Don't try to figure it out, girl,* she told herself. *There's too much you don't know. Just pay attention. It'll sort out for you.*

* * *

After lunch, Varia was taken to Connir A'duaill, who stood as they entered. *The interrogator?* she wondered. A'duaill looked as young as most ylver—yet didn't, the difference lying in his aura, and in eyes that felt as if they'd seen everything, or near enough. She had no doubt he was a master magician like Sarkia; it fit both his aura and eyes. Though he could hardly be as old as the Dynast.

The room had no window; that troubled Varia at once. Light came from a skylight shaft and several oil lamps. And the doors were thick; she could scream herself hoarse without anyone hearing.

On the other hand, the appointments were more or less aesthetic, not threatening at all. There were no straps or ties on the table, no whips or tongs or pan of coals, no Xader or Corgan. Besides herself there were only A'duaill and Cyncaidh, and an ylvin scribe with stacked vellum, and a row of sharpened graphite sticks wrapped in paper—effectively pencils.

Musing, she'd hardly heard Cyncaidh's introductions; hadn't even caught the scribe's name. When he'd finished, he looked at A'duaill. "I presume I'm to go now."

"If you please, Your Excellency." A'duaill turned to Varia as if he'd sensed the flash of fear that came despite herself. And said the right thing: "You'll not be harmed, physically or in spirit. That's not something we do here, and in any case we value you for much more than whatever knowledge you may have."

That again. She peered closely at him. "Then why no windows? I could scream myself to death in here without being heard."

"Ah. It's not to keep sounds in, but out. Sounds and more than sounds would hamper what I do here." He turned to Cyncaidh, who hadn't left yet. "Your Excellency."

Cyncaidh nodded to A'duaill, then to Varia, and left. When the door had closed, A'duaill motioned to an upholstered chair across the table from himself. "If you please, my lady." When she was seated, he took the plain wooden chair across from her.

"Why do you call me 'my lady'?" Varia asked.

"It's a matter of status and courtesy. You're the Cyncaidh's guest."

"Why am I his guest? Beyond whatever information you may get from me."

"My lady, much will be made clear to you after this interrogation's over, I'm sure. I hope to complete it this afternoon," he added pointedly. "And when I've questioned you, I promise to receive your questions in turn. Tomorrow, if you'd like. Now, was your lunch adequate?"

She looked curiously at him. "More than adequate."

"Good. And I believe no ale or wine or spirits were served?"

"Nothing stronger than a tea of some sort."

"Fine. Have you relieved yourself since eating?"

"Just before I came here. What...?"

"When we've begun, it's much better if no interruption is necessary. Now. Do you have anything on your mind? Anything pressing?"

She peered at him quizzically. "Right now I want very much to know what you're going to do."

"Good. Let's find out. Start of interrogation." He said the latter as if it were a formal opening.

"First we need to find your memories and open them to recall. Think of them as being buried. Deeply. Deeply. You'll need to go deep to see them. Imagine they're so deep, you can only get to them by a deep spiral staircase, going down and down...."

She recognized hypnotism; she used it herself. But she relaxed, letting it happen, letting his voice take her more and more deeply.

* * *

In time she woke up groggy, remembering nothing. "Thank you, Varia," A'duaill said. "Welcome back to the waking world. We did well; you've been very helpful. Now, look around the room and tell me something you like."

I don't remember a thing, she thought. She was—not muzzy, but disoriented. A'duaill repeated himself. "Look around the room and tell me something you like."

She scanned slowly, noticing what was there. "That rug on the wall," she said, gesturing. She hadn't noticed it when she'd sat down; *preoccupied*, she told herself. "It's quite handsome."

"Ah yes," said A'duaill. "Look around and tell me something else you like."

"Hmm! The—carving? Sculpture?" She pointed. "The dwarf on the shelf."

"Either term is appropriate. It's carved soapstone. Tell me something else you like."

She looked and frowned. "In that glass pitcher. Is that ice?"

He laughed. ">From our own pond. It's cut each winter and stored in a deep bed of sphagnum moss, in an ice house built of logs. In our northern climate, it lasts from year to year."

Varia frowned. Ice wouldn't last in that pitcher very long. "I didn't notice it before." How long had it been? At least an hour, she decided. Surely that long.

A'duaill smiled. "It wasn't there when you came in. When we finished, I allowed you to rest a few minutes; to 'settle out' as we say, before I brought you back to the present. I had it delivered then. It's a bit after supper, but cook will have something for you. He knows we're done; he sent the ice." He held up a bottle. "Would you like some wine poured over it? There are those who consider that barbaric, but I like it, and the Cyncaidh does too."

After supper!? They'd begun shortly after lunch! She accepted the offer. He poured her only a little, perhaps three ounces. It was as good as Sister-made, she thought, pink and dry, at the edge of sweet. What had he asked? What had she said? The scribe was gone, but presumably he'd written it down, or the gist of it. She doubted anyone could write fast enough to make a verbatim record.

When she'd finished her wine, A'duaill led her to the dining room and left her with the second steward. There she discovered she felt more than hungry. She felt empty! Neither Cyncaidh nor Mariil had eaten with the soldiers; they came in now to eat with her. To the detriment of conversation, she ate like Will after a winter day in the logging woods. And when she finished, felt desperately sleepy, despite having slept, or at least lain unconscious, all afternoon. Something in the wine? A serving girl led her to her room. She was too groggy to bathe. Fifteen minutes after eating, she was in her bed asleep, leaving her clothes for the girl to hang up.

* * *

She slept till well after sunup. The first part of the night had not been restful. She'd dreamed strong unpleasant dreams that brought her half awake repeatedly, only to slip back into continuations. The Tiger barracks had been part of it. And a troll, stalking her babies; when she ran to rescue them, the troll turned into Sarkia, who smiled a loving smile and turned her into a frog. Then Cyncaidh had ridden up and cast a spell that turned her not into a woman again, but into a woman-sized frog. He tried several spells, and she grew larger and smaller but remained a frog. Finally he kissed her and said he loved her, and that he'd take her home with him even if she was a frog.

She recalled being reunited with Curtis, too, only to find

the body on top of her was Xader. That time she'd wakened completely, and gotten out of bed shaking. The oil lamp showed her a small wine bottle, but when she'd raised it to her lips, what she swallowed wasn't wine, but something faintly bitter, some medicine. She'd made a face and stumbled back to bed, this time to sleep deeply and unbrokenly.

* * *

Whatever the drug had been, it left an unpleasant taste. She poured a glass of water and rinsed her mouth, then drank. Her serving girl, an ylf maid named Ardain, came in from the adjoining room.

"Good morning, your ladyship," Ardain said. "I hope you rested well."

Varia assessed how she felt. Neither good nor bad. *A sort of medium gray,* she decided. "Well enough, I guess," she said, and wondered if this girl read auras. Not likely. She also wondered again what A'duaill had learned from her the day before. He'd said he'd answer her questions today. Or no, that wasn't it. He'd said he'd *receive* her questions. *Pin him down,* she told herself.

She bathed, the ylf maid scrubbing her back. What would Liiset say if she could see? She knew what Idri would say, or Sarkia, who as long as Varia could remember, had portrayed the ylver as evil, depraved. She reminded herself then of General Quaie, who'd made the slander convincing. Not that most of the Sisterhood needed convincing; if Sarkia said it, it was so.

I'm well out of all that, she told herself. *The trick now is to get out of* here, *a much more pleasant prison.*

Clean clothing had been put out for her, including a frock hanging at her dresser set. Ardain suggested she wear it this morning. It was lovely, a pale green; she was surprised this house had one so suited to her coloring. *If my hair were long,* she told herself, *I might put it on,* then rejected the thought. It wouldn't do to look too pretty, not where Cyncaidh would see, so she dressed in uniform.

She'd expected to eat breakfast with him, and perhaps Mariil. When they weren't there, she told the steward she'd like to see them after breakfast. Mariil, he answered, usually slept through the morning, and the Cyncaidh was out inspecting the property. *That,* Varia told herself, *could take awhile.* "Then I'd like to speak with A'duaill," she said.

"I'll leave your message with his scribe," the steward answered politely, "but just now, he can't be disturbed."

Varia wondered if she was being put off. It smelled that way. She ended up asking a reluctant Ardain to eat with her, clearly not the sort of thing a serving girl was supposed to do. But perhaps she could answer some questions.

"Why am I being treated so well?" Varia asked. "I was brought here a prisoner, you know."

"A prisoner? No ma'am, I didn't know that." Ardain seemed to doubt the claim.

"Why do you *imagine* I'm being treated so well?"

Ardain was uncomfortable now. "The Cyncaidh is a gentleman, and thoughtful, my lady."

He's that, all right, Varia told herself, *but it doesn't answer my question. Besides, Ardain sweetie, you know something you're not telling me.* She tried another angle. "Ahain told me Mariil would be happy to see me, or something to that effect. Why would he say that, do you suppose? She'd never met me."

The ylf maid's discomfort clearly was growing. "I don't know, my lady."

But you suspect, Varia thought, then told herself to leave the girl alone; she'd hardly tell anyway. "Are you from around here?" she asked.

"Yes, my lady, from Salmon Cove. My family fishes. And harvests seals in their season."

"That sounds interesting. How did you come to work here at the manor?"

"My uncle's been with the Cyncaidh's household troops since he was eighteen. He's first sergeant now," she added proudly. "So I got interviewed by Lady Mariil. I've been here since I was fifteen."

"I'll bet they like you; I do. How old are you?"

"Seventeen."

"Suppose you want to get married? Or are those things arranged for you?"

Ardain blushed. "Noble girls get husbands arranged for them sometimes, though they can refuse. For folk like us though, fisher folk or farmers, it's usual to marry a lad who catches your eye." She laughed. "The boy's supposed to ask the girl, but a girl can get him to, if she wants."

"And do the lords ever, um, impose on a girl who works in the house? A lord or his sons?"

Ardain darkened. "Never!" she said.

"I don't mean you, Ardain, or the Cyncaidh. I was thinking about households less well regulated. Less honorable. I'm a stranger in your land, you know."

This mollified the girl somewhat. "I've heard of such, I'll admit," she said, "but it wouldn't happen here. If the Cyncaidh had sons, and they—troubled a serving girl, he'd discipline them severely, I have no doubt."

If the Cyncaidh had sons. "I suppose he would. He's considerate of others." *A noble without sons, whose wife is far beyond child-bearing.* "Thank you for answering my questions, Ardain. I think I'll go to the study now."

Vordan, the second steward, took her, and at her request, showed her the shelf on local and family history, then left her to herself.

* * *

Varia ate in the small dining room. Would have eaten alone, if she hadn't again requested Ardain's company. The second steward acquiesced gracefully. Clearly there was no taboo connected with it; it was simply something out of the ordinary. Varia could see the value of not hobnobbing with the help. If the staff was like part of the family, there'd be little privacy, and the distinctions between duties and personal relationships could get badly blurred. But she was a guest, and wanted company.

When she and Ardain sat down alone, she asked Vordan when she might talk with the Cyncaidh, or A'duaill, or Lady Mariil. Vordan brought the steward, who promised to get her a more specific answer. He was back before she'd gotten to dessert. The Cyncaidh, he said, was with A'duaill and the Lady Mariil in

A'duaill's office, where they'd had lunch as they worked, and would remain till they were finished. She'd be informed at once when they were.

In the study again, Varia did as much thinking as browsing. She'd found nothing about any gate in this part of the world. Were there gates in the empire? If there were, Ylver could safely pass through, at least those with talent. What regulations and policies might they have?

From auras she'd seen in the empire, most ylver had only modest talents, probably because among commoners, breedings weren't arranged. Apparently they weren't among noble families, either, but nobility might originally have been a function of talent. In which case, if nobles married nobles more or less exclusively, most noble children would be born with substantial talent, and no doubt be trained to use it.

Fertility was a problem among the ylver; that was well known to the Sisterhood. Sarulin, the founder and first Dynast, had been ylvin, a sorceror's daughter in the court of a high noble. At least in those days, ylvin nobles sometimes warred on each other, took other ylver captive and made slaves of them. And if the story was true, Sarulin had been such a captive. Beautiful red-haired Sarulin; among the mostly black-haired ylver, she'd been conspicuous. Her captor, who was also red-haired, had raped her—impregnated her at any rate—and the story was that he'd been an exceptional magician.

Sarulin had already decided to escape and start a rebel movement, and with her powers, she'd known almost as soon as it happened that she'd conceived. So she'd undertaken to manipulate the microscopic creature in her uterus to produce a multiple birth, something that had never been tried before, and she'd succeeded. Then she'd run away with her master's discontented son, also very gifted.

Or so the story went, and the truth might well have been something like that.

Varia wondered again what A'duaill's questions had been. Had he learned how fertile her clone was? That among the Sisterhood, multiple births were a learned skill? Had he learned how it was done? Was that why she'd been brought here?

* * *

She had her audience with him that afternoon, and didn't ask any of those questions. Perhaps later, but just now...Her loyalty to the Sisterhood had been battered since her kidnapping from Farside. But on the other hand, while clearly the ylver were not an evil race, they had their Quaies in high places. Thus she didn't want them learning to do what Sisters routinely did—produce litters.

If A'duaill hadn't learned about this already, to ask would result in another interrogation. Then he'd surely know.

So she asked instead how such interrogations were done. When the person was deeply enough in trance, he said, they'd answer any question, if it was skillfully put. The trick was to ask the right questions. This he did by reading the aura. A skilled questioner could see and interpret its responses to questions, and use them, along with the answers, to guide further questioning.

"And what will the result be of our session together?" Varia asked. "What is my status here now?"

"My lady, you are still the Cyncaidh's honored guest. Beyond that, you'll have to ask him."

"Honored guest? I'd thought of myself as his well-treated prisoner."

A'duaill seemed honestly pained at that; troubled at least. "I can see why you might think so, my lady. Let me suggest you speak with Lady Mariil about it. The Cyncaidh is involved for the rest of the day, and I know Lady Mariil hoped to talk with you after supper, her strength permitting. She's resting just now; sleeping I suspect. The day has taxed her quite severely."

Varia returned to Cyncaidh's study looking forward to the evening. It seemed to her she was getting close to learning what she needed to know. The trick would be to make an ally of Mariil. Perhaps they'd agree to let her go through and bring Curtis back with her. To the empire. If they wanted her as a brood mare, maybe they'd be interested in another unusually fertile blood line—fertile by the standards of ylver and the Sisterhood. She'd promise it, if necessary. But what she and Curtis decided when they were together again might be another matter.

* * *

The book she pulled from a shelf was *The Western Empire, from the Reign of Braighn the Red to the Time of Troubles.* She found it fascinating; not least to learn that among this raven-haired people there'd been redheads well before Sarulin and her captor, notably Braighn the First. Who was fascinating, although the ylver he ruled might have used another adjective. If Sarulin was of Braighn's lineage, it would explain her ruthless strength as well as her red hair.

From time to time, Varia encountered something in its pages that brought her own situation to mind. Affairs and jealousies had played significant roles in ylvin politics then. Probably they still did. And apparently, Cyncaidh wanted, intended, to make her his mistress. Apparently Mariil knew it—apparently the household staff did too—and approved. Certainly the family Cyncaidh would want an heir, preferably male, and preferably of fertile lineage, with demonstrated talent. From what she'd read these last two days, adoption was often resorted to, though historically, adopted sons were less readily accepted in matters of political power.

What would the Cyncaidh and Mariil think of Curtis Macurdy as a sire to adoptive children? Unfortunately, Curtis showed no clear ylvin traits, aside from his untrained talent and minimal body hair. Her tentative optimism of earlier that day looked—unwarranted—given what she'd just read.

Still she'd present the idea, and see what the response was.

* * *

She wasn't good company for Ardain at supper. *Being company for Ardain isn't your job,* she reminded herself, then wondered what was. When they'd finished dessert and she still hadn't heard from Mariil, she decided to have a hot bath, and dismissed Ardain for the day. When she'd finished bathing, she dressed in her uniform again, and was sitting on her balcony appreciating the sunset, when someone rapped. The steward this time.

"Lady Varia," he said, "the Lady Mariil would be pleased

to have your company in her suite. In twenty minutes, if that's suitable."

Why not now? she asked herself. *As if I haven't waited long enough already.* She shook the thought off irritably. *Don't be petty, Varia Macurdy. She gave you the twenty minutes so you could be ready without hurrying.*

"Thank you. Do I go myself, or—?"

"Annith will come for you, if that's all right my lady."

"That'll be fine."

He turned and left. Twenty minutes. Her eyes lit on the dress that had been hung for her that morning; she'd had Ardain leave it out. *That,* she thought. *I'll wear it. Dressed as a soldier, I invite orders. Let her see me as a woman like herself.*

She took off her uniform, then her underclothes, and looked at herself in the mirror. She'd grown up among Sisters where youth seemed almost eternal. But among them, on the onset of decline, a Sister was removed from the community, sent to spend her remaining five to ten years at a retreat "in the south," where no one visited. A practice that grew out of Sarkia's unwilling-ness to confront the loss of vigor and life, Varia thought wryly. At least the ylver honored their elderly.

As for herself—her critical eyes could find no fault with what she saw. Mother of forty-three, wife of two, and abused re-peatedly by a squad of Tigers for how many months. The correct ylvin genes, unhindered by counter-beliefs, healed most wounds short of mutilation or death. *You still look twenty,* she told her-self. *Except for the eyes and aura, I suppose, and most don't confront the one or see the other. So here you are, coveted as a brood mare by an ylvin high noble.*

She dressed and looked again. It wasn't a formal gown, but a dinner frock. Still, she'd never had so nice a dress in her life before, not even for her first wedding. She didn't pirouette in it though, just looked. *God,* she thought, *I'm beautiful after all. Truly beautiful, except for that wretched short hair. Curtis, oh Curtis, I wish you could see me in this.*

She felt the damned tears begin to well, and would have changed back into her uniform, except for the knock at her door.

"Come," she said. Mariil's nurse opened it, and Varia left with her, to the east wing and Lady Cyncaidh's suite. Mariil looked up when they entered, and her expression softened visibly when she saw Varia in the frock. She didn't stand, but motioned Varia to a chair in front of hers. "You are truly beautiful," she said softly. "More beautiful than I realized."

"You wanted to talk to me."

Mariil nodded. "To you, with you, about you. I've read the transcript of your interrogation, and there was much personal history in it. You are—even more remarkable than I'd appreciated. Even stronger. Raien had already told me what he knew of you—how he found you after your flight through the wilderness; of your assault on him when he wouldn't free you to find your Curtis; and of your swim. I was impressed. But the things we learned through A'duaill…"

"I trust there was more to it than my life history."

"Much more. Much of use to Raien in planning."

"Planning?"

Mariil shook her head. "We could talk about that for days. And will, I hope. Just now I want to talk about you and Raien."

"Your husband."

"My husband. The man I've loved since I first saw him when he was what he looks now to be: a youth in his early twenties." She smiled at Varia then. "I was seventy-two, and quite lovely. At least I thought so, and I'd been hearing it all my life. My first husband was a pleasant and thoughtful man, if a bit careless with the maids, but Raien— And Erig was in decline.

"Raien, it seemed, was as smitten with me as I with him. I was much older, of course, and we knew that barring violence or accident, the time would come…" She gestured to herself. "The time would come that has."

Varia kept aloof, as best she could. "And you've produced no heir in those thirty or so years."

"Twenty-nine years last equinox."

"You've had the man you love for twenty-nine years. I had mine for a few weeks."

The reply seemed to shrink Mariil, and for a long moment

she didn't answer, then nodded. "But it wouldn't work," she said, "even if you could reach him. Your Dynast knows only that you fled. And where to? To Curtis Macurdy or your death." Again Mariil paused. "Your Dynast is ancient and unrelenting. She doesn't easily give up what she thinks of as hers. She'd send someone after you. Idri perhaps."

The thought jarred Varia. She'd recognized the possibility once, then pushed it away out of sight. Oregon. Suppose they went to Oregon. Could Idri sniff her out so far? Could a tracker?

"Your Dynast still has allies," Mariil was saying. "She'll have sent Idri to Oz, with a strong escort from some friendly king, probably Gurtho of Tekalos. With a request to hold you, if you showed up. But not to Ferny Cove; that would be too dangerous."

Mariil's expression was bleak, grim. "Then Idri would go through the Oz Gate with three or four guardsmen to hunt you, and if you'd gotten through, you'd be taken, you and your Curtis. Unless he fought. Then he'd be killed."

Unless he fought. And he would. But he wasn't trained to it; and probably they'd catch him with no weapon. Varia felt herself taut, vibrating like a fiddle string.

"The Cyncaidh could take me there," she said. The words tumbled out of her more rapidly than she'd intended. "With a company of soldiers. Let me get Curtis and bring him through. Then we could live here—you could let us have a servant's cottage—and produce sons and daughters for you. You could choose one of them to adopt. Or more than one."

Mariil shook her head slowly. The discussion and emotions had taxed her strength. "It wouldn't work," she said. "Not for the Cyncaidh, and not for you. It was possible for him to slip around in the Rude Lands with a few half-ylver who could pass as locals. But to ride in with a company—they'd hardly come back alive, certainly not from Ferny Cove. Your captured Sisters weren't the only ones savaged there. The fighting was fierce, and Quaie took no prisoners. Vertorus was quartered, and his body thrown to the dogs. His sole surviving son, Keltorus, has sworn his enmity forever, though being an ill-tongued drunkard of a short-lived family, his *forever* might be shorter than he thinks. He's ordered no Sister be allowed within the borders of Kormehr, and any trespass be referred to him for punishment. I can guess what it would be—death, but not quick."

Frowning, Varia gnawed a lip. "And you want me for a brood mare, for Cyncaidh himself to sire his sons on."

"We want you to be Lady Cyncaidh."

Varia stared. "His wife?"

"His wife. I'm in the process of dying, as you see. And he needs more than heirs. To have a blood heir is desirable, but Raien wants and deserves more than that, believe me."

She paused, seeming to gather strength. "Besides, my dear, he loves you." Again she paused. "I'm an old soul, Varia, with many earlier lifetimes whispering to me. Wisps of wisdom, when I manage to hear and recognize them. And I have no doubt you were born to this. I'll be dead within months. I've been declining for more than seven years now, and am very near the end. The Cyncaidh, on the other hand, is fifty-three, and his line tends to longer lives than most."

She paused, looking piercingly at Varia. "Not that I'm useless yet; certainly not to you. I'm a healer of the spirit, and yours has cruel wounds, not healed, just scarred over." She waved a hand as if impatient with herself. "Back to the issue. Like myself, the Emperor's Chief Counselor has reached his decline, though he may continue in office for another year or three. And the Cyncaidh is likeliest to replace him, for when Paedhrig was Chief Counselor, and Raien his aide, they were haft and blade, two parts of one instrument.

"Our Emperor is eighty-four himself now, and the Diet most often elects the Chief Counselor to the throne, if he's served well. But meanwhile, as Chief Counselor, Raien would start a healing. More than a healing: the spread of trade and learning and peace in the Rude Lands—something made more difficult by that lunatic Quaie. Peace even with the Sisterhood; Sarkia can't live forever. And closer at hand, he'd promote civility within the empire."

Varia shook her head, not disagreeing but overwhelmed—

this was too much too fast.

"Meanwhile he's taken no mistress during my decline, though I've suggested it to him. Until he knew you, there was none he wanted." Mariil got laboriously to her feet. "Come, Varia. I'm tired. Even talking tires me these days. And a go-between should take such matters only so far. Let him ask you himself."

As if hypnotized again, Varia stood. "There is something else I must tell you," Mariil said. "Something he cannot and would not. That he is a very good man: kind, considerate, and loving. He is still loving to me. Not in bed of course, bag of bones that I am. Let him remember what I was like in bed in decades past: smooth and supple and full of life." She put her hand on the door handle. "Hmh! I ramble."

Together they walked down the hall to the Cyncaidh's private apartment, and Mariil knocked.

"Come!"

Before she touched the handle, she turned and kissed Varia's cheek, a quick dry touch. "I hope you'll be happy, whatever you decide." Then she opened, turned away, and left Varia standing there alone. The Cyncaidh had gotten to his feet and started to the door. He too had exchanged his uniform for less formal wear.

He stopped in his tracks. "God," he breathed. "Varia, you're beautiful!"

She looked down at herself, then at him.

"Come in! Come in!" he said. She did, and he closed the door behind her. "Mariil's told you what I want?"

"Yes."

"That I want you as my wife, when she's gone? And as my mistress now?"

"The first, yes. The latter she implied."

Reaching, he touched her cheek. "I fell in love with you when I first saw you on that mountain pass, deep inside the Rude Lands."

Varia's voice was quiet, almost emotionless. "There are beautiful ylvin women who'd bring a dowry of wealth and connections."

"I know. Since Mariil's decline became known, a few have

courted me, or their fathers or brothers have. But it's you I want to spend my life with. I have no doubt it's our destiny, for I wanted you before I really knew you." He chuckled. "I wanted you when your face and clothes were grimy, and your hair only this long." He indicated half an inch.

Varia failed to smile. "Before you really knew me. Do you know me yet? Really?"

He sobered. "I think I do. I've been on the trail with you. Seen you under stress, seen your aura, and read the transcript of A'duaill's interrogation. And beyond that, there's a knowing that goes deeper than seeing."

"You know I love someone else."

"I do know, and I'm content with it. He must be good, for you to love him."

Good and innocent. But I wonder how Curtis would feel to share me with you. Though I've been overshared already, if not of my own will.

The Cyncaidh put a hand on her waist and gently but firmly drew her close. She did not resist. "It is my wish," he said, "to love you so long as we both shall live."

So long as we both shall live. She'd heard those words before, in English. Had said them. Tears began to flow, silent as always. Cyncaidh kissed first them, then her lips, and she responded the way she'd feared she might.

She did not return to her room that night, nor on any night thereafter.

Chapter 16: Reflections in a Prenuptial Bed

General Lord Raien Cyncaidh lay on his side, staring motionless at the glowing coals in his fireplace. This far north, a night fire was usual in summer, and rather often, when he was at home, he let watching it lull him to sleep.

Tonight, though, he felt no sleepiness at all, despite more than an hour of love-making. Good love-making, it seemed to him. It had gripped him, lifted him, held him aloft, then spent him. Twice. The first time it hadn't worked for Varia, though it had started well; Curtis Macurdy had gotten in the way. But the second time she'd climaxed despite herself, with urgent movements and sharp cries, her strong clutching fingers digging hard in his back.

Then his joy had turned to dismay, for her climax ended in tears and bitter sobbing. "Curtis," she'd wept, "oh Curtis, I'm sorry. I'm so sorry." Over and over, till she'd run down and slept.

Earlier, when they'd stood in his parlor and kissed, when they'd come into this room and undressed, and gazed at each other, and when he'd caressed her and she'd begun to move beneath his hands, it had promised to be one of the most beautiful, fulfilling nights of his life. And when at last they'd merged in climax, it seemed the promise had been met.

He hadn't imagined it might affect her as it did. He'd thought that once she'd consented, everything would be beautiful. And she did love him; over the weeks, he'd seen it in her aura. But not tonight; tonight there'd been first despair, then yielding, participation, and at length passion. But not love. And afterward—afterward guilt and grief. Obviously, as she saw it, she'd betrayed not only her husband on Farside, but her dreams and her sense of loyalty.

They'd caught her between them, he and Mariil, in a sense had trapped her, then worked on her from both sides. They'd broken her dream of reaching Curtis Macurdy, taken away her hope, then had set himself before her as her only option.

Even Mariil hadn't foreseen the result, he was sure.

After all that had happened to her—imprisonment, fists, knife tips, raped nightly for months—they hadn't imagined that this evening with him, whom she loved, would cause her grief. But in the Tiger barracks, helpless and brutalized, she'd withheld herself in mind and spirit. While tonight she'd *given* herself: body and soul. That was the difference, he had no doubt. It was giving herself that spawned remorse and grief.

He'd rushed things, overridden her uncertainty and scruples, taken advantage of her vulnerability and despair. Perhaps—hopefully—it had been for the best, but...He'd back off now, apologize honestly, let her evaluate and adjust. When she felt ready...

To a degree they'd lied to her, had exaggerated the hopelessness and danger. In part to keep her from harm, for in fact she could well be killed trying. Given Keltorus' hatred of the Sisterhood, she'd almost surely have been killed, brutally, if she'd continued alone to Ferny Cove. But their primary motive had been to convince her to stay and marry. The odds, he judged, would have been no worse than even—probably better—if he'd sent a squad riding with her to Oz, there to smuggle her to the gate. Volunteers wearing wadmal like tribesmen. He could have. He still could.

But he wasn't going to. Certainly not now.

He turned his attention from his thoughts to the lovely woman sleeping at his back. Listened to her quiet breathing, then carefully turned his head and looked at her. Her aura remained somewhat shrunken, though the colors had cleared a bit, pulsing lightly in dream. Apparently a healing dream. Resilient! She'd had to be to get through this past—what? Sixteen months. Looking at her, he felt love and compassion. And commitment.

In the morning he'd tell Mariil what had happened tonight. No one healed the spirit more skillfully than Mariil, and she admired Varia as much as he.

I love you, Varia, he thought to her, *and I'll make you happy. I swear it. I won't try to make you forget your Curtis, but I'll do all I can to make you happy with me.*

Her aura didn't react to his thought; she was too deep in dream, perhaps of Curtis Macurdy. He wondered what the Farside farmer was doing, after more than a year. How ironic—reasonable but ironic—if the man had settled down on his farm with a new wife. Had he known, really, what a remarkable—what an admirable woman he'd married?

PART 3: The Lion Grows Claws

Chapter 17: Sword, Spear, and Bow

After work, three days later, Hauser sent Macurdy to Arbel's workshop. Seemingly casual, the shaman stood up when the slave came in. "What is my mood?" he asked.

Macurdy's attention focused. "By your eyes, you seem relaxed. By your aura—you're hiding something. Not unpleasant, but—" Macurdy shrugged.

"Fine. Of course, you've been concealing something from me recently, too. Nothing discreditable, but you've been doing something and not saying anything about it."

"Yes sir. Almost every day recently, I've been visited about noon by a tomttu and a great raven. We've exchanged stories and information about our worlds."

The shaman's eyebrows arched. "Ah! You've been privileged! I've never met a tomttu myself. Nor exchanged as much as a greeting with a great raven; they are highly respected, you know. The popular belief is, they're the spirits of shamans awarded a lifetime of freedom from cares and human limitations. It's said that even goshawks don't molest them." Arbel chuckled. "We shamans tell our people to put meat scraps out when a great raven is in the district. Looking to our own future, you see. Though seemingly they prefer to scavenge for themselves.

"But I believe they're gone now. Right?"

Macurdy nodded. "Maikel left to winter in the Diamond

Mountains with his family. Blue Wing went east to sheep country; more scavenging there."

Arbel laughed. "Well. I have news that may or may not please you. Please you, I trust. But first, light my fireplace."

Macurdy went to it, knelt, and with a pass of a hand, caused the kindling to burst into flame.

"Good. And your reading of auras is developing nicely—a rare and useful skill. With use, it should improve without further instruction. Anything else you've noticed?"

"In the way of magic? I saw through the tomttu's invisibility spell. I heard him laugh, and when I looked, there he was."

"Hmh! Very good. You can expect similar surprises from time to time. In many respects you have proven an excellent student, but as a healer…"

Macurdy recalled the sick and injured farm animals Arbel had had him try to heal. In a few there'd been healing or marked improvement, but usually not. And twice he'd been assigned to heal humans—once a severe rash and once a wry neck, examples of things that, according to Arbel, were readily healed by magic. When the patients returned the next day unrelieved, Arbel had taken them into his workshop one at a time, for ten or fifteen minutes each, and banished their conditions then and there.

"It seems clear to me," Arbel continued, "that being a shaman is not your destiny, but neither is the slave crew. So we will try something else and see what happens. You will continue at your present work, living with Charles so he may continue to help you with our language. You use it well enough now for ordinary purposes, but I see in you—possibilities I cannot identify. So I want you truly fluent. And instead of my working with you in the evenings, you will train with our militia, in the skills of war."

The shaman raised an eyebrow. "I see that pleases you. Good. It was no little trouble to get approval for this; you are, after all, a slave. Sergeant Friisok spoke for you, or I would certainly have failed. It was he who captured you when you came through the world gate. He said you showed presence of mind, toughness, boldness, and measured judgment. And Captain

Isherhohm, in turn, values the sergeant's judgment."

Arbel paused, his gaze calm. "Wolf Springs is a proud district. And as we are not satisfied with an ordinary shaman here, neither are we satisfied with an ordinary militia. Captain Isherhohm demands diligence and strict obedience, and our militia is the best of any in Oz, including Oztown itself. But from your aura, I have no doubt you will excel in this training, and who knows what good may come of it."

* * *

The district militia were infantry, and consisted of three categories: novices, youths, and veterans. The novices, who trained four evenings a week, included all able-bodied fourteen-year-old boys, and worked primarily on weapons skills. Youths aged fifteen to twenty trained twice a week on weapons skills, and twice on fighting drills and tactics. Veterans trained only once a week.

The novices already had four months training when Macurdy joined them. Emphasis was on the spear and sword, as most had been practicing with the bow from age four, as play, and were skilled with it. Among them, Macurdy was a giant in strength, and the story of how he'd almost killed a guard, the day he was captured, was already known around the district—thanks to the man's family, which had asked approval to kill or at least maim the new slave. But their brother had a reputation as a sadistic idiot, and good slaves were valuable, and when the father hinted he and his sons might take matters into their own hands, the headman had threatened floggings and ruinous fines.

As a novice, Macurdy quickly demonstrated excellent weapons talent. His coordination and quickness to learn were outstanding. Within weeks he showed more skill than any other novice with spear and sword. And with the shield, which was worn slung on the back, and used only in sword drill.

From the beginning he could draw the heaviest bow, and after only a month, his accuracy approached ordinary for novices. While he matched almost any of the veterans in the number of practice arrows shot successfully into a target area in a given time—timed by a small sand glass. When the target area was at extreme ranges, he was almost unmatched.

At the end of four weeks, he was promoted to the youth level. However, on two additional evenings he was required to continue his weapons training under a hardbitten, partially disabled sergeant whose usual job was to coach and browbeat those who needed extra sessions.

By late winter—the end of Two-Month—Macurdy showed substantially higher skill with both spear and sword than anyone else at the youth level, and his accuracy with the bow was quite good. As for tactics, he'd already seen improvements that could be made, but diplomatically kept them to himself. His reaction time and concentration became notorious, yet no one showed resentment, for there was no vanity or arrogance in him, only good nature.

Arbel had given Hauser the use of a large, heavy-bladed knife to cut branches of shrubs and trees whose leaves or buds, flowers or inner bark, had medicinal value. At Macurdy's request, Hauser loaned it to him in the evenings, and Macurdy practiced throwing it at a log shed for ten or fifteen minutes in the dark. Always, as Hauser told Arbel, returning it razor sharp. Although the knife was not at all balanced for throwing, Macurdy was soon able to stick it reliably and deeply into an area the size of a man's torso, at distances out to twenty feet.

While at his lunchtime in the forest, he almost always spent a few minutes throwing the axe at some large-boled tree. And like any Ozian woodcutter or Hoosier logger, carried a file and stone to remove nicks and dullness. By winter's end, he could reliably sink this unorthodox weapon deeply into the wood at the height of a man's chest.

He felt good about it all. It wasn't the sort of thing he'd been brought up to, certainly not by his mother. The Macurdies didn't much hold with violence, except in games. Or self defense, and the need was rare, given the Macurdy reputation for size, strength, and quickness.

But this wasn't Washington County.

In fact, he found himself exhilarated by his emerging skills. He had no doubt at all that when summer came, he'd leave Wolf

Springs. Run away, travel eastward to the Kingdom of the Silver Mountain, and take Varia away from Idri or whoever had her. He was a warrior now, and if someone tried to stop him, too bad for them.

Once they were back on Farside, there'd be time enough for peace. Peace and love and children. But first, he told himself, he'd have to bring it about. Earn it.

* * *

With the last new moon at hand before the spring equinox, Captain Isherhohm took him aside. "Macurdy," he said (as a slave, it was all the name Macurdy had there), "we're sending you to Oztown. It's where the Chief has his house and farm. He also has a company of Heroes; a hundred, more or less. Only the best from the districts are chosen for it, and Wolf Springs already has more than any other in its ranks."

Macurdy's brows rose. He'd heard the Heroes talked about, but hadn't thought a slave could be chosen. And they were cavalry. Though trained to ride to battle, then dismount and fight, they were also trained to fight in the saddle. This was an opportunity to expand and improve his warrior skills.

"Both Friisok and myself were Heroes in our youth," Isherhohm went on. "You serve for six years, then usually return to your village. Heroes have no other duties than to train, and to serve the chief as his personal troops. You can bring credit to Wolf Springs, and when you return, you'll be a free man. Given a good farm with oxen and good saddle horses, and slave girls to father children on. If you bring home a spear maiden, it'll be a large farm, with slaves enough, you won't have to lift a hand in labor."

He paused. "Captain," Macurdy said, "I thank you. I'm indebted to you for all you've taught me." *And to repay you,* he added silently, *I'm going to run away before the summer's over. Probably make you look bad, and kill the chance of any slave being chosen in the future. But if there's some way I can make it up to you later, I will.*

He couldn't even imagine what that way might be, but his intention was honest. If it was possible, he would.

* * *

After a day's ride, Macurdy arrived at Oztown, escorted there by Friisok. There were perhaps twenty Hero candidates loitering outside the split plank building that housed and officed the company's officers: Captain Palkio, the commander; his aide; and the two platoon commanders. The captain tested each candidate, requiring a demonstration of spear forms and sword forms, followed by sparring with one of the Heroes assigned that day for the purpose. Macurdy was passed without hesitation, despite Palkio's eyebrows rising at a slave being sent. It seemed to Macurdy the Ozmen were pretty sensible about their slaves. Property was property. You took decent care of it, and used it to good advantage.

All but one of the candidates passed. Macurdy was assigned to 2nd Platoon, whose recruits fell in behind their corporal, and marched to the longhouse that would be their home.

Chapter 18: House of Heroes

When the recruits arrived at the 2nd Platoon long house, the platoon was absent, except for the corporal who'd guided them, and three men who'd helped test them. There Corporal Jeremid talked to them about their new life. They would, he said, become not only the best fighting men in the tribe, but the best in the world. And they had the toughest sergeant in the world; he'd beaten a man to death with his bare fists once, for backflashing him.

In the Rude Lands, most months are divided into four weeks of seven days each, with freedays at the end so that each month begins with the new moon. (Twelve-Month and One-Month are trimmed and patched so One-Month begins on the New Moon nearest the Winter Solstice. The system lacks elegance, but suits their needs.) On six days of the standard week, the Heroes trained to improve their weapons and tactical skills, and the novices learned horsemanship.

Most Ozian farmers owned no more than a single horse—some plowed with their milk cow—and few new Heroes were satisfactory horsemen. So each morning of their rookie month, the novices were taken out to ride across rough pastures and through forest. At no more than a trot to begin with, later at a canter and eventually a gallop. When they could gallop break-neck through forested hills without losing control, they were ready to hunt.

Jeremid's eyes glistened in the telling. Hunting, he said, was the high point of training. They'd ride behind hounds, pursuing whatever game they put up—fox, wolf, bear, the great and small cats—with the Heroes hurtling after them. Most deaths or cripplings in training were from hunting accidents: a neck or head broken by a low branch, a horse failing to clear a blow-down, even a jaguar brought to bay and charging. Heroes were forbidden to use a bow against large prey, he went on; it was considered cowardly. The spear was the kill weapon, with only one man wielding it.

The training days, he told them, started at sunup and con-tinued till dusk. During the week, drinking was forbidden, ex-cept for a large mug of ale served nightly with supper. But after supper on Six-Day, the slave girls were brought in. Slave girls selected for Heroes, good-looking girls who considered it a priv-ilege. So the corporal said. It was a party for the girls as well as the Heroes, and it gave them favored status, sparing them the more disagreeable jobs between parties. And on Six-Day night, there was all a man could drink, spirits as well as ale. Seven-Day was given to recovering.

As the corporal described it, Macurdy decided he'd have to sneak out. He'd be true to Varia in spite of all.

Meanwhile it was One-Day. He had five days to come up with a strategy.

* * *

He found it easy, adjusting to a Hero's workday life. You just did it. Riding was the aspect he'd felt concern over. He'd ridden horses all his life, both in the saddle, and bareback on work horses. But back home, riding had pretty much amounted to plodding. Now and then, mainly as adolescents, they'd raced on a road or in a pasture, hopefully when no one's pa or ma or sister was watching, but that was about it. So the notion of gal-loping headlong through forest and brush was sobering.

All the new trainees were skilled with weapons, though probably few at throwing the ax, or even the knife. (Hauser and Arbel had given him the knife he'd learned on, as a parting gift.) But here they learned additional techniques, with spear, sword, and shield, techniques well beyond those taught to militia. And from the first, the infantry tactics they drilled included tactics more refined than he'd learned before. Thus Macurdy discovered he hadn't been as skilled as he'd thought.

On the other hand, the horsemanship training wasn't as hair-raising as he'd expected. Most of the other new Heroes were no more skilled in the saddle than he, and the training was pitched accordingly.

* * *

By the end of his first week, he'd improved a lot—and had his strategy for avoiding the Six-Day evening orgy. It was simple enough: Heroes had access to the several Oztown shamans, which gave him somewhere to go. So he told his platoon sergeant his back was seizing up on him. Sergeant Zassfel scowled but gave his approval, and Macurdy left. On the premise it was best to go to the top, he'd already learned which shaman was regarded as most powerful. When he got there, though, he said nothing about his back. His hope was to be accepted as a student on Six-Day evenings.

He told the shaman an edited version of his history with Arbel, but this man was no Arbel. He was haughty and unimpressed, and sent Macurdy on his way. Bumpkin soldiers and rural shamans were beneath his interest. So Macurdy found a decrepit, abandoned outbuilding not too far from the longhouses, and spent the rest of the night there.

At early dawn he awoke from cold, not for the first time, and went to the 2nd Platoon longhouse. The place buzzed with snoring, and smelled of vomit and rut. By dawnlight and the glow from the fireplaces, he saw the bodies of Heroes and slave girls, most of them naked, lying singly or more or less entwined on low beds, floor and tables. In some obscure corner, two of them had reengaged, grunting and moaning, the sound stimulating Macurdy sexually. *Yes,* he thought, *it's a good thing I wasn't here last evening. I'd have never held out.*

* * *

Next Six-Day, not having come up with a better strategy, he again used that ancient military complaint, the bad back. Zassfel eyed him skeptically. "Again? If this keeps up, I'm sending you back to the slave crew. Heroes don't have bad backs."

The man's aura reflected irritation and hostility, but not suspicion. "Yes, sergeant. I never had it before, and I'd just as soon never have it again. If this time doesn't take care of it for good, I'll tell you so you can get rid of me."

Zassfel, who was larger than Macurdy, jutted his jaw. "All right. This one time. Jeremid says you're the best of the new men, otherwise I wouldn't put up with it. Now get out of my sight!"

Macurdy got. He tried a different shaman, but the man's aura showed little psionic talent; he might or might not be a competent herbalist. This time Macurdy spent the night in a hayloft, which risked discovery by someone at morning chores but was a lot better sleeping.

* * *

Many in the new training class found themselves attracted by Macurdy's charisma. All his life his peers had tended to look up to him, more so since Arbel had freed him of the false modesty imposed by his upbringing. In addition he was older than the other rookies, twenty-six compared to their twenty or twenty-one.

Macurdy, in turn, particularly liked Corporal Jeremid, a third-year Hero from Oztown itself. Jeremid was nearly as tall as he, and if somewhat less powerfully built, was exceptionally athletic. His principal duty was teaching horsemanship to the recruits.

The next Six-Day was the first time the rookies hunted, riding with the veterans, galloping recklessly through woods and brushy bottomlands, while the hounds bayed on the trail of a jaguar. Finally they brought it to bay in a broad-crowned oak, to snarl down from a branch well up in the crown. The hounds circled, necks craned, their trail song become a clamor.

Zassfel looked around. "Macurdy!" he shouted, "take your spear and drive him down out of there."

Even the veterans found the order hard to believe. "Yes sergeant," he called back, mind racing. *Drive him down out of there!* he echoed mentally. *What an ass!* It seemed to him he'd better take his shield, too, so he left it slung on his back.

"Gester," he said to one of the others, "hold my spear till I get up in there." Then, while the others watched, he rode to the oak. Leaning his hands on the thick trunk, he stood up on the horse's back, grasped the only branch he could reach, and pulled himself up, then regained his spear from Gester. Sliding it through the back of his sword belt left both hands free, and he began to clamber up through the branches, doing his best not to catch the spear on a branch, or dislodge his shield.

No one spoke, not even Zassfel. *Not even any horseshit advice,* Macurdy told himself grimly. *They don't have any more idea of how to do this than I do.* He stopped about fifteen feet short of the cat, which had been hissing at him the whole way. *So far, so good,* he thought eyeing it, *but if you come for me now, I don't have a prayer.* He withdrew the spear, an awkward job. "One hand for climbing, one for the cat," he muttered. "This is the shits!" Sweating with tension, he climbed one branch higher, paused, and reaching with the spear, poked at the jaguar. Its hiss swelled, and swatting, it cut its paw unexpectedly on the blade, almost knocking the weapon from Macurdy's hand. *Shit!* he thought, *got to get closer.* His heart drummed in his rib cage, but his hands were steady. *One branch more and see what happens.*

The cat began to back out on its branch, flattened to it. *Just what I need: two hundred pounds of spotted cat out on a limb, with me between him and the trunk.* He stopped on a branch about five feet below the cat, stood on it, and edged outward. The cat moved up one, but didn't take the opportunity to move to the trunk again. *Okay,* Macurdy thought, *give me a chance at your belly.* He rested the spear on the branch overhead, like a pool cue on a bridge, ready to stab upward. The cat reached down, slapping in his direction with a broad hook-rimmed paw, slaps so quick he couldn't have counted them, and Macurdy realized even more how overmatched he was. Again his spear darted, stabbed a muscled shoulder, and after squalling, the cat moved in to the trunk, to begin backing down. Hopefully to continue downward, because now it was Macurdy who was out on a limb.

When it got to his branch, it paused. Macurdy jabbed again, the blade slipping past the jaguar's guard, slicing into the muscles of the chest. The cat screeched—the sound freezing Macurdy's heart—partly lost its hold, then recovered. Macurdy had drawn the spear back; now he jabbed again. This time the paw was quicker, striking the spear aside, and now the cat stepped out toward him, inside the spear's reach. Hands almost spasming, Macurdy gripped the branch next to his head, the cat hardly six feet from him, jaws wide, the sound from its throat like the steam hose at the creamery.

He tossed the spear away, drawing cries from the men on the ground, but at such close range, he couldn't use it one-handed. Then, holding the branch above with his right hand, he rolled his left shoulder enough to slide his shield down onto his left arm, shifting it between himself and the cat.

He couldn't crouch—the branch he held for balance was too high—and he could only bend a little. If the cat chose to, it could easily attack his lower legs. But he thrust the shield toward it, and that held the cat's focus. "Haah! Haah!" he shouted. A paw struck the shield before he could see the movement, struck so hard it almost dislodged Macurdy, who nonetheless inched another step forward. "Haah! Haah!" The cat backed away. For a moment it crouched with its hindquarters against the trunk, then with a quick scrabbling began to back down the tree again. When it reached the next to lowest limb, it paused, then launched itself, clearing the men near the tree, landing on last fall's dead leaves.

Its impact and horizontal momentum caused its legs to collapse for just an instant, and two of the hounds were on it before the cat could streak away. It twisted, raked one hound off, then other dogs were at it, and the action, with squalling, yelping and growling, was too swift for Macurdy to follow. A spear drove, taking the cat in the flank, another spear struck, and another, and the dogs swarmed over it, tearing.

Shit, thought Macurdy. *Whatever happened to the rule that only one man wields the spear?* It was just as well though, he told himself; saved wear and tear on the dogs. He reslung his shield until he reached the lower branch, then tossed it to the ground.

On the way back to town, most of the trainees were still

exhilarated from the kill. Macurdy, on the other hand, was grim and angry. He'd hunted all his life, perhaps not with great enthusiasm, but it was what men did, and he'd found pleasure in it. But this time—

* * *

He sat beside Jeremid at supper. The young corporal was still somewhat excited. "You've got to stay for the party tonight, Macurdy," he said. "There's not only the slave girls; there'll likely be a spear maiden or two, maybe more. Probably try someone out. A good-looking guy like you, one of them may even take you home with her for the night. Get her pregnant, and you've got a life of ease, making babies with her. With luck she'll even let you hump slave girls on the side." Jeremid laughed. "Especially if she doesn't know about it."

Macurdy had heard about spear maidens. Other nations didn't have them, he'd been told. The daughters of Heroes were trained from girlhood with weapons, the best being honored as spear maidens. They almost always married Heroes. No doubt the practice had been started deliberately to breed up warriors.

Marrying a spear maiden was nothing he wanted to do, but to leave with one, then pretend to get too drunk—

So he waited around, sipping at an ale to pass the time. There was cheering from the doorway, and laughter, male and female. Slave girls came prancing in, wearing nothing but little aprons in front and behind. Thirty or forty poured through the door in a brief flood, dispersing through the room, pairing off, men grabbing them, kissing and pawing. One, a blond with bold breasts, had spied Macurdy's large body and fended off other Heroes to reach him.

"I never saw you before," she said, and grabbing him, kissed him roundly while rubbing against his erection.

Good God! he thought, *talk about brazen!* "Sorry," he said, "I'm waiting for a spear maiden."

"Come on, Muscles, don't be that way. Let's you and me hump, and *then* you can wait for a spear maiden."

His powerful hands gripped her shoulders and removed her, holding her at arm's length. "When she comes in," he said, "I want to be ready and loaded. You're a great looking woman, and there's lots more guys here. You'll get all you want."

She tossed her head, insulted despite the compliments, and turning, walked away, reaching back to flip up her rear apron and expose her buttocks to him. Macurdy sighed. This could be a trying evening. Not a dozen feet away, one of the Heroes already had a slave bent over the table, his buttocks driving. More, though, were drinking and laughing with their girl of the moment, kissing between swigs.

Then he saw another woman enter, broad-shouldered, dressed in decorated calfskin breeches and shirt, wearing a short sword on one hip and a knife on the other. Just inside she paused, scanning the chaos with half a smile. Macurdy waved to her, and she started over. None of the unpaired Heroes grabbed at her, though several spoke as she passed. She answered without looking aside, her focus on Macurdy.

Half a dozen feet away she stopped and looked him over, seeing a man taller than most, lean and hard, with wide heavy shoulders and a strong, good-looking face. Macurdy, on the other hand, saw a woman as tall as an Ozman. Eighteen or twenty years old, he guessed, and long-legged, with shoulders that made her waist look small, and large muscular hands. She had a warrior aura. Her brown hair bordered on blond, and her face, dusted with freckles, suggested straightforward honesty.

She smiled at him before she spoke, and her teeth were strong and even. "I haven't seen you before. Where've you been?"

Suddenly Macurdy felt stupid. He couldn't tell the truth, it seemed to him, yet anything else would sound lame. "Visiting a couple shamans," he said.

"Shamans? On Six-Day evening?"

"When else?"

She cocked a critical eye at him. "My name is Melody."

Melody. With a sword and knife, fully clothed at an orgy. "Mine's Macurdy,"

"Macurdy? Never heard of a name like that. And you've got an accent. Where are you from?"

"I came here from Wolf Springs. Before that—I came from a far place."

"Sit down," she said, and motioned to a long bench built along the south wall. They went to it, and sat side by side. "Wolf Springs sends more than their share of Heroes," she said. "My dad's from Wolf Springs, and got my mother pregnant with me. She was a spear maiden too. Now tell me about this far place."

Without examining the wisdom of it, Macurdy began to talk on the premise that truth is usually safer than lies. "You've heard of the wizard gate there?"

She frowned. "Sure. What about it?"

"I came through it."

"Are you lying to me?"

"Nope. I came through a year ago. Got made a slave, and then the shaman's apprentice, till he found out I didn't have a healing touch. So he had me put in the militia. Now I'm here."

"A slave in the Heroes! I never heard of such a thing. You must be something, to have gotten sent here."

While they'd talked, a grinning Jeremid had come over with a slave girl, one of his hands kneading a breast. "He's a Hero, all right. We got a big jaguar up a tree today, and he climbed up and chased it down! It's true! Better grab him, Melody. He's going to be one of the all-time best!" He led his partner to his sleeping pad then, where she began undressing him. From nearby came the urgent, passionate grunts of some Hero's orgasm.

"This place gets me horny," Melody said, and getting up, sat astride Macurdy's lap, her face in his. "Let's you and I get acquainted. Where's your bed sack?"

"Uh, Melody, I'm married."

"Married!? They don't send married men here."

"Married on the other side. Through the gate."

Both her eyebrows raised. "On the other side doesn't count," she said. "The gate is one way. Guys have tried to go through it, but no one's made it except Sisters. Like swimming against a strong current, and the closer they got, the stronger it got." She put her arms around Macurdy's neck and kissed him, soft and moist, lingering. "The other side's lost to you, Macurdy," she murmured. "While I'm here, and I like you. I want to try you out. Who knows? Maybe I'll marry you."

He reminded himself to breathe. This woman was a lot more enticing, compelling, than the big blond. "I promised her to take no other woman as long as we both shall live."

She stared. "Even when she's somewhere else? Why would you promise such a thing?"

"It's part of the marriage agreement."

Melody frowned. "Crazy! Do the men there actually live up to it?"

"Most of them."

She kissed him again. "Think about it," she said. "Think about us naked on your bed." She got graphic then, describing sound, sight, and feel. Taking a long quavering breath, he put a hand on her shoulder. "Please," he said. "You're making this hard for me."

She laughed. "That's how we want it. The harder, the better."

"I'm not the one for you. Really. I'd like to be, but my wife is on this side too." It occurred to him that he might be saying too much, but he went on. "She got stolen and brought through. That's why I came through. And I love her more than my life. If I ever have a chance, I'll find her."

Melody stood up frowning. "Macurdy, you're a strange one, no doubt about it." She backed away a step. "I'll ask you again sometime. I don't give up easily." She turned then and walked away, his eyes following her to the door. When she reached it, she stopped and looked back, as if to see if he'd changed his mind and followed her. Instead he waved, once. She turned away again and disappeared.

By this time all the slave girls were sexually engaged, Hero haunches bobbing everywhere Macurdy looked. He took a deep quavering breath, walked to the narrow rear exit and left. No one would notice, he felt sure.

Outside, he ran off down the road, through the dusk, determined to run himself exhausted before he came back.

* * *

The next morning, Macurdy was lame. He'd alternately run and walked three or four miles the night before, and unaccustomed to it, was sore from buttocks to calves. "What's the matter with you?" the sergeant asked.

All around them were men hung over, or sleeping off exhaustion. "I'm sore," Macurdy answered.

Zassfel scowled. "Someone said you turned Melody down last night, then left. You never screwed anyone at all, did you."

His aura was hostile. To Macurdy's surprise, he found himself feeling better. Hostility was something he could deal with. "You don't know what I did," he said, "or what I can do."

Zassfel's eyes sharpened. "Is that some kind of threat?"

"I don't threaten anyone. Least of all the platoon sergeant."

"Don't play games with me, Macurdy. I can ruin you. Any kind of ruin you can think of."

"Sergeant, I'm the best new man you've got, and by the time the leaves turn, I'll be the best new or old. There's no need to get on me."

Zassfel's face froze in a grimace, and his hand moved as if to the hilt of the sword he wasn't wearing at the moment. "You son of a bitch," he growled softly. "You better be careful. Real careful."

Macurdy nodded pleasantly. Later he'd be astonished that he'd felt no fear, no upset or anger. "Just remember who went up the tree yesterday," he said, "and how it worked out."

Then he walked outside and sat in the sun, to occupy himself with a dream of rescuing Varia.

* * *

The week went well enough. Mostly Zassfel ignored him, as if he'd forgotten about it, but whenever his glance passed over Macurdy, Macurdy could literally feel it, and see the anger in the sergeant's aura. Not until Six-Day before supper, though, was anything said. Then Zassfel walked over to him.

"Macurdy," he murmured, "tonight we'll see whether you're a man or a pansy. Don't leave the longhouse unless I say so, or I'll put you on punishment. Bad punishment."

Macurdy nodded without speaking, wishing the uncanny

calm of the previous Seven-Day would come back to him. As it was he ate his supper, but his stomach churned.

Afterward the men sat around, waiting for the slave girls, some of them telling what they were going to do. To Macurdy, they sounded like a couple of eighth graders he'd known in the one-room Oak Creek school. Then Zassfel stepped into the middle of the floor and called for quiet.

"Men," he said, "we've got a pansy among us, someone who's been here four weeks now and hasn't humped a single girl, let alone half a dozen a night like a real Hero. So tonight we're going to test him. When the girls come, I'm going to set Maira on him. He turned her down once; she told me so. If he can satisfy her..." His pause was met by knowing laughs. "If he can satisfy Maira, we'll keep him around. Otherwise, the slave bastard goes back to the potato field.

"So when the girls come in, nobody grabs one. Nobody." He looked around. "That includes you, Margli. I'm going to take Maira to Macurdy, and he's going to hump her on this table in front of all of us." He grinned at his victim. "We'll see how he does. The rule is, he has to satisfy her. My bet is, he won't even be able to get it up."

When Zassfel identified his victim, the laughter stopped. Macurdy was liked—admired—especially since his climb up the tree. Now his pulse pounded like a triphammer, while his guts kept churning. A long few minutes later, the watchers outside the door began their cheer, answered at a little distance by female voices.

Macurdy became aware of Jeremid behind him. "Ride her rough, Macurdy," the corporal whispered. "Really bang her! It's your only chance; Maira likes it rough. And whisper to her that you'll sneak out and go to her during the week. Maybe she'll fake it for you. Usually she humps one guy after another. Long after everyone's had enough, she's pawing guys in their sleep, trying to get a rise out of one."

Macurdy heard, but his mind had frozen with determination. The girls trooped in subdued, aware now of something unusual pending. The sergeant ordered the men into a large oval around the central table, while he held Maira by an arm. "Macurdy," he said, "drop your pants."

It felt to Macurdy as if his throat was coated with cotton batting, but surprisingly his voice seemed normal. "No thanks, Sergeant. You've got no authority to do this."

Zassfel grinned. "Strip him, boys."

Most of the men stood unmoving. The four men Zassfel had prearranged things with were his closest friends, four of his own year in the company. They'd stationed themselves close behind Macurdy, and two of them grabbed him now.

"Zassfel!" Macurdy shouted. "If you're such a Hero, fight me!"

The room fell absolutely silent for a moment. Then Zassfel's grin grew wider. "Ho ho ho!" he said. "It seems like every now and then I have to beat someone up. Otherwise people forget." He waved the crowd back at his end of the oval, then stripped off his shirt and stepped forward. "All right, Macurdy, we fight. And when I'm done, we tie what's left of you to the tree out front, with a sign telling people what you are." He raised his hands; apparently this was to be with fists. "Let's do it."

The four let Macurdy go, ready to pounce if he tried to run. He didn't. He stripped off his own shirt, raised his fists, and stepped to meet Zassfel.

When Mr. Anderson had taught Oak Creek school, he'd brought boxing gloves, and had given the boys lessons with them. He had, he claimed, been the Golden Gloves champion of Indiana. Whether or not he actually had, he'd impressed them with his moves and style, and taught them how to jab, to throw a right cross, a proper hook, an uppercut.

And clearly, Zassfel had never heard of any of them, certainly not the jab. What he did know was the crushing roundhouse swing, grabbing the hair, the use of knee and elbow—all things Macurdy expected and watched for. Meanwhile Macurdy introduced him to the jab and all the rest of it. Within a minute, Zassfel's mouth and nose were bleeding, one eye was swelling, a cheek was cut, and he was raising himself to a sitting position, purple with rage. "Kosek! Ardonor! Kill the son of a bitch."

They were on Macurdy in an instant, not only Kosek and Ardonor, but the other two, grabbing, slugging. When they were done, they threw him out the front door, to lie semiconscious and bleeding in the dirt street. After a bit he was aware of someone, two someones, helping him to his feet and supporting him an uncertain distance to—somewhere, then letting him down onto a bed.

He recognized a voice: Melody's, and opened the eye that would, enough to see lamplight. "Thanks, Jeremid," she was saying. "I'll take care of him now. Tomorrow I'll tell the captain what happened, and you'll back me on it. He might or might not do something, but what Zassfel did in there didn't fit any law I ever heard of."

"He's legally a slave," Jeremid murmured. "You can do anything to a slave, as long as you don't reduce their value."

Her words were crisp. "He's also a Hero. There are laws about what anyone can do to Heroes."

After a minute, Macurdy felt a wet cloth dabbing at his face, and winced.

"You're awake."

His mouth felt ragged, his lips swollen, and he knew he had teeth missing and broken. He began to answer, then thought better of it and nodded. That was a mistake too. She continued dabbing and wiping, hissing now and then, occasionally swearing. Briefly she plucked pieces of broken teeth from his lips. "We'll fix his ass, Macurdy," she said. "My father was captain in his time. He has influence, and he spoils me. When I tell him—"

She stopped there. It seemed to Macurdy she didn't feel much confidence. He was a slave; it would come down to that. He felt her fingers prod his ribs, his collarbones. The ribs on one side hurt, but not enough that he flinched.

"Open your mouth."

He did.

"The filthy bastards!" He could hear her breathe in and out through her nose, controlling herself. "You'll be all right here," she said. "I'm going to the shaman and get some things."

She left. For a while he drifted in and out of consciousness;

then she was back. He could hear her doing things, he didn't know what. Preparing poultices from something the shaman had given her, because now she was placing damp cloths over each eye, on a cheek, on his mouth, crooning as she did so. Then she stroked his forehead with gentle fingers, and left him.

He slept. And sleeping, dreamed of the jaguar. And of Varia, who kept changing into the spear maiden. Sometime in the night he felt hands tug down his breeches, fondle him. Felt himself swell and harden. Felt someone straddle him, insert him, ride him gently…And when it was over, felt his good cheek very gently kissed. "I love you, Macurdy." The voice was Melody's, not Varia's. "Don't ask me why. I only talked to you once. Maybe I'm crazy."

Then he drifted into sleep again.

Chapter 19: Pillow Talk

Pain half wakened him occasionally, and now and then the delicate replacement of a poultice. Gradually he awakened fully, and carefully peeled the poultice off one eye. The swelling seemed mostly gone; his vision through it little restricted. Then he peeled off the other; he could see through it too, though it was still pretty swollen. His mouth, on the other hand...Gingerly he touched his split, still-swollen lips, and decided it was best he had no mirror, otherwise he'd be tempted to look at his teeth. His exploring tongue told him all he needed to know about them.

The evening before, and the night, were all there for him; the concussion hadn't been severe enough to block recall. Sitting up, he looked around. Melody dozed on a mat, curled beneath a blanket. He pulled his breeches back up and got out of bed, staggered a bit, then steadied. Found his boots and pulled them on. Before he left, he looked back at Melody. She'd wakened, was resting on an elbow looking at him. On an impulse, he tossed a kiss at her, then left, wondering if she knew the gesture.

He didn't walk to the longhouse, he trotted. The jarring hurt—not his head, but his mouth and ribs. Trotted limping on legs still sore from running on Six-Day night. It was already half light outdoors, but seen from the road, the village could have been deserted. He stopped on the longhouse stoop and peered inside, which was darker than he wanted, but he was in no mood to wait. Besides, even from the door he recognized Ardonor sprawled nearby, naked on a bed not his own.

He went to him, grabbed a handful of hair and lifted. Waking, Ardonor squawked in pain and indignation, grabbing at Macurdy's left wrist. Macurdy's right fist hit him on the nose. Cartilage gave, and Macurdy let him fall to the floor, then kicked him heavily in the ribs, once, twice, and felt them give too. Ardonor keened weakly, so he kicked him in the belly.

Then looked around for the others who'd beaten him. He saw Maira sitting astride a Hero, motionless now, frightened. Both had watched. He winked at them, raising a finger to his swollen lips as if saying hush, then spotted his next victim and headed toward him. Belver lay sleeping on his own low bed, snoring coarsely. Crouched above him, Macurdy locked both hands on the man's throat and squeezed, at the same time sitting on him. The snoring stopped and the eyes popped open, to stare in horrified recognition. "I'm back," Macurdy growled, then chuckled deliberately. Belver clawed at his wrists, but Macurdy just squeezed harder. After the body went slack, he got off, grabbed the man's ankles and dragged him from the bed, across the floor and out the door onto the stoop. By that time Belver was recovering consciousness. Macurdy kicked him in the leg. "Stand up."

Belver just stared. Macurdy kicked him in the belly this time, not too hard. "Stand up or I'll burst your gut with the next one." Carefully, fear in his eyes, Belver got unsteadily to his feet, then Macurdy struck him as hard as he could in the mouth. The man flung backward, hit his head on the wall and slid down it like a sack, stunned.

Hoisting him on one shoulder, Macurdy took him back inside and dumped him heavily beside Ardonor. Then he kicked Belver in the ribs, hard, and Ardonor again, before looking around. The naked Maira was trying desperately to waken Zassfel, who wasn't responding. Macurdy ignored them and headed for Kosek's bed. Kosek wasn't in it; he'd rolled off in his sleep. Macurdy knelt astraddle of him, held his head down by the hair, and began clubbing his face with a fist, shouting hoarsely now through broken teeth as he hit him. "When you"—*sock, sock*—"beat on someone"—*sock, sock*—"like this"—*sock, sock*—"you can't get good leverage"—*sock, sock*—"so you've got to use technique." When he stopped, Kosek's eyes were glazed, his face a bloody smear.

By that time a dozen or more men were sitting up or standing, watching. Zassfel was on his feet now, Maira crouching behind him. Macurdy took Kosek's ankles and dragged him toward Ardonor and Belver, pausing however near Zassfel. "Sergeant," Macurdy said, "are you ready to fight again?"

Zassfel already looked pretty well beaten up. "I had enough last night," he answered hoarsely. "Enough to know you're ready for promotion to corporal."

You're not talking too well this morning either, Macurdy thought, and moved in on him. "You told those piles of shit to beat me up. Are you ready to get down on your knees and beg forgiveness?"

Zassfel looked around wildly. "Kill the slave son of a bitch!" he yelled. "That's an order!"

No one moved except Macurdy. He slammed Zassfel right on his swollen, already broken nose, and again the blood flowed. The sergeant fell backward over the crouching Maira, to lie unmoving, tears flowing from the pain. Macurdy kicked him in the ribs then, hard enough to feel them give, leaving the man openmouthed and gasping. That done, he dragged Zassfel and Kosek, one after the other, to where he'd left the first two. There was another around somewhere, but he wasn't sure who. Dieser, probably, but he'd let it go at that.

Instead he went to his bed, buckled on his belt with its Hero-issue saber and Arbel's gift knife, and stuffed his few other personal possessions in his saddle bags. Then he rolled his blanket, slung his bow and quiver, grabbed his spear, and stalked from the building. All eyes followed him, but no one said anything or moved to interfere.

Melody had watched from the road as Macurdy had beaten up Belver, and from the door as he'd beaten Kosek and Zassfel. Now, as he came out, she stared half in awe, half in concern. "Come on," she said, "you've got to get away from here," and tugging on his sleeve, pulled him toward 2nd Platoon's stable. *Melody, I know that much,* he thought. *I'm not totally out of my skull.*

"Hurry," she said. "Saddle up and wait inside. I'll be right back." Then she left running.

Macurdy was cinching down the girth on his horse, when someone came into the stable. His head snapped around. It was Jeremid, also carrying his personal gear. The man said nothing, just grabbed a saddle blanket and began to saddle a horse.

"Saddle two, if you're coming with me," Macurdy said. Jeremid said nothing, working quickly. When each had a mount and spare ready, Macurdy stopped Jeremid inside the door. "We wait here."

"What for?"

"Melody."

Mouth open, Jeremid stared at him. The longhouse was still quiet, but there had to be activity inside. Presumably, Macurdy thought, no one had seen where he'd gone, but if any of them were thinking at all this morning, they'd surely guess. His heartbeats counted down two long minutes before he saw Melody riding toward them, a remount tethered behind. Seeing him, she beckoned. "Now," he said, and leading his mount out the door, swung into the saddle.

Like the two men, Melody had her spear in its saddle boot. Together in the growing light, the three of them trotted their horses eastward out of town, Macurdy's ribs, swollen face, sore haunches feeling every jar. He took the lead, setting the direction, though he knew nothing of the road eastward beyond the first hours' ride.

Eastward. If the others wondered why, they didn't ask.

* * *

Their horses were strong and splendidly conditioned. Thus for more than an hour they jogged without a break, then changed mounts and trotted another hour before slowing to a walk. They stayed on the road; to leave it would only slow them. And pursuers would undoubtedly have hounds which could track them easily in the forest. For the first three hours, the land along the road was as much clearings as woods, with a small village in every major opening. Finally they entered low forested hills, and having heard no sign of hounds, dismounted to lead their horses awhile.

In those three hours, no one had spoken, aside from functional suggestions and Macurdy's few orders. For one thing, Macurdy's ruined mouth made talking painful. Melody's and Jeremid's thoughts were mostly on the possibility of capture, and why on Earth they were doing this. Macurdy's were on escape, and on how hard he dared push the horses. He was willing to wear them out, if it resulted in pursuit being abandoned, but he dared not break them down. Because of his size, he'd taken two of the company's larger horses, but even so, he was a heavy burden for them.

When a meadow came into sight ahead, Jeremid said they'd best stop and let the horses graze a bit. Macurdy agreed. They took time to hobble them; there were hobble straps in every set of equipment, and they couldn't risk losing a horse.

Their pursuers would undoubtedly have a pack horse carrying a sack of oats, Jeremid said, which meant their mounts would hold up better. And the White River lay less than an hour's ride ahead, if they kept pushing. There they'd have a choice of either swimming their horses downstream or up, or straight across. Which with luck would confuse and delay pursuit.

So they rested less than twenty minutes. At the White, they swam upstream, even though it was harder on the horses. Then, instead of coming out on the other side, where their tracks would be looked for, they came out on the west bank again, and followed it upstream for several miles, on foot again, leading their horses to rest them. The hope was their pursuers would overlook the west bank option.

At length they reentered the water, crossing this time. Then Macurdy led off eastward through untracked forest. Until, abruptly, a voice froze them. "Macurdy! Macurdy!"

None of them spoke. Their eyes scanned the woods.

"No no, Macurdy! I'm up here! Blue Wing!"

They looked up in unison to where the great raven sat in a tall, thick-boled walnut tree.

"I saw you crossing the river, and wondered why humans would be riding so far from any road or trail." Blue Wing paused.

"Why are you?"

"We're in trouble," Macurdy said, "and we think men might be following us. Soldiers with hounds. We're trying to leave a trail they won't find."

Blue Wing said nothing to that, and it seemed to Macurdy the bird comprehended neither his problem nor his strategy. A raven's solution to danger would be flight, he supposed. "I wonder," Macurdy called, "if you'd do me a favor?"

"Ask and find out."

He described the road they'd fled on, and the form any successful pursuit would take. "I will look and see," Blue Wing said, and with a thrust of legs and wings, lifted into the sky.

They rode on then, not hurrying, for this was old forest, long unburned, and though the hills were mild, the ground had gotten pocked and humped, over the centuries, from the tipped-up roots and moldering trunks of wind thrown trees. Only once did they pause, to shoot and gut a turkey. Three miles farther, they came to a small isolated clearing, more or less level, with a cabin and outbuildings of logs. From a little distance, their roofs looked more or less intact, but saplings were already invading the clearing. There was still abundant grass though, beaten down and grayed by winter's frosts and rains, and tinged green by the new growth beneath it. Macurdy wondered why the place had been abandoned.

By then the sun was low. They rode over to the buildings and dismounted, hobbling the horses and leaving them to graze. Inside the cabin, things had been smashed, and bones were scattered around, the broken skulls human.

"Troll work!" Jeremid breathed the words, sounding spooked. The stock shed had been similarly vandalized. There too bones lay scattered and broken, with skulls of a cow, a calf, a horse.

By the time they'd looked it over, Blue Wing had found them. "No one is following you," he said. "I flew above the river to the road, and then westward quite a distance. With the trees still bare, I couldn't possibly have missed anyone. I saw not more than two riders together, and no hounds at all."

Jeremid looked at Macurdy. "What now?" he asked.

"We camp," Macurdy said. "There's plenty of wood in the woodshed. We'll take turns standing watch and keeping fires going, in case the troll's still around here somewhere. We can picket the horses inside them."

Without anyone actually suggesting it, they made their beds in the hay shed, where there were no bones, fluffing up the hay in the driest corner. The decaying roof wouldn't hold out serious rain, but it would hold heat somewhat, and protect against a shower.

Macurdy selected eight fire sites close outside the cluster of buildings, and they carried a pile of firewood to each. There was a well in front of the cabin, its white oak shoring still intact, and they raised water from it. Blue Wing announced he would sleep on its sweep. Then, in front of the hay shed, Macurdy lit the cook fire with the pass of a hand. Jeremid stared big-eyed.

"Where did you learn to do that?" he asked.

"The shaman at Wolf Springs taught me. He said I had talent, and trained me in the evenings for a while."

"Could you have, uh, set fire to Zassfel this morning?" Jeremid asked.

Macurdy shrugged. "I never thought to try."

As they roasted the turkey, dusk began to settle. Eating wouldn't be easy for his damaged mouth, so Macurdy had taken an iron pot from the cabin and was stewing turkey in it. *Rust stew,* he thought drily as he raked coals around it.

"It's hard to believe no one's chasing us," Jeremid said quietly. "Could the bird be lying?"

Macurdy shook his head. "We're old friends from Wolf Springs."

"I believe him," Melody said. "My father was commander in his time, and a councilman since. We grew up, my brothers and I, being lectured by him. A platoon sergeant can get away with a lot, but what he did last night?" She shook her head, then cut off a slab of half-roasted turkey breast. "Of course, what you did was damned extreme, too, but you were justified."

"Justification's not all I had," Macurdy mumbled. "I had to

try getting away without getting chased and caught. So I humiliated him, and pretty much crippled him for a while. That way,
one of two things would happen. He might go crazy, and order
the men out to get me at all costs—or he might cave in and order nothing. Or maybe he was in too bad a shape to give orders.
After that it would depend on the captain, but he wouldn't send
men out till after someone took the story to him. Or he might
write it off and bust Zassfel."

Inwardly he grunted. *Face it, Macurdy, you wanted to get
even. It felt good, beating them up like that.* Whatever; the good
feeling was gone now. Heavily he got up and circled the buildings, lighting the watch fires.

Jeremid had volunteered to take the first watch. Now, as
dusk thickened, he left with spear and sword. Using mostly his
back teeth, Macurdy gnawed briefly on a piece of stewed turkey,
his eyes watering from the pain. Eating, he decided, would be
more of a problem than he'd feared. After a few minutes, he and
Melody went into the shed and made nests in the hay. "It's going
to be a cold night, Macurdy," she murmured. "We could keep
warmer if we lay close together. The way you lit those fires, you
could keep us both warm."

He sighed. "Melody, I'd like to. I really would. But I told
you my marriage vows."

She frowned. "I never heard of anything so ridiculous. For
a wife, yes, but for a husband?"

"For a husband it should be the same."

"Not for a husband who's a Hero."

"Maybe not, if he's an Ozman. But I'm not a Hero any longer anyway." He paused. "If I was married to you, would you
like me to, uh, hump other women?"

That stopped her only for a moment. "I wouldn't care. It's
expected. As long as I had you when I wanted you. But you
wouldn't, because I'd give you all you could handle.

"Your vow's already broken," she went on. "Last night at
my place. You remember; I know you do. You weren't unconscious; you couldn't have been. Even beat up like you were, you
were pushing, helping out."

He almost said he couldn't help himself—that he'd been confused from his beating. Then asked himself, *Who do you think you're kidding, Macurdy? You were confused when she put it in, but when you realized, you could have pushed her off.* Instead he nodded. "I remember. I let it happen; it was too good to stop. But that was once. Doing it once doesn't make it right a second time."

He thought she might get angry, but her mouth didn't tighten and her aura didn't darken. She lay thoughtful a minute. "What's she like, Macurdy? This wife of yours."

He didn't actually think about it, but answered on the premise he needed confederates, and that she'd need to know sooner or later. "She's a member of the Sisterhood, Melody. She'd run away from them. Then, one day when I wasn't home, they came and stole her. Brought her back to Yuulith. But she had time to write me a note, and put it where I'd find it, so I followed her."

Melody's eyes reflected belief. And concern. "That's where we're going, isn't it," she said. "That's why we're going east instead of some other direction: to get her back."

He nodded.

"What's her name?"

"Varia."

"Varia." She tasted it. "Does she love you?"

"Yep."

"I've heard stories about the Sisters. If they stole her back, you know what kind of life she's leading now. In spite of any vows."

"I don't know."

"They put them with studs, like you do mares, but not just one stud. Different ones hump them till they're pregnant. And when they've weaned their kid, they send the studs around again. And the story is, they like it, like the slave girls do who get taken to the House of Heroes."

His face was swollen and discolored, but she could read the bleakness in it, even in the failing light. "Forget I said that, Macurdy," she murmured. "I was being an asshole, and I'm sorry. You've been a real Hero, not like some of those others. What I said is true, or at least it's what people believe, but—shit!"

She sighed gustily. "I ought to wish I wasn't in love with you, but I am." She raised herself on an elbow, and reaching, caressed his better cheek with her fingertips. "If you change your mind, I'm right here beside you. And I don't think your Varia would be mad at you for humping me."

She turned away, and Macurdy went to sleep thinking maybe Varia wouldn't be angry, but a vow was a vow. He wondered if Melody would try anything after he went to sleep, and found himself half hoping she would.

* * *

He woke to Jeremid's hand tugging his foot—his turn on watch—and got up quietly, his stomach complaining with hunger. Outside the horses looked at him briefly, then returned to grazing. The cook fire was stone cold. Cautiously he touched the pot, then reached into the still-warm water, scooped out a piece of turkey cooked soft by long boiling, and chewed painfully as he walked to the nearest watch fire. They were burning strongly; Jeremid had fed them before coming in.

The thin moon had already set, but he guessed it was still somewhat short of midnight; three hours would be about right for his shift, he decided; maybe three and a little bit. Recalling something Mr. Anderson had taught them at school, he found the Big Dipper; it was supposed to circle the North Star once a day. So in three hours, the dipper should go a quarter—no, an eighth of the way around the North Star. Which meant when the pointer stars got around to—about there—he'd go wake up Melody for her watch.

He stayed on his feet, walking the perimeter to stay awake. Paying only occasional attention to his surroundings—the horses would tell him if anything was prowling. Part of the time he occupied his mind with Varia and Melody. Jeremid was a good-looking young guy; maybe Melody would decide it was him she wanted. At least she might settle for him. *Hell,* he told himself, *they could be humping in the hay right now, for all you know. They're Ozians, and she sounded horny enough.*

A twinge of jealousy surprised and irritated him. Briefly he examined his feelings, and there was no doubt: Varia was his love. Melody was—nice and kind and tough. And crazy to have run off with him; reckless at least. In Oztown she'd been someone important and privileged, and she'd thrown it away, apparently because she wanted to be humped by him, even though he'd already turned her down. *Or could she actually love me?* He examined the possibility to no conclusion.

The watch wore on. Several times he added wood to the fires, twice went back to the cook pot, and occasionally checked the Dipper before deciding his three hours were up and returning to the shed. Crawling, he groped, finding a bare foot that could only be Melody's. It pulled away with a rustling of old hay.

"Macurdy?" she whispered.

"Yes."

She rustled around some more, finding her boots, then got up and went outside to put them on. He felt an urge to follow her, talk with her, learn more about this girl who said she loved him. But his mouth hurt, and besides, it felt dangerous. So instead he found his blanket and settled down, leaving his boots on as before, in case of emergency.

* * *

It was daylight and the sun about to rise when Jeremid woke him. "Macurdy," he said, "Melody and I talked last night."

The words brought a pang: *They've decided to pair up, to leave me and go back.* But that made no sense. They could hardly go back now. "She told me about your wife," Jeremid went on. "What does she look like?"

Macurdy frowned. An odd question to be asked on waking. "She's beautiful. Long red hair and green tilty eyes."

"And the people with her? Do you know?"

He's seen her! Macurdy's mind focused. "Another good-looking woman, and a man. The woman's name is Idri; her hair is auburn, and she's got tilty eyes too, only not as green."

"God! That was the name: Idri. The other was Varia. They came into Oztown about a year ago, with a bull of a guard. The chief loaned them an escort, and I was one of them. Your wife was a prisoner."

Macurdy's throat was dry now. "Right. I had to wait a month before the gate opened again and I could follow them."

Melody had come to the door, and stood looking in at them, listening.

"We took them east, across the Great Muddy," Jeremid said. "They got other escorts there, and we came back." He shook his head. "Your wife's the prettiest woman I ever saw. And dangerous! Her guard tried to rape her one night. I don't know what she did, but he screamed the worst scream I ever imagined. I ran over with a torch, and they were both there with their breeches off. Your wife looked at me and said never to try raping a Sister, or I'd end up like him. He was doubled over with his hands in his crotch, hardly able to whimper. Then the other Sister came with a saber and ran him through."

Melody spoke, her voice flat. "Sounds like she's worth saving, Macurdy. Congratulations." Then she turned and walked out of sight.

Jeremid's story shook Macurdy so, it took him several minutes to get up and come out of the shed. Varia had got through that experience seemingly unhurt, and Idri had killed the guy, but what a terrible damned thing to almost happen.

* * *

They ate more turkey, then left the rest for Blue Wing. Breaking camp amounted to little more than catching their hobbled horses and saddling them, taking the cook pot and ax they'd found there. The sun was still low when they rode away eastward, shielding their eyes from it with a hand. Here there was a clear trail to follow. After a bit, Blue Wing caught up with them. *I suppose this is interesting to him,* Macurdy thought. *He can share it with the rest of his people.*

Later that morning they hit a rutted cart road, and followed it south to the eastbound road. There they rode well strung out, as if they weren't together; there seemed less chance they'd be remembered or reported that way. Only occasionally did they meet other travelers—farmers and other locals going about their business.

In late afternoon they reached the Great Muddy River, running wide and smooth, but powerful. Both Melody and Jeremid had coins in their purses, and when the next ferry crossed, the three of them were on it.

Chapter 20: Four Become Seven

During the first three days east of the Great Muddy, they traveled in a kingdom named Miskmehr, land hillier than they were used to, with farms in every significant bottomland. It was a lovely season, the forest canopy washed pale green with opening buds. At a village they bought a cheese and hardtack for basic rations. Their breaks they took in moist roadside woods, eating the wild leeks that grew there till they reeked of them. Macurdy was healing rapidly; his mouth was healed enough, he ate what the others ate, though he soaked his hardtack first.

Their road trended more south than east now, and this troubled Macurdy, for his understanding was the Silver Mountain was east from Oz. But Blue Wing explained it angled south to strike the Valley Highway, the great road that paralleled the Green River. The highway would take them up the valley all the way to the Great Eastern Mountains, and the dwarvish kingdom named for one of them. No, he had no idea how many days ride they had ahead of them; humans traveled so slowly, he didn't see how they could stand it.

The valley and its margins were kingdoms instead of tribal territories, Blue Wing said, with far more people, towns and villages than the lands they'd seen so far. Its farms were famous for their fertility.

On the fourth day they rode out of the hills into the valley, to the Highway, which was better than any road Macurdy had seen in this world. But the land where the two roads met was nothing to brag about—brushy forest, with half its trees tipped over or broken off by some twister.

Blue Wing, who'd been foraging, was waiting there for them, perched in a swamp white-oak. "Macurdy," he called, then spread his broad wings and hopped off, gliding down to the roadside. "There are men and dwarves just ahead beside the road. They've been fighting each other; there are bodies. It may be dangerous for you there."

"How many men? And dwarves? Alive, that is."

"Numerous. We have trouble with numbers. More men than dwarves though. The dwarves are surrounded."

"How far from here? On which side of the road?"

"You know I don't know your distances!" Blue Wing said, then paused. "If they were shouting, you could probably hear them from here. They're on the south side of the road, but their horses are farther on, on the road itself, with a man guarding them. Another man watches the road in this direction."

"We can bypass them through the woods on the north," Jeremid said. "They'll never know."

Macurdy thought for a moment before answering. "Jeremid, you take the horses off the road and stay with them. Melody, your clothes are harder to notice in the woods. Sneak through the brush on the north side of the road until you see their horses, then stop and keep your eyes open. I'll ride down the road and find out what the situation is. It'd be useful to have dwarves as allies."

He thanked Blue Wing then, and started eastward down the rutted, hoof-packed highway, while Jeremid and Melody disappeared into the forest. He'd ridden perhaps a hundred and fifty yards when a man rose up from behind a fallen tree. His left hand held a bow, and his right a nocked arrow; at twenty yards he could hardly miss. "Stop right there," he called. More loudly than need be, Macurdy thought, unless he wanted his own people to hear him.

Macurdy reined in. "I've been sent to talk to your leader," he said, also loudly.

The man scowled uncertainly, peering at Macurdy's face, still purple and green with bruises. Then a voice called from the woods nearby. "Send him in. I'll listen to him."

Macurdy swung down from his horse, and after tying the reins to a clump of willow, walked into the woods, leaving his spear and bow, but keeping his sword at his waist. The blow-downs were old enough decay had weakened the branches, allowing many of the trunks to settle to the ground or onto other fallen trees. The heavy opening of the forest roof had allowed the undergrowth to thicken, and saplings had sprung up twenty or more feet high.

A mess, Macurdy thought. *At home these would have been cut up for logs and firewood, except for the elm.* He picked his way around and over blowdowns in the direction the voice had called from, not trying to keep a low target. A man crouched behind a thick elm, bow ready, his gaze shifting from the woods in front of him to the approaching Macurdy, and back again.

"Are you the leader here?" Macurdy asked.

The man looked at him suspiciously. "I am."

"What have you got pinned down in there?" Macurdy called. Loudly enough, he thought, the dwarves would hear too.

"What business is it of yours?"

"It's my master's business. I act on his orders. He's a magician, and he says it's dwarves you've trapped here."

The bandit ignored the question. "What the hell happened to your face?" he asked. "I never saw anyone beat up so bad."

Macurdy fingered the hard welt on his broken left cheekbone. "I displeased my master."

They were, he decided, being held off by dwarvish marksmanship. The bandits might have an advantage in numbers, but it seemed to him they had some disadvantages, for at least the leader's quiver looked light for a siege, and he carried a longbow. While according to the lore Macurdy had learned from Maikel and Blue Wing, the dwarves' long-range weapon was the crossbow, whose bolts, short and heavy, would be less deflected by undergrowth.

Meanwhile the bandit had turned to face Macurdy, his bowstring half drawn. At ten feet, Macurdy told himself, the arrow could pass through his breastbone and mostly out his back. He ignored it, lowering to a crouch himself, moving in closer with a hand cupped to his mouth, as if for private conversation. But his voice, when he spoke, was loud.

"Excuse me for shouting," he said, "but your men need to hear me, too. My master's not known for his patience, and your lives mean even less to him than mine. He does business with dwarves from time to time, and considers himself a dwarf friend. He orders you to make terms with them."

The man's eyes bulged in angry reaction, then abruptly Macurdy lunged, his left hand chopping sideways, deflecting the bow while his right drew his knife. He backed the bandit against the elm, the man staring not in anger now but fear, for the knife blade was at his belly.

"If you knew my master," Macurdy told him loudly, "you'd understand I fear him much more than I fear you. Tell your men you're going to make terms. Tell them to be ready to leave when you've got an agreement with the dwarves."

He twitched lightly with the knife, slicing the man's home-spun shirt, and the skin beneath it.

"You heard what he said!" the leader shouted.

"Lords of the Mountain!" Macurdy called. "Will you agree not to shoot at these people while they withdraw?"

The answering voice was a deep, accented bass. "Yewr mad if ye think ye can fool us so easily! Ye'd shoot us down in cold blood!"

"What's your name?" Macurdy asked the bandit quietly.

"Slaney."

"Slaney," Macurdy said loudly, "step out here!"

"What?! They'll shoot me!"

"Louder!"

"I said they'd shoot me!"

"I don't think so. But it's a chance you take, being a high-wayman, and if you don't step out, I'll spill your guts on the ground right here. I'll count to three: one…"

Slaney stepped away from the elm, Macurdy with him, the heavy knife still at the bandit's belly. "We're not highwaymen," the bandit muttered. "But rebels have to eat, and with Gurtho on the throne…"

Macurdy's left hand reached, drew Slaney's knife from its sheath and tossed it away. "Hold your bow against the tree."

He did, and Macurdy cut the string. "How many men do you have here?"

"In the woods? Fourteen alive and fit. Three others are dead by those vermin, and two badly hurt."

"Plus two on the road," Macurdy prompted.

The man nodded. "Plus two on the road."

"Tell them to cut their bows with their swords, lay them on a tree and chop them. So I can hear it happen." With a flick of the knife blade, Macurdy made another slit in the man's shirt, another thin red line on his belly. "Tell them!"

Worms writhed in Slaney's face. "You heard what he said," he called. "Chop your bows in two."

Several seconds passed before Macurdy heard the first chop. A moment later he heard a second, then more, though how many had actually struck a bow…"Anyone who walks out of here with a whole bow will answer to my master!" he shouted. "With his life!" There were three more chops, then a fourth.

"Lords of the Mountain!" he called, "does that convince you they won't attack if you come out?"

"And what's to prevent *yew* from fillin' us with arrows?"

"Because we're dwarf friends." Macurdy raised his voice to full shout. "My lord! Send the great raven to vouch for us!"

Blue Wing, who'd been circling well above the trees, spiraled down to perch among the upper branches of one. "Lords of the Mountain," the bird called, "these are honorable men! Trust them!"

"Yew!" the dwarf called out, "the man who's taken it on himself to intercede here! What's yer name?"

"Macurdy."

"Macurdy, why don't ye just kill the boogers?"

"My master is a magician and warrior, not a butcher. And these men haven't harmed us."

"What will they pay for our dead and wounded? And our ponies, and the tallfolk groom they killed?"

"Nothing!" Slaney bellowed, then paled chalk-white as Macurdy's knife slit again, this time through skin and shallowly into the muscle beneath it. Blood oozed, flowing down his hairy belly.

"They'll pay the contents of their purses," Macurdy called back, "whatever that may be. And their horses, keeping enough to ride home on, doubling two on a horse."

Macurdy heard the brief bass rumble of dwarves conferring. Then their leader called again. "All right. Have them hold their purses above their heads. We're comin' out with bows at the ready. We'll not shoot if not threatened, but…"

"Do you pledge that on the honor of your sons?"

"On the honor of our sons through three generations!"

Long generations, Macurdy thought. According to Maikel, dwarves lived longer than Sisters, though they aged more or less gradually, and seldom had children before age forty.

"Careful now, Slaney," Macurdy called. "If even one of your men plays false, you all die. Yourself first." Then he shouted at full voice again. "My lord, send in someone to collect their purses for the Lords of the Mountain."

Blue Wing flew off with the message, in case Jeremid hadn't heard. It took several minutes for the Ozman to get there. With saber in one hand he made the circle; the purses he stuffed in his shirt mostly felt empty, or near it, and not every man even admitted to one. Eight dwarves came out, two of them limping. They wore mail shirts that seemed too light to stop a sword blow, but by their shimmer, Macurdy suspected they were more than ordinary steel.

The bandits, it turned out, had more dead than they'd realized. With a well-aimed arrow, Melody had killed the bandit who'd first challenged Macurdy, shot him when he'd started in from the road as if to intervene. Then she'd gone on to the horse guard and shot him too. Her marksmanship impressed Macurdy; both her arrows had pierced the victims' hearts. Her casual willingness to kill people also impressed him—shocked him a bit despite how warlike the Ozians were.

It was dwarves with their crossbows who stood guard over the bandits and chose the horses with which they'd be paid—the ten best of nineteen. Two others had been wounded during the original skirmish, and run off. Meanwhile the dwarves searched the bandits for valuables they might have transferred from their purses, and found little. Another visited the dead bandits, collected their bows and swords, and chopped their spears in two.

Slaney stepped over to Macurdy. "The truth between the two of us," he growled, in a tone not to be heard by his men. "There is no master, right? There's only the three of you."

"Right and wrong," Macurdy lied. "There are seven of us, but I'm the leader and magician. The other four don't want their presence known in this country. Also I am dwarf friend, and couldn't let them die here."

Slaney didn't know what to believe, and said nothing more; his aura was thick with hate. He and his men mounted—two to a horse except for himself—and without looking back, headed east down the highway.

* * *

Dwarves do not ride full-sized horses; Macurdy had learned that from Maikel. Their legs are short, they require special saddles, and there's the problem of climbing on and off. They ride ponies specially bred—short of leg and very tame, with a quick-footed gait.

This party had been traveling with two saddle ponies each, plus spares and pack ponies, and enough were left that each survivor had one to ride, with several left over. With tallfolk help, they loaded their goods on compensatory horses, on pack saddles lashed together from stout ash saplings. Their dead, including the tallfolk groom they'd hired, were also loaded across horses. Macurdy wondered aloud if it might not be better to build a pyre and burn them, this being the tallfolk custom in Yuulith. The elder dwarf answered there'd be no decay, and he'd have strong coffins made at the nearest village where a proper cart could be bought.

That said he put his hand on each corpse, one after the other, concentrating and muttering, as if preserving them with a spell.

The dwarves didn't look forward to tending a string of horses—they preferred to not even tend their ponies if they could hire some tallfolk to do it—but they seemed not to doubt they could if they had to.

Their biggest problem was that four of them, venturesome youths by dwarvish standards, wanted to join Macurdy, whom they believed would be doing more bold adventurous things— things they hoped to be part of. This, however, would leave their leader with a party of only four, of whom two had been wounded, though one but slightly. But those who wanted to leave claimed the right to do so. They hadn't been part of the original party; had attached themselves to it because they were also from the Diamond Flues.

Old Kittul Kendersson Great Lode disagreed. He pointed out, as a member of the ruling council, he had the authority to take command in emergencies. On the other hand, young Tossi Pellersson Rich Lode, eldest of the four cousins, claimed the emergency was over. And a tallfolk could be hired at the next village to tend the animals.

Old Kittul was apparently not a typical dwarf. He undertook a compromise, for he saw the Pellerssons would leave despite him, which could give rise to ill feelings in both clans. And at any rate the younger dwarf's arguments had merit. While Tossi, though young, understood the politics of the Diamond Flues. The upshot was one of the cousins would leave with Kittul. And Tossi, if he lived long enough, was to personally deliver, to the King In Silver Mountain, a report of the events here. He was also to send one in writing, for the king should be apprised travel entailed risks in this region.

Tossi's three cousins drew straws—Tossi, as senior, held aloof from the risk—the short straw to ride west with Kittul.

When Kittul's party was in the saddle, he called Macurdy to him. "And yewr people," he said, "and yewrs, Tossi Pellersson." When they'd gathered, Kittul cleared his throat and began.

"Macurdy," he said, "ye haven't told me where yer goin' nor why. But yewr a born commander, both in yer manner and yer thinkin', though ye don't flaunt it. And I have no doubt at all that whatever yer about, it's honorable.

"As for yew, Tossi, I suspect yew and yer wild cousins will

find adventures enough to last yer lifetime. Which I hope will be long enough to have children to tell them to."

He looked into the crown of a roadside tree. "And yew, great bird," he called. "Knowledge of yer folk is part of our lore, though it's at second hand from the tomttu. We're too much inside the mountain to know ye first hand. But it's well known yewr kind has a penchant for doin' that which, from time to time, influences events. Sometimes for good, sometimes not, but always honestly. Yer connection with this man is a favorable omen, and I wish ye well."

He turned in his saddle. "Macurdy, hand me your blade."

Macurdy did, and Kittul lay it across his lap (dwarves ride with their knees high), then sat with his eyes closed for a long minute, head back, beard jutting, his ruler's aura swelling upward like pale, purple-blue flame. Then he took Jeremid's saber, frowned a moment over it, and repeated the performance. And then Melody's. When he was done, he looked long at Macurdy before speaking. "It's a hazardous road you've chosen. That much I know, even if I don't know what it is. Much will happen that none of us can foresee. But what I've done with these will help." He gestured at Macurdy's sword. "There is more to re-finin' weapons than just forgin'. And though it's not dwarf made, like theirs"—he gestured toward the cousins—"still it's better now than others made by tallfolk."

With that he tossed his head in a dwarvish farewell, turned his pony, and trotted off westward at the head of his party.

With Blue Wing scouting ahead, Macurdy, Jeremid, Melody, and the three young dwarves rode eastward in the direction of the Silver Mountain, the Sisterhood, and he supposed Varia. Before long they crossed a modest river, and shortly afterward, saw where hooves had left the highway on a narrow, well-worn trail that disappeared northward into the forest. It seemed safe to bet they'd never see Slaney and his crew again.

Chapter 21: The Inn

Within an hour of leaving the skirmish site, they rode out into cleared farmland, the most Macurdy had seen in this world, with woods only here and there. A couple of miles southward, a dark strip of forest stretched from east to west as far as he could see, with more farmland on the other side. The river woods, he supposed. Northward at the edge of seeing were high hills dark with forest.

As they rode, he questioned the dwarves about the country they'd pass through. Tossi, being the eldest of the three, did most of the answering. This, he said, was the beginning of Tekalos, whose king was Gurtho. The oppressive ruler the bandit chief had mentioned, Macurdy realized.

Occasionally they met traffic, most seeming local. There were numerous tiny hamlets—clusters of farmers' huts and out-buildings—and here and there villages. Near evening they saw a rather large village ahead.

Tossi trotted his pony up beside Macurdy's. "Macurdy!" he said, "there's a decent inn ahead. I suggest we stop for supper, and spend the night."

"Feel free, you and your cousins, Tossi Pellersson," Macurdy answered. "The three of us will eat here, but our money's too short to stay under a roof at night. We'll camp by the road east of town, and meet you in the morning."

"Ye don't understand," Tossi said. "We folk who live in the mountain seldom travel without money. I'll pay for the rooms, and the meal too." Macurdy began to decline, but Tossi cut him short: "Think where I'd be tonight, if it wasn't for yew three.

Dead in the woods, likely."

"Say yes, Macurdy," Melody broke in. "They probably have a bath house, and ale."

Macurdy agreed. And there was indeed a bath, but only for men. Melody said she'd share, but the innkeeper refused, looking worriedly at Macurdy's discolored face. He had a number of guests, he said, all of them male, and he feared if she bathed with them, there'd be fights, which could result in his being fined for encouraging disorder.

"How does your wife bathe?" Melody asked.

"In summer, in the walled courtyard behind our apartment, in a big tub. Otherwise in her own kitchen. If the lady would care to, you can use the tub in the garden."

Tossi offered to hire their clothes laundered, along with the dwarves', but they had nothing to wear while their clothes were being washed. So before supper, they went to the shop of a clothier, who sewed clothing of several sizes on speculation. Cottons were cheap enough Melody and Jeremid covered the cost for the three of them. Macurdy had also hoped to buy an old dog from someone, some blind and feeble hound for a copper, to take out of town and shoot for Blue Wing. But the great raven had left when they'd arrived at the inn, so he let it pass.

* * *

Supper was better than he'd expected—a beef stew with assorted vegetables not cooked to pieces, and oatmeal mush with honey, cooked somewhat stiff, with bits of dried apples stirred in after cooking. By local standards, he supposed it was quite good. The pot room was well occupied, seemingly as much by locals as travelers, the ale as popular as the food. But their table, in an out-of-the-way corner, they had to themselves for a while, though it had seating for more. Macurdy wondered if his discolored face was the reason—that and his size and brawn. People might take him for a troublemaker. Or was it the dwarves they were leery of?

Later, while they ate, a man came and sat across from Tossi, and when the potboy came over, ordered supper and ale. Macurdy paid little attention to him till the man spoke to Tossi.

"Excuse me, sir dwarf lord," he said quietly. "Do you deal in weapons?"

"Some in my clan do. What, specifically, are ye interested in?"

"Swords."

"Indeed? How many? When circumstances permit, I might speak to someone who could discuss the matter with ye while passin' through."

"Ah. How many indeed. It would depend on the price; my friends and I have limited resources. Probably not many."

Macurdy looked the man over. By Arbel's system of evaluating auras, this was a ruler of sorts, someone whom others tended to defer to. He wasn't sure how meaningful that was though; Arbel had said *his* was a "ruler's aura," yet he'd been a slave at the time. Just now, Macurdy decided, the stranger lacked money. He was more wishing than anything else. Although his aura reflected inner power.

The conversation ended with Tossi giving him an estimate. "I can't speak with authority though," he finished, "not bein' in the trade myself." The man thanked him and turned to his supper, and the dwarves left, saying they seldom drank more than a single ale in public. And when Jeremid and Melody had finished a second tankard each, the three refugees from Oz went upstairs to bed.

* * *

The dwarves shared one room and the tallfolk another, with a single large bed in each. Jeremid suggested they draw straws to see who slept in the middle, and Melody drew the short. After they'd lain down, she raised herself on one elbow and leaned over Macurdy. He could smell the ale on her breath. "Macurdy," she said, "your mouth looks well enough for kissing now," and lowering her face to his, kissed him sweetly, long and lovingly, while groping him. "Make love to me, Macurdy," she murmured.

"Melody, I can't," he said, moving her hand away. "You know that. And anyway we're not alone."

"Would you if Jeremid weren't here?"

"God, Melody, I'd like to, but it wouldn't be right."

She lay back down exasperated. "I've never in my life heard of anyone so damned difficult," she said.

Jeremid spoke then. "Spear maiden, there's a Hero on the other side of you who'd happily hump you all night long."

"You're not the Hero I want humping me."

He laughed. "Then you're as damned difficult as he is."

"Go to hell, Jeremid."

He laughed again, and after a moment, she did too.

Macurdy didn't. After a bit he went to sleep, but awoke some time later to quiet sounds. He was the only one in bed, and the sounds were of panting and moaning on the floor beside it. He lay without moving, feeling miserable. The sounds speeded and intensified without growing appreciably louder, peaked, then died. A minute later, Macurdy heard Jeremid's whisper: "How'd you like that, spear maiden?"

"You're good, Hero," she whispered back, "you're very good."

"It's here for you whenever you want it." Jeremid's chuckling was a series of soft aspirations. "I'm better than Macurdy'd be, I'll bet."

"Hard to say. His horn is bigger though, that's for sure. He's a real horse."

This time Jeremid didn't chuckle. "How do you know?"

Melody told him of mounting Macurdy on the night he was beaten.

"Then all that stuff about loyalty to his wife…"

"He wasn't awake when I slid it in. And even then he didn't start pushing for a while."

Neither spoke for a minute or so, till Jeremid said, "Why did you follow him? Just to get humped by him? I always thought that recklessness of yours would get you in trouble. And he's not even good-looking anymore, with his teeth all broken out."

"I'm in love with him. That's not something you'd understand. Humping's as far as it goes with you."

Jeremid didn't respond. Despite his own state of mind, Macurdy wondered what the Ozman was thinking.

"Why did you follow him?" Melody asked.

"Don't know. I guess—I admire him. He's got more guts than anyone I've ever seen. And he's honest. And smart, damned smart—except when it comes to you." Jeremid chuckled again. "Besides, where he is, interesting things are going to happen."

Their conversation lapsed, and Macurdy wondered if they'd gone to sleep there on the floor. Then one of them began to breathe a little raggedly. "Damn you," Melody whispered, "I said only once."

Again Jeremid chuckled. "Here we are naked, and who knows when we'll have this good a chance again."

After a moment, Melody said, "Just a minute."

Between half closed lids, Macurdy watched her go to her gear. In the dimness, the vague sight of her bare buttocks made the breath stick in his chest. Half a minute later she was back out of sight, on the floor with Jeremid. Before long he could hear them having sex again. His torment lasted considerably longer than the first time, and Melody was harder put to keep her climax quiet.

This time when they'd finished, there was no conversation. They put their cottons back on and came carefully back to bed. It was quite a while before Macurdy slept again.

Chapter 22: Decorations on a Town Square

On the road next morning, Macurdy did not feel refreshed. His dreams had been restless and troubling, though he couldn't remember them. He had no trouble at all, though, recalling what he'd heard when he'd wakened in the night. He supposed he should feel complimented by the things they'd said about him, while by the standards of Oz, or at least the House of Heroes, their couplings had been unobtrusive, even modest.

These realizations didn't help. He felt—deprived and jealous. Feelings which he realized were totally unjustified. Jeremid wanted Melody as much as he did, and had as much right to. As for Melody and himself—clearly all he needed to do was say yes.

And how had Varia spent last night? he wondered. Being bred by some stud? Enjoying it? She'd been more than enthusiastic when they'd been together. He imagined her groans, her cries almost yelps, her strong fingers digging his back. Whose back now?

While he imagined, Melody trotted her horse up beside his. "Macurdy," she said, "we need to talk. Privately."

He dug heels in his horse's ribs, and they pulled farther ahead of the others. "You woke up last night, didn't you?" she asked.

He nodded without speaking.

"When I got back in bed, your breathing didn't sound like you were sleeping. And this morning—it was pretty obvious."

Yeah, he thought, *I suppose it was.*

"What did you hear?" she asked.

"All of it, I guess. The first time, and the second, and the talk in between."

"Macurdy, I love you, you—jackass. And it's damned hard to be around you without having you."

"It's the same with me."

"I suppose it was bad for you, listening to us go at it."

He grunted. "That's not your fault. Not your problem."

"I know it's not. But I don't like having caused you pain. I'd rather cause you pleasure."

"Suppose you get pregnant?"

"I've got lamb bane in my gear."

Lamb bane. Of course. He'd heard of it from Hauser, who collected it in season for Arbel. It didn't keep anyone from getting pregnant, but both sheep and women, if they ate it early enough, miscarried with no trouble. The two of them rode without speaking for several chains. "Look," she said finally. "I can't promise I won't hump with Jeremid again. But I do promise not to do it where you can hear us. Will that help?"

By Oz standards, he realized, that was downright thoughtful. Even sweet. He looked at her earnest face and found himself smiling. Fondly! The realization startled him, left him mentally gawping. *You're in love with her, Macurdy!* he told himself amazed. *You are! You're in love with this girl!* "Sure," he found himself saying. "It'll help a lot. And Melody, I don't want you to feel bad about it; I really don't. Because I love you, too."

She stared at him, surprised, then annoyed. "Macurdy," she said, "you're an exasperating bastard." And pulling aside, fell in a little distance behind him.

Leaving Macurdy wondering what he'd said wrong. But the question was fleeting, giving way to the matter of being in love with two women at once. Truly in love with them. He'd never thought about such a thing before, had grown up accepting you could only love one at a time. Yet it seemed to him both loves were real. His love for Melody was different than his love for Varia, but it was love, he had no doubt.

The difference that counted, he told himself, was the vow he'd taken. And he'd abide by it in spite of all.

* * *

The weather had turned nearly summery. Gnats were out, though not a kind that bit. The elms along the road were pale green now, with countless millions of disk-winged seeds, while the new leaves of various species were expanding.

This plain, this Green River Valley, was pleasant to Macurdy's eyes. Tekalos was good farmland. Talbott and Hauser assumed there was a geographical equivalence between Yuulith and Farside, and as closely as Macurdy could figure, if there was a gate here, it would open into Tennessee. Western Tennessee or maybe west-central. From all he'd heard, Tennessee was mostly hills and mountains, and he wondered if it had any area of farmland to compare with this.

In midafternoon, Blue Wing caught up with them. He'd flown back to the site where the bandits had attacked the dwarves, and filled his belly and crop with dead horse meat. Or so he said. But Macurdy was aware that even vultures, with their hooked and powerful beaks, let dead horses and cattle lay longer than that for the hide to soften. It seemed likelier that some dead bandit had been Blue Wing's meal.

The dwarves slowed their progress. Their ponies were slower, and they took breaks long enough to make fire and boil water for sassafras tea. They felt no urgency. And while Macurdy's experience with horses hadn't included long cross-country trips, he told himself this was probably a more sensible speed anyway. Besides, more than a year had passed since Varia had been kidnapped; what difference would a few days make now? She was no doubt safe enough.

And it seemed to him the dwarves were much more important to him than the time they were costing; they were his passport to the King in Silver Mountain. Meanwhile they were good companions; it was one of them who shot a possum with his crossbow, then carried it along as supper for Blue Wing.

Still, from time to time he felt restless.

Near dusk, the six of them made camp in a pleasant woods, along a river not much more than a creek. It allowed them to bathe again, which they did naked, though the dwarves used a stretch of riverbank screened from the tallfolk by undergrowth. Naked, Melody was prettier than he'd realized, though muscular for a woman. Breaking the spell, he jumped from the cutbank into the river, to conceal his developing erection. The cold water killed it utterly, and he grinned as Melody waded tentatively in, her arms wrapped around herself.

"Shall I splash you?" he called.

"You hadn't better," she answered, then launched herself, gasping as she surfaced. He did splash her then, and she charged him, splashing back. In a moment they were tussling and laughing, their wet bodies twisting against each other.

Abruptly Macurdy let her go and backed away, chagrined, and at the same time pleased with himself. Melody smiled. "That's a good start, Macurdy," she said softly, and reaching, touched his cheek. Then she turned and waded out of the river. Macurdy watched first her departing back, then her buttocks and legs, while his fingers touched his cheek where hers had. Varia had touched him like that.

* * *

That evening, fireflies were out by the hundreds in their camp, yellowish glowing lights bobbing and circling in the twilight and dark. Melody went to where Macurdy squatted, and squatted beside him, their arms and shoulders touching as they watched. But only for a little. Then the three tallfolk bedded down near each other, Macurdy feeling as if, for the first time in his life, he had a girl friend. His relationship with Varia had skipped that stage.

* * *

The next day brought a thundershower by midmorning, and a prolonged thunderstorm in late afternoon that drove them to cover at a crossroads inn. It wasn't as large as the inn they'd stayed in before, nor as clean, and Macurdy decided this was a good time to exercise the magic Arbel had taught him for killing fleas, lice, and the like.

It seemed to work well; either that or there'd been none to start with. And no one had sex out of sight on the floor, because there was no bed, only three straw-filled sacks unrolled side by side.

* * *

About two hours into their ride next morning, Blue Wing's voice called from overhead: "Macurdy! Macurdy!" Macurdy reined in and waited, looking up. The great bird spiraled sharply down and reached for the roadside with long legs.

"What'd you find?"

"There's a town ahead, not far from the highway."

"Aye," said Tossi. "Gormin Town. I recall it. It's a reeve's town, a shire seat, walled with a palisade. There's a better than usual inn at the crossroads nearby."

Macurdy nodded, looking at Blue Wing, waiting.

"The town has an open space near its center," the bird continued. "With poles standing there, and men hanging on them."

"Hanging?"

"By their wrists. Some appear to be dead. Others were just then being fastened up."

"Sounds like a good place to stay away from," Jeremid suggested.

Macurdy spoke as if to himself. "Men hung up from poles." He focused on Blue Wing again. "How many?"

"You know I'm not good with numbers," Blue Wing said a little testily. "You are six, right?"

"That's right."

"At least twice that many, I would guess."

"If we spend a day or two there, what will you do?" Macurdy asked. "I may need you."

"There's a slaughterhouse nearby, with a place where the offal is thrown. They'll very likely put out some choice pieces for me: a head already skinned perhaps, and some organs. And I can keep track of where you are by the dwarves' ponies. There'll hardly be anything else like them there."

"Thanks. Keep an eye on me for a while, if you would. I may have questions."

"As you wish."

The raven took to the air, running and hopping a few strides

for his takeoff, as if his crop was full; perhaps he'd already visited the slaughterhouse. Macurdy nudged his horse with his heels.
"Gormin Town doesn't sound like a good place to be," Jeremid
said.

Macurdy's lips pursed thoughtfully. "To get Varia away
from the Sisterhood, it could be useful to have armed men with
me. Not to take inside the dwarf kingdom, but standing by."

It was Melody who answered. "What do men hanging in the
square have to do with that?"

"I'm not sure. But—why hang men up like that? Are they
bandits? Rebels?"

She waited for the rest of it, and when there was no more,
rode on frowning. An hour and a half later they came to the inn,
at the crossroads a half-mile outside the town's north gate. Macurdy stopped outside the courtyard, and looking up, spotted Blue
Wing high overhead. He waved until the bird tilted and started
down. Then Macurdy gathered the others close around him. In
a minute, Blue Wing arrived to perch on the top rail of a fence
beside the road.

"Tossi," Macurdy said, "would you take a room at the inn
for Jeremid, Melody and me? But not for you three?"

The dwarf gnarled his brows. "What have ye in mind?"

"I'm not sure. But it may be I'll want you to take a place in
town for yourselves."

"In town?"

"Can you make swords?"

"What?!"

"You told Kittul Kendersson you wanted adventure. It might
be we'll find some here. If I decide it's the thing to do, would
you hire a room at the inn for the three of us?"

"Aye, I would. But as for making swords…We could, any
of us, but they'd not be of first quality. Better than tallfolk make,
but…Every dwarf lad is taught to work metals, from gold to
iron, but we'd rarely be called on to do it without a master smith
at hand to supervise."

"Good enough. Making swords would only be an excuse
for hiring a place in town. Let's leave our remounts and pack

animals at the stable here and ride in. We won't take rooms yet; I have to see what's going on first."

* * *

At the town gates, Macurdy felt the sentries eye his spear, and those of the two Ozians, but didn't stop them. The dwarves, he decided, had been their pass. Inside the stockade, the cobbled main street was wide enough for wagons to pass easily, though buildings overhung it. The six visitors walked their mounts briskly, the quickstepping hooves of the dwarves' ponies a sharp counterpoint to the louder clopping of the horses, and shortly they came to the town square.

It was decorated with the bodies of men dead or dying, or soon to be—fourteen of them, standing or hanging with their wrists lashed overhead, the sun beating on them. Above each was a sign in blood red: REBEL. Two were conspicuously dead, had begun to swell, and flies swarmed on them. Six others were either dead or too weak to stand, hanging on their tethers, their hands swollen and black. Another six stood grimly, their weight on their feet instead of on their wrists. Three guards stood by. Most bypassers avoided looking. A stray dog, in slinking mode, approached one of the dead and sniffed. Spear leveled, one of the guards ran it off.

"Stay here," Macurdy murmured to the others, and dismounting, walked up to a guard. "We're strangers," he said. "From the Kingdom of the Diamond Flues." He gestured toward the posts. "What sort of men are these?"

The guard looked sourly at the posts, then at Macurdy's discolored face, but his speech was civil. "They're from the hills off north," he said. "Part of a rebel band." He wrinkled his nose. "The dead'll be cut down this evening."

Macurdy thanked him and returned to the others, to continue slowly on around the square. Here and there were benches, mostly unoccupied. Macurdy looked over the auras of the few who sat there, and shortly pulled up and dismounted again, walking over to a man who was old by Rude Lands standards, his mouth a sunken, lipless crease.

Sitting down near him, Macurdy spoke quietly. "A hard way

to die, on those posts."

The old man said nothing, as if he hadn't heard.

"We're from over west of the Great Muddy, traveling east to the Silver Mountain. Came in to buy some goods, and saw those poor devils hanging by their wrists."

Still nothing.

"Why would men rebel, in a country as fertile as this? Surely there must be plenty to eat."

The toothless mouth seemed hardly to move, but words came from it now, low and monotone. "There are kingdoms where men are pressed down by cruelties and demands. Where the man who swings the scythe may have too little bread to eat and where he'd best not have a pretty wife or daughter. Or pride."

"Ah. Then why so few rebels?"

"The commons have no generals, no strong and able leaders. Nor weapons, most of them, nor any place to hide."

"And yet those men..." Macurdy gestured.

The old man took a slow breath. "They're Kullvordi—hillsmen from off north. Their not-too-distant grandfathers were tribesmen who lived in their own way. Even now they have bows and spears; some even have swords. And forests to hide in, where soldiers hardly dare to go. But if a rebellion grows troublesome, the soldiers burn some farms, drive off their livestock, and kill hostages. And after a bit, the rebellion dies as if it never was, leaving only a few hard men living off what game they can shoot, and by thieving. Until someone gives them away for a purse."

The old man stopped then, and Macurdy asked no more. After a minute he lay a paw on a bent shoulder and squeezed lightly, then got up and left.

* * *

The six of them rode back to the inn for the midday meal. Afterward, Macurdy, Melody, and Jeremid took a room with money Tossi provided, then rode northward, killing time with exploration, while Blue Wing flew high, learning the land far more widely than they could.

Meanwhile the dwarves, with their ponies and a pack horse,

returned to town to carry out their part of the plan. When they'd finished their business for the day, the youngest of them, Yxhaft Vorelsson Rich Lode, rode back out to the inn, where he sat in the pot room nursing a short mug of ale till the tallfolk got back. After a supper of pot roast and boiled potatoes, they all went to the small room the three tallfolk were to share. Tossi, Yxhaft said, had seen to everything agreed on. As for security—during the day there'd been a single guard in each of the rather widely-spaced watch shelters on the town walls, but it was logical to expect two or more at night, to keep each other awake. He also mapped the whereabouts of the ground-floor apartment Tossi had rented. "If yer uncertain," he finished, "there'll be a small sign by the door, with dwarf runes in charcoal, tellin' those who can read it—and I doubt there's one such in all Gormin Town, except ourselves—that 'here dwell three sons of the Rich Lode Clan.' "

He grinned at Macurdy then, for he was a youth as dwarves go. "It has a cellar hole," he went on, "and its own weed patch in back, with its own privy. We've put the anvil block on the cellar lid, and strewed sand over the floor, as one might to prevent fires startin' from the forge. It's a poor place for smithin', but who'd know except a smith?

"Oh! And Tossi got a letter of retainer from the reeve, which no doubt we can use, if we need to, as a pass to get through the gate. Should they start keepin' folks in, which I expect they will."

Then Yxhaft left, riding back to town.

* * *

According to the innkeeper, the town gates closed at sundown, or on cloudy days when dusk began to thicken. And because of recent disorders, there was a curfew. So when the sun was low, Macurdy, Melody, and Jeremid walked the half-mile to town, chatting and laughing deliberately as they approached the gate. They entered without being questioned, and strolled the perimeter street, still chatting while Macurdy unobtrusively examined the palisade. Each stair-flight up to the archery walk ended at a watch shelter, and even as they walked, a column of guardsmen marched past them, pausing to send three to each shelter, replacing the one on day watch.

"We'll have to figure out some other way," Jeremid said. "We can do the job tomorrow night."

Macurdy shook his head. "Tomorrow night's too late. We need to free them while they're able-bodied."

"Maybe we can use a rope with a hook," Melody suggested. "Throw it onto the archery walk, and climb."

Macurdy nodded, thinking the odds of success were not good. Maybe Tossi would have some ideas. It wouldn't do, though, to be seen going into the dwarves' apartment, so when twilight came, they sheltered in the shadows of an unpaved alley nearby. Once they heard the hard-booted feet of a street patrol, but didn't see it. After the curfew bell tolled, Macurdy sent Jeremid out; he'd yowl twice like a cat if everything was clear. A minute later they heard the yowls and slipped out of their alley. Jeremid beckoned, and when they got to him, Kittul Kendersson stood with the door ajar. "In! In!" he rumbled softly, then closed it behind them.

The room was lit by the usual lamp—a bowl of oil with a wick on one side. Kittul took them into the room fitted as a smithy, and grinning, waved around. "The reeve provided all of it: forge, anvil, tongs, hammer, quenchin' tank—everything."

They're hungry for dwarf steel here, Macurdy thought. There were coarse sacks of charcoal, too, and from behind them, Kittul took a rope with knots at intervals. At one end was a triple grab hook that he held up chuckling. "Just made it. Thought it might be useful."

"Good. We've been talking about that. And the crossbows?"

"They're in the sleepin' room." Kittul paused. "I've been thinkin' though. 'Tis us should do the shootin'. We're used to crossbows; we'll not miss."

Macurdy shook his head. "I don't doubt you're better marksmen with them," he said. "But if anyone saw, even in the night, they could tell the patrolmen it was dwarves. While with us—in the dark we look like anyone else around here. And if there's a chase, our legs are longer.

"Besides, Jeremid and Melody have used crossbows, and in my world, we use weapons called guns that you aim pretty much the same way."

"Ah. Well," said Kittul thoughtfully, "there's no doubt we'd be recognized, even if just glimpsed. So then. Best ye start while the moon's still up." He led them into the bedroom, and standing on tiptoes, took two crossbows from pegs on the wall, crossbows that were cocked using a stirrup, and a hook on the belt. Macurdy had thought to use one himself, but the belts were too small to buckle around him.

He handed it to Jeremid, saying, "Try it on." Jeremid did. It buckled in the last notch. "You and Melody will do the shooting," Macurdy told him.

* * *

They got ready and left, walking to the square via an alley that opened onto it not far from the posts. At the alley's mouth they huddled in darkness, eyes sorting through the moon shadows around the post area.

Macurdy's eyes made out four guards now, one each on the southeast and southwest corners, while two stood conversing quietly within a few feet of one another on the north end, near where the main street hit the square. He wondered how alert they were. Did they think someone might try a rescue? Or was guard just routine, another dull watch?

He led the others back a ways. "Melody," he murmured, "circle 'round and come out the next alley south. Jeremid, circle north, cross the main street where they won't see you; come to the square on the other side. You two will kill the two in back, the corner men." He paused. "Melody, tell me what I said." She did. Then Jeremid repeated the instructions.

"Good. I'll take the two in front. After you've had time to get in position, I'll go out to one of them. I've got no bow, no spear, and no sword, and my knife's around back of my hip, so they shouldn't be too leery of me.

"Keep a close eye on me. I'll pretend I've been drinking, and walk up to him and start talking. Then I'll knife him and jump the other one. That's when you'll shoot your men and reload. Got it?"

They both stared at him. *I know,* he thought. *I can't believe we're doing this either.* They'd discussed the broad features back at the inn, and it had felt spooky enough then, in daylight and safety. "Good," he said. "Go!"

It took them three or four seconds to turn away, leaving Macurdy where he stood. *Come on,* he told himself, *it's for Varia. Let's get going.* He took another alley, moving quickly but quietly, eyes and ears fine-tuned. Asking himself how this could be for Varia, or how it could possibly work. But not wavering.

Shortly he reached the main street. The moon was low and the whole street in shadow, when he turned quietly onto it. He was in mid-block when he heard what had to be a patrol, and pausing, looked backward. They were turning onto his street from a cross street a hundred yards away. With torches.

Hell! he thought. Some of the shops along the street had small marquees over their entrances, perhaps to protect them from slops thrown from windows above. Striding a few quick steps farther, he jumped, grabbed a marquee, and pulled himself up. It took his weight, and he lay as low and flat as he could. If they'd seen him...

But the shadows were dark, and the torches had little reach. He shielded his face with his arms. The patrol passed so close below, it seemed to him they should have heard his heart pounding. Passed and continued along the street, hard-soled boots thudding and scuffing on the cobblestones. After half a minute he raised his head enough to see them from behind. Eight or ten, it seemed, fewer than he'd thought. At the square, instead of turning west or east to pass it by, they walked directly to the poles and stopped. Faintly he heard commands being given; seconds later they turned and started back his way. Again he lowered his face, shielding it, and again they passed beneath him, marching back north up the street, turned onto another and were gone.

Changing the guard! he thought. *Gentle Jesus thank you! If I'd been three minutes sooner...* He stayed where he was for several minutes, giving Melody and Jeremid more time, then dropped quietly to the cobblestones and moved on. *That was an omen,* he told himself, *a good one!* And tried to believe it.

The square opened before him, the nearer guard about thirty yards away, and he scarcely hesitated, emerging from the shadows, walking unsteadily. It only then occurred to him they might shout or blow a whistle or something—maybe kill him—because he was breaking the curfew.

The new guards stood about five yards apart, instead of side by side like the previous two. Both pointed their spears at him, ready to thrust long or short. He walked up dangerously close to one of them, pretending drunkenness. "'Scuse me," he said. "I'm lookin' for a frien' I used to have. Name is Lucky. Someone said he was one of these guys." He waved broadly at the pole-bound captives.

Both guards laughed. "Nobody here's called Lucky," one said. "Not anymore."

Macurdy peered as if to penetrate the night, stepping nearer, weaving, and spoke confidentially. "He owes me five coppers. Did you know that?" Then lowered his voice further. "Are they dead?"

"They cut the dead ones down at sunset, and took them away. These are all alive."

Macurdy leaned. "Lucky," he called hoarsely, "are you there?"

And moved, his left hand closing on the spear shaft, shoving it aside and pulling it past him, drawing his knife as he strode into the guard, plunging it under his ribs, in and up and back out, letting the man fall, catching the other with his eyes. The second guard's reaction was slow; he took an uncertain step toward Macurdy, and the heavy knife, thrown hard, struck him in the middle of the chest. With a weak bleat, the man slumped and fell. Macurdy was on him in an instant, ignoring the third and fourth guards, who were Melody's and Jeremid's responsibilities. Gripping a shoulder, he turned the man over and grabbed the knife hilt. It had gone through the breastbone to the hilt and was slippery with blood. He'd probably stepped in blood, too, he realized.

Then Melody's voice hissed at him. "Macurdy! Hurry! A

patrol's coming!" He looked around, feeling just an instant's prick of panic, then strode to the nearest rebel and cut the thong that held his arms overhead. The man fell unmoving, and Macurdy realized he'd been dead weight on his bonds. The next was standing, and he freed him. "Stay with her," Macurdy husked to him, and went to a third. He became aware Melody was also cutting men free. When they were done, six rebels stood. Three others lay still. Without hesitating, Macurdy cut their throats; he couldn't take them, and wouldn't leave them for further torture. Only one gushed blood. The other two had died already.

"Come *on!*" Melody said.

"You take them," Macurdy answered. "My boots are bloody; they'll leave marks. Go!"

He heard a command shouted from near the south end of the square, and ran not north with Melody and the rebels, but west, scuffing his feet in the grass and dirt to wipe off what he could of the blood. Crossing the street, he ducked into an alley, wondering where Jeremid might be. Somewhere off southeast someone was shouting, and he wondered what that was about. Around a corner he stopped, and pulling off his boots, tied them together, slung them over a shoulder, then trotted off barefoot.

The cobblestones were rough-surfaced, and he was limping when the dwarves let him in. The front room was dark, crowded but quiet. Men sat on the floor with cups and bowls, and the place smelled of stew—supper reheated. Melody gripped Macurdy's sleeve and pulled him into the kitchen. "You did it!" she said, and began to unbutton his bloody shirt. "We need to rinse this before the blood sets."

He dropped his boots and stripped it off. Melody immersed it in a small tub, surging it up and down while the water reddened. "The boots too," Macurdy said, looking around for more water. Apparently it had to be carried from some public well.

"I need to get the blood out of your shirt, first."

"Where's Jeremid?" he asked.

"The last I saw, he was running toward the patrol. Probably to draw them off."

Macurdy's face was stiff with tension. He'd hoped to pull

this off and get over the wall without an uproar. But now...Now the whole damned police force would be out, and any soldiers garrisoned there. The gates were already closed, and the guards in the watch shelters would be wide awake now, alert as hawks. "Where's Tossi?" he asked.

"Right here." The dwarf had come in behind him from the front room.

"Will your cellar hole hold six men?"

"If they don't mind dark and discomfort."

"Anything will be better than what they've just been through. But they'll need air and water."

Tossi frowned. "I can leave the trapdoor open most of the time. If someone bangs on the door, one of us can answer it while another closes the trapdoor and slides the anvil block over top of it." He paused, peering intently at Macurdy. "How long will we be stayin', with the six of them under the floor?"

"I'll try taking one or maybe two out with Melody and me tonight. And Jeremid, if he gets back in time. Police and soldiers will be searching house to house tomorrow—maybe even later tonight—and it'll look suspicious to have tallfolk here, even if they're not the prisoners. But these men need to stay somewhere, until things quiet down or I get them out somehow."

"One or two tonight, you say. The danger's great, I'm sure ye know. It'll be buzzin' like a beehive out there."

"It'll be worse a little later, when the confusion settles and they get organized. Let me trade shirts with someone, to wear while this one dries. Then we'll be on our way."

* * *

Ten minutes later, Macurdy was out in the night again, with Melody and a rebel named Verder. Macurdy carried twenty-five feet of slender, knotted rope wrapped around his waist, concealed by a tunic the canny Tossi had bought for the purpose. He carried the grapnel in his hand for lack of a better place. At the first corner, not a hundred feet away, they turned down an alley, moving at an easy jog.

It took a minute for the sound to register on Macurdy, but when it did, he stopped. The night, the town, held a diffuse droning. Melody and Verder were listening, too.

"What is it?" Verder asked.

"People," Melody said in a hushed voice. "People off south."

Then it struck Macurdy. He knew as if he'd been there and heard it happen! Striding to a shutter, he banged on it with the grapnel, shouting: "Have you heard?! The guards were killed in the square, and the prisoners cut free!"

Melody and the rebel stared shocked. "Macurdy!" she hissed. "What—"

"The people you hear," he answered. "They know! It must have been Jeremid. He must have run through the streets yelling what happened, and people are coming out. They don't like their rulers here; that's why there's a curfew. And if enough people come out, it'll keep the street patrols tied up." He turned and trotted off, still shouting, pausing now and then to bang on shutters. Melody and the rebel trotted after him, both of them shouting too. Voices answered from indoors, some questioning, some angry. When the alley opened onto a street, they turned east on it and trotted three more blocks shouting, before they saw five youths run into the street ahead of them from an alley. They were shouting too.

"The guards in the square are killed!" Macurdy yelled again. "The prisoners are freed!" Just ahead was a broken fence enclosing a weedy garden, and abruptly he stopped to yank staves loose from it. The youths watched, uncertain but alert. Melody realized at once what he was up to, and began piling the staves in the middle of the street. Verder helped, and now the youths, catching on, kicked and shoved on the supports of a rickety porch till the roof fell. Macurdy ignited the pile of fence staves, then ran on. They'd gone hardly more than a block before they heard shouts of "Fire! Fire!" behind them.

He shouted no more, nor stopped again till panting, they reached the perimeter street. The half moon was low in the west, but by its pale light, Macurdy could make out guards in and by the watch shelters. The sound of people was growing. To the guards it must seem dangerous, threatening.

"Let's go for it," Macurdy said. "If they see us, they still might stay where they are. If necessary, we'll run across the street again."

"What about the others?" Verder asked.

"I'll lower you two from the wall and go back for them. Melody knows where to take you."

The perimeter street was bare dirt, very wide by Rude Lands standards, about forty feet, but in dense moon shadow all the way to the palisade. Macurdy had opened his tunic while he'd talked, and unwound the rope. Now he dashed across, twirling the grapnel, and flung it up to the archery walk midway between watch shelters. It caught, and he started climbing, wishing the rope was thicker and gave a better grip. *Thank God for the knots*, he thought. After a moment's pause to look, he pulled himself onto the walk. There was a tug at the rope, and he hauled the rebel up, then repeated the performance with Melody. Still no one seemed to notice them. In another minute he'd lowered first Melody, then Verder down the outside.

Only then did he turn and look over the town. He wasn't the only one who'd set fires, and some hadn't taken care to light them in the middle of the street; south of the square, part of the town was burning. He rehooked the grapnel on the planking and lowered himself to the street, then with a few flips of the rope, dislodged it.

For a moment he considered leaving it there, finding it again when he came back. But afraid of losing it, he wrapped it around himself again, buttoned his tunic, and ran back up the street. It was starting to fill with people, and more porches were burning.

* * *

When he arrived at the dwarves' apartment, Jeremid was there, grinning excitedly. In a hurried conference, it was decided the dwarves should leave too. Their ponies were lodged at a stable on the main street, near the north gate, and it seemed likely that considering the fires, the gate guards would let them out. They were dwarves, after all, and had a letter of retainer from the reeve.

They'd take Jeremid with them, posing as their servant, to help them handle their personal gear. The smithing gear they'd leave behind. They'd gotten it on credit anyway, using the reeve's letter of authorization.

Macurdy left with the five remaining rebels, taking alleys to bypass fires, and in minutes they'd reached the stockade. It was burning too, though not vigorously; the guards had abandoned their posts, and fires had been lit in some of the watch shelters. Moments later, Macurdy and his five charges were on the outside. Leaving the rope and grapnel hanging, he led his rebels north past the town.

Chapter 23: The Rebel Commander

When he'd left the northeast corner of the stockade behind, Macurdy took his little band through a field of some spring-seeded small grain—whether oats or barley, he couldn't tell in the dark. It was heavily loaded with dew that had already soaked his boots.

Well before he reached the road, his rebels were getting strung out, too weak to keep up. "We'll stop here," he said, and at once, three of them sank to the ground despite the cold dew. Southward, the sky above town was ruddied by fires, here and there flames tall enough to be seen above the town walls. Macurdy felt a certain guilt at his role in the burning. But the townsmen, he told himself, had been ready to rise up, to riot, and the fires had been inevitable.

Rebellion, he told himself, was the easy part. The hard parts would be winning, and replacing their government with something better. But that was up to them. What he needed to do was work this to somehow help him rescue Varia.

Meanwhile he had allies now, or so it seemed. He looked them over. All but one had what Arbel had taught him to recognize as warrior auras. The other had an artisan aura; he'd be good at making things, and maybe at coming up with ideas. "I guess you know my name's Macurdy," Macurdy said. "What are yours?"

They told him, stepping on one another's lines. It turned out they were from two different districts. Three were from north, up the road not many hours' ride; the others were from three day's ride northeast.

"Anyone here injured?" he asked.

They'd all been beaten after their capture, and the two from the northeastern band hadn't eaten for four days, except what the dwarves had fed them. Macurdy realized he was pretty hungry himself. "All right. We're going north another quarter mile or so. There's an inn there. I'll hide you near it and go see about horses."

One of the rebels spoke then—one of the northeastern group—a rangy, tough-looking man who'd given his name as Wolf. "Where are you from?" he asked. "You don't sound like Tekalos, neither hillsman nor flatlander."

"From off west," Macurdy said, "the other side of the Great Muddy. A country called Oz; I was a soldier there. Two of us were, and the woman's father was a commander. She's one of a caste of warrior women, weapons-trained all her life. She's killed two men since we left there."

"How'd you get mixed up in our trouble?"

Macurdy laughed wryly. "We didn't get along with our troll's spawn of a commander. So one morning about daybreak I tromped the seeds out of him and three of his bully boys. Then we grabbed some horses and took off. Kept ahead of them long enough to cross the Muddy."

Macurdy realized his story sounded unlikely, but it went with the lingering discoloration of his face, and his missing and broken teeth.

"That doesn't answer my question," Wolf said. "How'd you get mixed up in the troubles here? Why'd you cut us loose?"

"Any king, or count, or reeve who'd hang people up like that, deserves all the enemies he can get. We decided we'd give him six more."

"How'd the dwarves get mixed up in it? I never heard of them mixing in tallfolks' troubles before."

"They're young westerners, feeling their oats."

"Umm."

It was apparent Wolf still had reservations, but he'd go along for the time being. The rest were probably too grateful, Macurdy decided, and too hungry, to question their rescuer's motives. "Okay," he said. "Let's get moving. We've got to get well away from here before daylight."

They walked slowly, keeping to the grain field to avoid people riding away from town and the fires. His rebels were rural, automatically considerate of growing crops, and stayed in single file to lessen damage. After a bit they crossed the Valley Highway and continued well past the inn, then angled northwest across pasture. Northeastward, Macurdy could make out horses grazing, probably rental animals belonging to the innkeeper. Scattered along the north-south road were spreading trees that would have inhibited dew formation, and he steered toward one of them. When they got there, they found a thin fringe of shrubs and saplings growing along the rail fence, screening the pasture from the road. The rebels sank to the ground.

"I'll leave you here for a while," Macurdy said, "while I see what horses I can scrounge. Wolf, come with me. I'll be back before long." Then he headed toward the inn.

The dwarves had come in just ahead of him. The town gates had been opened, and the last room already let when they'd arrived, so they'd crowded in with Jeremid, Melody, and Verder, in the small room Macurdy had rented earlier.

"I've got the others waiting north up the road," he told them. "They're not in very good shape; haven't been eating, and two were beaten up pretty badly. I'll take them north up the road to the nearest rebel camp, but I need horses for them."

"Simple enough," Jeremid said. Melody was nodding agreement even before he explained. "Just take some from the stable. Saddle what you need and go."

Macurdy shook his head. "There's the stable boy, and whatever guard or guards the innkeeper has there. We'd have to manhandle them; tie and gag them. And the only enemies I want in this country are the king and his henchmen."

Tossi spoke before Jeremid could argue. "As I count them," the dwarf said, "we need only three more. I'll hire them from the innkeeper in the mornin', or buy them if he'll sell."

Macurdy was relieved. He'd decided the dwarves had deep pockets, but hadn't been sure Tossi would go for another expense like this. Now he gave instructions: He, Melody and the rebels would leave at once. Jeremid and the dwarves would follow at dawn.

Within a few minutes, they were headed north up the road in the moonless dark, Macurdy and Melody on their own horses, the six rebels doubled up on three others. None of them knew where they were going. The men were either from Wollerda's Company, off east, or Dell's Band, which had been broken. There was another band off north, Orthal's Company, but they didn't know where it was. Macurdy grunted. "We'll find it," he said.

It took some four hours to reach forested hills; fifteen or twenty miles, he guessed. By that time there was a hint of dawn in the eastern sky. Half an hour later they left the road at a creek, splashing westward through gray dawn-light, heavy forest on both banks. When they'd gone a hundred yards or so, they left the stream, pushing through a fringe of osier and willow onto dry ground.

"We'll rest here a few hours," Macurdy said. "Tie your horses and get dry wood for warming fires." He and Melody helped, and after they'd piled a stock of branchwood, he built and lit a pair of fires. Then the two of them walked back out to the roadside, carrying the oiled leather rain capes that were part of their saddle gear, and picked their careful way up the slope to an overlook forty or fifty feet above the road.

At the top, Macurdy sat down on leaf mould just within the forest edge. "What do you think?" he asked.

"About what?"

"Anything. Our evening's work. Our rebels. How we're doing."

"Macurdy, you're a magician, and I'm not talking about how you make fires. Things go right for you." She shifted closer to him. "All that excitement made me horny. If you had to separate Jeremid and me tonight, the least you can do is kiss me. The very least."

She held her face toward his, perhaps a foot away. He didn't close the gap. "Melody," he said. "I like sitting here with you, but…"

"I know. You're married, with some kind of strange Farside vow." She sighed. "All right, I won't push it. Who takes the first watch?"

"I will."

"Wake me up if you get too sleepy. I don't want to miss the others." She paused and grinned wickedly. "Especially not Jeremid. I may not be in love with him, but he knows how to please a woman."

Macurdy managed to grin back at her. "So do I. Take my word for it."

"Take your word?" Melody sputtered. "Bastard!" He could tell she wasn't serious though, and as if to prove it, she chuckled, the sound reminding him of Varia. "You know, Macurdy, I loved you from the first, before I knew you well enough to like you. Now I like you, too."

Then she wrapped herself in her rain cape and curled up on the cold ground. When her breathing and aura said she slept, Macurdy put his own cape over her and stood up. He was getting sleepy, and considered doing calisthenics to stay awake and warm, then decided he was too tired. Instead he fingered his gums and broken front teeth. They'd begun to hurt. He'd assumed they'd start to rot in time, but hadn't thought it would be so soon. Presumably they had tooth butchers in this world, but he was willing to bet they were a bloody, painful lot.

He sat down again. They were back barely within the trees; the sun, when it rose, would shine in his face. It ought to be all right to sleep till then. He should have three or four hours before the dwarves arrived.

* * *

The sun rose, but by then he'd turned his back to it, as Melody had. An hour later it was Blue Wing's raucous voice that wakened him, from a limb almost directly overhead. "Macurdy! Macurdy!"

He jerked abruptly to a sitting position. "Huh? Oh! Blue Wing!" He turned to Melody; she was sitting up too.

"The dwarves are on their way," the bird said. "Tossi sent

me to tell you. Where are the others?"

"In the woods, up the creek a little ways."

"Have you slept?"

"A little bit."

"Humans are strange! Go back to sleep. I'll wake you when they get here."

He didn't need to urge them. They lay down again where they were, backs to the sun, letting it warm them. It didn't much make up for the cold, hard ground, but they quickly fell asleep again.

* * *

The next time Blue Wing wakened them, Macurdy could see the dwarves coming, a quarter mile south down the road, Jeremid riding a little ahead as if impatient. Their pack animals trailed behind, along with three new horses. Macurdy waved, getting their attention, then he and Melody scrambled down the side of the ridge and led them to the rebels, who still slept beside cold fires.

While Macurdy and Melody stacked a new fire, Tossi brought out a huge summer sausage, along with some potatoes that weren't too badly sprouted. The activity had wakened most of the rebels, who watched impressed as Macurdy lit the fire. They'd seen him do it the night before, but they'd been half unconscious then; it could have been a dream.

"Are you part ylf?" Wolf asked.

Macurdy laughed. "I used to be a shaman's apprentice. Learned to start fires and kill bugs in the bedding. That's pretty much it."

They seemed comfortable with that.

Now Macurdy raised his face. "Blue Wing!" he shouted. "Blue Wing!" The rebels looked at him as if he'd lost his mind. "Huh! I hope he hasn't flown off out of hearing." Not many seconds later, the great raven landed in a tuliptree, perching on a branch about sixty feet overhead.

"What do you want, Macurdy?"

"We need to find a band of men. Rebels. There'll be quite a few of them, and they'll be armed. Men that may resemble the men we found with the dwarves a few days ago."

Blue Wing didn't say anything for a long moment. "Can you tell me more? What direction? Anything?"

Macurdy looked at Verder. "What can you tell him?"

Verder stared impressed at the big bird. "I suppose they'll be somewhere north and west of here not many miles. Probably where there's open ground with grass for the horses; a burn maybe, a year or two old. There's likely to be lean-tos and tents."

Blue Wing didn't ask for clarification on "not many miles." Probably, Macurdy thought, he'd taken it to mean not too far away. The great raven launched from the branch, big wings thrusting, lifted through a gap in the forest roof and out of sight.

He was back in half an hour to describe a camp he'd found. "I'll bet that's it," Verder said.

They got on their horses, three of the rebels riding bareback. (The innkeeper had been unwilling to sell any of his saddles; the saddle makers in Gormin Town might have been burned out the night before, and he didn't know when he could get more.) Over the next hour the bird guided them west and north, then landed in a tree. "Macurdy!" he called, "it's only a short way farther. Leave the ridge and follow the draw on your right. You'll come to a large grassy area."

"Thanks!" Macurdy called back, then turned to Verder. "They're not going to know us. Could there be any trouble?"

"I don't know why. They ought to welcome volunteers."

Macurdy's eyes scanned down the line of horses and ponies. "String your bows," he said, and waited while the dwarves dismounted to draw their braided wire crossbow cords.

He followed Blue Wing's directions then, and in the draw found a well-used trail. Before long they were challenged. He stopped, and a sentry came out on foot, sidling toward him, bow half drawn. "Who are you?" the man asked. "What are you doing here?"

"We came up to join, if we like the look of things."

Another voice called from out of sight behind a thicket. "Kahl, take them to Orthal. He'll decide what to do with them. And you! Strangers! All of you off your horses! On foot!"

Macurdy looked back. "Do it," he said.

Another, presumably Kahl, rode out on horseback then, and herded the newcomers to a broad meadow. As they crossed it, a heavy-set man sauntered to meet them, a man with considerable fat over thick muscles. Orthal, Macurdy decided. In one hand he carried a roasted joint of some animal, a deer maybe, or calf. His face, hands, and hairy belly were slick with grease. His aura marked him as a natural ruler, a man born to give orders and be obeyed. It also showed him to be brutal. Most of his command seemed to be loafing, and Macurdy got the sense of people who didn't know what to do next—men without a clear objective or plan or strategy.

"Captain," Kahl said, "these people were coming up the trail. Thurgo told me to bring them to you."

Orthal scowled at the newcomers. "What do you want here?"

"We came to join," Macurdy said.

"Who in the devil's name are you?"

"My name's Macurdy, and these are Jeremid and Melody. We're from Oz. These dwarves are sons of the Rich Lode clan, from the Diamond Flues. These others are rebels from other bands, men we rescued from the reeve in Gormin Town. I don't know all their names."

None of it seemed to register on Orthal, who looked them over slowly, his eyes stopping on Melody for a long moment before returning to Macurdy. Meanwhile, more and more of Orthal's band gathered around, bows nocked or spears in hand. Jeremid kept his own arrow casually directed at Orthal's greasy chest, the bowstring half drawn. Orthal was very aware of it.

"Who do you know here that can speak for you?" Orthal asked.

"Here? No one of yours. But these…"

Orthal waved him off. "They don't mean shit to me. I never saw them before."

"I'll tell ye who he is," said Tossi angrily. "He's the one that killed the reeve's guards in the square in Gormin Town. He and those tew. And cut these others down from where they'd been hung up to die in public. And led a public riot against the king, that set the town burnin'.'"

Most of Orthal's men were staring hard at Macurdy now, unsure whether the claims were true, but feeling a certain awe. Macurdy could sense it.

Orthal grunted. "Huh! Sounds like bullshit to me. What's your name again?"

"Macurdy."

"Macnurley!" His mispronunciation, Macurdy guessed, was deliberate. "I've got foragers out, and they bring news as well as food. If the things this halfling says are true, we'll welcome you. But for now...For now you'll have to give up your weapons. And your horses."

Macurdy felt his people tighten. He was also aware Orthal had reestablished his authority; his men were ready to let their arrows fly, their spears thrust. One of them even stepped in front of his captain as if to shield him. Macurdy looked back. "Do what he says," he ordered. "If we're going to be part of this, we need to take orders." He slipped his sheathed saber from his belt and lay it on the ground; unhappy, the others followed his example with bows and swords. Meanwhile rebels had moved in, taken the reins of the horses and ponies, and were leading them away.

No one but Macurdy paid attention to the heavy knife still behind his hip. They were led to a place in the shade and seated in a cluster, unbound but guarded. After a little, the rebels ate their midday meal, offering their prisoners neither food nor water. Jeremid gave Macurdy dirty looks. Before the meal was over, a sentry rode up. "Captain! There's men coming up the trail from Three Forks. Slaney and his, I think!"

Macurdy swallowed bile.

Other rebels mounted horses and rode off southwest, clearly not in hostile reaction, but to confirm and greet.

"Slaney?" Jeremid murmured. "Isn't he the one...?"

"He's the one," Macurdy murmured back.

"Shit! What do we do now?"

"Wait for our chance. Don't do anything till I tell you."

Six or eight minutes later, Slaney rode into the clearing at the head of about twenty men. Macurdy got to his feet, the rest of his party rising too. As the newcomers rode up, Slaney's glance stopped on him.

"Well! What have we got here?" he said. Reining up, he dismounted and swaggered over. "Looks like you caught yourself some prisoners, Orthal!" He laughed then. "Yes, you surely did."

"You know them?"

"Oh yes. Yes, I know them. I know them real well. This one especially." He pointed to Macurdy, then actually rubbed his hands together. "I never forget a face, and that one I'd remember in hell."

He told about the affair at the blown down timber then, his account more or less factual, but incomplete. Finishing with, "He took our horses then, and our loot and weapons, and rode off with it."

"Slaney," Macurdy said, "you're a liar as well as a coward. I left you horses enough to leave on, and what I took, I gave to the dwarves, as blood money for their cousins you killed. Anyone with even half a brain knows better than to start a war with dwarves."

Slaney flushed, and with an oath drew his sword. Macurdy's knife struck him just below the breastbone, and the bandit took one wobbling step before falling on his face. Rebels crowded around Macurdy then, punching and kicking, getting in their own way, until Orthal bellowed to let him be. Probably, Macurdy thought, he had his own ideas for punishment.

Then someone else spoke, Slaney's second-in-command. "Are these the ones Burney told us about when we were riding up? That want to join?"

Orthal took a moment before answering. "That's right. What about it?"

"What their leader said is true: They could have killed us all, or left us afoot. And if they want to join...When we stopped at Stoney Creek, Bekker told us recruitment's down to nothing, since Dell's band got massacred."

"That's us!" Verder said. "I was one of Dell's. Some of us were taken alive. Dell and Liskor were hung up on the spot and used for target practice."

Again there was uncertainty on many rebel faces.

"Counting the dwarves, there's twelve of them," someone added. "Enough to be worthwhile."

"Eleven," someone corrected. "The other one's a woman."

"I'm as good as most men in a fight!" Melody answered. "Anyone want to test me? Orthal?"

Orthal laughed. "Oh, I'll test you all right. On your back, after we've executed these filth. Starting with him." He gestured at Macurdy. "Then we'll all test you."

It was Melody, not Macurdy, Orthal walked up to, as if to grab her. Her right fist caught him flush on the nose, and blood flowed as he stepped backward in surprise. Then, with a roar, he drew his sword.

Macurdy's bellow stopped everything. "NOW WE SEE WHAT KIND OF SPINELESS COWARD ORTHAL IS!" he shouted. "TOO GUTLESS TO GIVE HER A SWORD AND FIGHT HER."

Orthal stared bug-eyed at him for a moment, then gradually relaxed and grinned. "Larny!" he called, "give the bitch your sword."

Some of the rebels laughed. Larny stepped forward, a massive shambling man not much taller than Macurdy but considerably heavier, mostly muscle. "It ain't right, Orthal," Larny said. "It's too big for her. She couldn't hardly lift it, let alone fight with it."

"Will you shut up, Larny! Just give her the damn sword!"

"Just a minute, Larny," Macurdy said, and stepped away from the spears at his back. "Let me see how heavy it is."

Before anyone but Macurdy realized what was happening, Larny handed him the sword, and Macurdy leaped. Orthal never got his own sword up before Larny's heavy blade thrust him through below the ribs. Macurdy wheeled then, sword ready. "What in hell," he shouted, "does a man have to do to join this humping outfit?"

Someone laughed, then someone else, then others, but most stood indecisively, till a voice called from overhead. "Macurdy! Macurdy! Men are coming on your trail!"

"How many?"

"More than ten!"

"Someone go see who they are!" he shouted, and several rebels ran to their horses as if used to taking his orders. They'd barely mounted when a man galloped up from the sentry post in that direction.

"Tarlok's coming! With recruits!"

The rebels seemed glad to turn their attention to this new development. They waited, and within three or four minutes, a dozen men rode into the clearing. Their leader trotted up ahead of the others. "Good news!" he shouted. "There's been excitement in Gormin Town! The reeve strung up a couple dozen of Dell's and Wollerda's guys in the square. Then someone killed the guards and cut the prisoners loose, and the whole town went on a rampage! Burned half of it to the ground! Including the stockade!"

"You see!" Wolf shouted. "I'm one of Wollerda's, and Macurdy's the one that cut us free. After knifing two of the guards himself."

Earlier, the matter of Macurdy and his people had focused the rebels. The arrival of the recruiting party had dispersed that focus. Now Wolf had returned it to Macurdy, in a manner of speaking; people were talking to each other about him, though leaving Macurdy pretty much to himself for the moment. Orthal lay ignored where he'd fallen.

Slaney's second came over to Macurdy. "You really want to join up?" he asked.

Macurdy examined the man's aura. It was the same general type as Arbel's; he was what Arbel called a student. Just now he was a bandit-rebel, and before that probably a farmer-herdsman, but beneath it all he was a student, perhaps of life. His aura seemed basically clean, with a zone suggesting a pragmatic nature. And he'd been Slaney's second, which meant he'd been accepted as capable, but took orders. Saner and smarter than Slaney though, and bigger, stronger-looking. So maybe not very aggressive.

Aggressive enough to make a pitch to Orthal, Macurdy reminded himself, *a pitch to save my neck. That took guts, with Slaney lying dead there.* He grunted. "Do I really want to join up? Not exactly. I want to command this outfit. Turn it into the core of an army that can throw Gurtho down once and for all. And I need someone by me who knows these people: what they want, what they need. What their strong points are, and their weaknesses. You want the job?"

The man didn't answer. Instead he said, "Don't be shy with them. They may not know it, but they're looking for a leader now. They want one. And they might accept a stranger. The right stranger."

They. They. That explained the aural coolness, Macurdy decided. The man was a local, one of the group, but inwardly held a little apart from it. *I believe I'm getting good at this aura analysis,* Macurdy told himself. "Thanks," he said. "Who'll take over if I don't?"

"Probably no one, with Slaney dead. And I expect they'll break up and drift home if someone doesn't take over."

Macurdy nodded. "What's your name? And the guy who just came in with recruits?"

"He's Tarlok. I'm Jesker."

"Thanks." Macurdy spotted Tarlok at the center of a large cluster of rebels, and started over. Some of the rebels from Gormin Town were there too; Verned glanced his way and beckoned. The cluster opened on Macurdy's side as if to receive him.

Let's do it, Macurdy told himself, and lengthened his stride.

"You're Macurdy?" Tarlok asked. "The one that killed Orthal?"

"I'm Macurdy. And yeah, I killed Orthal. Partly. Mainly he killed himself, by stupidity, and treating people like shit."

Tarlok's gaze was steady. Analytical. He had a warrior's aura, a fairly clean one. This was a man who'd take responsibility, and give loyalty where it was due.

"A couple of your people know a couple of my recruits,"

Tarlok said. "They tell us you killed the soldiers guarding them in Gormin Town, then cut them loose. And you're the one who lit off the uprising there."

"I'm from Oz, me and two others. We each killed guards, but I was the ringleader. Lighting off the uprising was easy. People there were ready; they hate Gurtho as much as you do. All they needed was someone to start something; they took it from there. I'd rather they hadn't burned the town, but it's their town."

"So what do you do next?"

"Let me ask *you* a question. I know what the people in Gormin Town want. They want to get rid of Gurtho. But what do you want? What are you up here for?"

Several men tried to speak then; Macurdy pointed at one. "You," he said. "What are you up here for?"

"Freedom for the tribe! Our grandfathers' grandfathers were free men. Then we lost a war with the flatlanders and had to swear allegiance to the kings of Tekalos. Obey their reeves and pay their taxes."

By this time, most of the rebels had gathered around to listen.

"All right," Macurdy said, "so you want freedom from lowland kings. Just don't replace them with somebody like Orthal, or you'll be as bad off as ever. You, Wolf! Is that what the rebels want where you're from? Freedom?"

"Pretty much. We want to rule ourselves."

"Anyone got something different?"

The only answers were shouts of "No!", or "that's it!"

"Then what were you sitting around for? You ought to be training for war! Learning to fight as a unit! Learning tactics! I came up here today and people were loafing! Did I get here on a holiday or something?"

No one answered.

"The only way to get your freedom is fight for it! And it's not enough just to fight! You've got to win!" He paused. "Now fighting's what I do. Fighting and winning. And I didn't come up here to waste my time. If you want to fight, and win your freedom, I'll organize and train you. Make a fighting force out of you. Lead you if you want. Otherwise I'll take my sword and my friends and go somewhere else. Tell me now."

There were several seconds of silence, long enough for Macurdy to wonder which answer he really preferred. Then Wolf said, "I've already seen him in action. He's smart, he's not afraid of anything—and he's *lucky!*"

Tarlok spoke next. "Orthal turned out to be a loudmouth bully, and Bono and I figured if things didn't get better, someone would cut his throat some night soon and we'd try a different captain. Maybe Macurdy's the man."

A number of voices shouted agreement, but it wasn't general. Jesker had followed Macurdy over; he spoke next. "Slaney'd been saying we needed to do something about Orthal, that as long as Orthal ran things, nothing would happen. Fighting with fists, he was the most dangerous man around, but for thinking? Then Slaney got crosswise with Macurdy over west, and Macurdy made a fool out of him; tricked him out of his boots. I know; I was there. Then here, when Slaney had the advantage of him, sword against knife, Macurdy split his breastbone. Now we hear what he did in Gormin Town last night. If we're not smart enough to make him commander after all that, I'm going home, and to hell with the rest of you! The gods sent him to us as our last chance. If we turn them down, we're finished. We'll deserve whatever happens to us."

Macurdy stood briefly stunned at the speech, and at the voices shouting his name now. Grinning men pushed up to him to shake his hand, and when things had calmed a bit, he raised his own voice. "Tarlok! Jesker! Jeremid! Melody! Tossi! Wolf, you too! I need to talk to you over by the cook tent! We need to get things started here!"

* * *

It took awhile. There were sixty-three rebels now, with Tarlok's new recruits, Slaney's band, and the six rebels Macurdy had rescued. None had been soldiers, and in Tekalos there was no militia training. All were good bowmen—many very good—and that was about the limit of their military competence. Most had also brought spears, such as hillsmen take when hunting bear or cat or razorbacks, and could stab a man with them if it came to it. But clashing spears with trained soldiers, they'd be in deep trouble. A few had swords, passed down through the family from tribal days, but almost none were trained with them, beyond the games boys played with sticks.

If competence was a problem, so was supply. With sixty-three mouths to feed, and located back in the wild as they were, foraging would be a problem. The nearest clusters of farms had been heavily drawn on already, and the camp had been there for only about a month, but getting food from farther away presented problems of transport.

Macurdy wondered again if this was a good idea, being here, doing this. To create an army out of a few thousand scattered hillsmen looked virtually impossible. And how was it going to help him rescue Varia anyway?

On the other hand, he reminded himself, he'd been operating on impulse, on intuition, ever since his run-in with Zassfel in the House of Heroes, and he'd succeeded beyond all reason. He'd been operating on "notions," like Will had, but bigger notions, and his had worked out.

Anyway here I am. And this makes more sense, or maybe it does, than just walking into the Sisterhood and telling them I've come to take Varia home.

* * *

With Tarlok's and Jesker's advice, he selected two platoon leaders, a sergeant at arms to enforce discipline, and a commissary chief. In the future, foragers would write chits for what they took, payable when Gurtho was thrown down. He named Jeremid his chief of operations, to see men got trained, and to schedule foraging and other work assignments. Melody would lead the actual training. Tarlok would still be the recruiter, along with Verder, who could tell firsthand stories about Macurdy, but they'd take only two men with them, instead of four or five. One of the older men, a smith himself, would travel around the district visiting smithies, to get production started on spearheads and arrowheads in quantities. Tossi and his cousins would find a suitable smithy and begin to train local smiths in the making of swords.

And Wolf would take Macurdy to visit the rebels in his district. They were a larger, considerably more effective band, and sooner or later coordination would be desirable.

When he'd worked these things out, Macurdy called a muster by shouting, reminding himself to see about getting bugles or trumpets or something. Squads were created, and assigned to platoons. Then, to inspire some enthusiasm for training, he had Jeremid and Melody give an exhibition of skilled spear fighting, first in slow motion, then at full speed, using training spears cut on the spot from saplings. It also prepared the men for taking instructions from Melody. When they were done, two of the dwarves gave an almost dizzying exhibition of swordsmanship, changing any perception of them as amusing halflings.

Macurdy had intended, when it was over, to send the squads out to cut practice spears for themselves. But before he could give the order, he saw three women watching from a little distance, and called them over. They were filthy, their clothes were torn, and their hair was matted with dirt and leaves.

"Who are you?" he asked.

It was the oldest who answered. The younger two were silent, eyes on the ground. "We're captives."

"Captives? Captured from who?"

"From our farms. From our families. A foraging party grabbed us when they came around to take food."

He realized why, but asked anyway. "What did they take you for?"

"They brought us here to hump us."

"Just the three of you? For all these men?"

The woman nodded grimly.

"And your family let them?" He knew the answer to that, too, but it loosened their tongues a little, or rather the older one's.

Their circumstances had differed, one from the other. The oldest was perhaps twenty-five, and married. Her husband had been away. The foraging party raped her on the spot, then tied her and took her with them. The younger two were sisters, fourteen and fifteen. Home alone with their mother, they'd been carried off and raped on the way to camp.

The rebels, standing around waiting for further orders, had listened to the whole exchange. Macurdy turned to them now, face dark with anger. "Those who were on those foraging parties," he ordered, "raise your hands."

Five hands reluctantly went up. "Orthal told us to," said one man.

Macurdy turned to the older woman again. "Is that all of them?"

"Yessir."

"All on one foraging trip?"

"Yessir."

"Which of the rest humped you?"

"Most all of them, I guess. Maybe a few didn't. They humped the young ones the most, I think because they cried. There was someone at them morning, noon, and night."

"Orthal said we could," one of the younger men called.

Macurdy's eyes found him. "What's your name?" he asked. His voice was a dangerous purr; the man paled at it.

"Parl, Captain."

"Parl, step out here." The young man hesitated. "NOW!"

He stepped, and Macurdy, standing close in front of him, barked a question in his face. "If Orthal told you you could hump your grandmother, would you do it?"

Silence. The commander seemed to swell. "GOD DAMN YOU! I ASKED YOU A QUESTION! WOULD YOU DO IT?"

Parl could barely get the words out. "No sir," he whispered.

"What would you demand of men who'd stolen and raped your daughter?"

"I—I'd want them punished."

"Punished shit! You'd want them killed!"

Parl almost fainted.

Macurdy looked around for Melody, and found her, her mouth a hard line. "Lieutenant Melody, talk with these women and come up with amends and punishments for the foraging party. And what the whole company can do for them before we take these women home again. I'll decide after supper."

* * *

Melody and the oldest victim came up with castration, to be followed by staking out over ant hills, naked in the sun. The girls couldn't bring themselves even to talk about it. Macurdy, though, wouldn't go along with such draconian and terminal punishments. The older victim relented before Melody.

He announced the amends the next morning at muster, and the punishments were meted. Each of the three captives was awarded 20 silver teklota or the equivalent, at the cost of every man but the newcomers, which virtually stripped the rebels of money. Some had to borrow from newcomers to pay their share. And remarkably no one grumbled, at least where Macurdy could hear. Beyond that, two conscience-stricken youths—brothers—asked leave to marry the girls, if they'd have them. The girls didn't say yes, but they didn't refuse, either, and Macurdy gave the youths a three-week leave, should the girls and their parents accept the offer. He didn't really care whether they came back or not. The girls, he thought, might need their reassurance more than he did their military service.

As for the foraging crew who'd stolen them, their leader was to receive ten strokes of the rod from each victim, and the other four, five each. The rod being unpeeled hornbeam about half an inch thick. But when it came down to it, the younger girl struck only the leader, twice, then burst into tears, threw away the cane, and ran to hide. Her sister wouldn't touch it. The older woman, though, laid it on with vigor, as if to make up for the unwillingness of the others, and Macurdy allowed her to strike for the younger two.

The results were an ugly bloody mess. Macurdy would let them suffer a day before trying the healing techniques Arbel had taught him.

The two girls were returned to their homes the next day, Jesker and Melody leading the escort to tell the families what had happened to Orthal, who'd ordered the capture, and to the foragers who'd taken them. Macurdy didn't think the girls could bring themselves to talk about it. The escort included the two volunteer bridegrooms, who didn't come back. Melody said they'd been allowed by the parents to stay.

The older woman remained with the company. "After what happened," she told Melody and Macurdy, "my husband would never have me back. And he's prosperous; he'll soon enough have another wife to keep his bed warm and mother our son." For a moment her mouth twisted, not with grief but bitterness, then she shook it off. "My father had no sons, and I was the oldest of three daughters. I'm strong. I worked in the field until I was married, behind the plow and with scythe and ax, rake and spade, pitchfork and pry pole. I never had a doll; I played with the bow. On summer pasture I've slept in the cow shed with a sword to hand, when there were tracks of cat or bear or troll around. I'm a good enough shot, I killed a wolf once, when they threatened the cattle, and another time I sent a catamount running off with an arrow in its flank.

"These"—she gestured at the camp and its men—"took my old life away from me. You can give me a new one now, and a spear and bow, and let me stay as a rebel. Afterward I'll see, if there is an afterward. These others are no more trained for fighting than I am, and women, more than menfolk, feel the curse of Gurtho. Some have even scarred their daughter's face, be she pretty enough Gurtho's agents might take her away as part of the tax."

With that, Macurdy lost any misgivings about leading these men.

* * *

After muster, he sorted out the things in Orthal's tent, stacking outside those he didn't want, for others to take. When he'd finished, he sat on a short section of log, elbows on his knees, face in his hands, his energy suddenly gone. Looking back at Washington County with greater appreciation than ever.

Chapter 24: Wollerda

He'd have gone to bed, but lacked the energy. Felt too tired to spread his blankets—Orthal's blankets—on the pile of dry grass. Then three men came to the tent. One of them, Tarlok, peered in at him.

"Captain?" he said hesitantly.

"What is it, Tarlok?"

"There are things we want to talk to you about, but they can wait if need be."

Macurdy got slowly to his feet, remaining somewhat bent because the roof was low. "No, let's hear them now," he said, and ducked out through the opening. The other two had come into camp with Tarlok. One was an older man who'd kept apart from the others at muster, like a bystander.

"Captain, this is Terel Kithro and this is Arva Bono, old friends of mine." He put a hand on the shoulder of a man about his own age, perhaps thirty. "Bono joined the company when I did. For the last eight, ten years, he's traveled around amongst the settlements, teaching the young to read and write and figure. Knows most everyone. He's been helping me recruit."

Tarlok paused as if ordering his thoughts. "I didn't tell you the entire truth, earlier. Bono and I'd planned to murder Orthal. Last night. Orthal and Slaney and a few others had a reputation for fighting and getting in trouble. Making trouble. Then the reeve came in with his bully boys and killed some people, burned some farms, and drove off livestock. For holding back on taxes, he said. When the word got around, folks were pretty upset, and Orthal and his buddies were naturals to recruit wild or would-be wild young bucks to form up a rebel band." Tarlok shook his head. "We didn't realize what a damned troll he really was. In the long run he was a hindrance for recruiting. Bono and I brought in quite a few men that afterward slipped off and went home—didn't like the way Orthal did things. It was their stories, more than anything else, that hurt recruiting. Looked like he'd turn the whole thing into banditry."

Macurdy interrupted before Tarlok could say more. "I'm worn out, Tarlok. What are you getting at?"

Tarlok nodded. "Right. We brought Kithro back with us because people know and respect him, and because he's a friend of Pavo Wollerda, the captain of Wollerda's company. Of the eastern clans. It's supposed to be a lot bigger than ours, and better organized and trained. And we figured when we had a better leader, maybe the two bands could work together."

"Who did you figure would lead, once Orthal was dead?"

"Well, I sort of planned to, if we couldn't talk Kithro into it. But now you're here, and we're all agreed you'd do a lot better job."

Macurdy grunted. "Kithro, do you think this Wollerda would be interested in working with us?"

"I think so. Otherwise I wouldn't have come up with Tarlok. I'm too old for a rebel. Old and spoiled by comfort."

Kithro's aura was pretty clean. Arbel would call him a warrior, in this case an overage warrior who'd go for his goals by other means than a sword: by focus and intelligence, and maybe other people's swords. "Tell me about Wollerda," Macurdy said.

Wollerda was of a lineage of chiefs, Kithro told him, and that still meant something among the Kullvordi, which was what the hillsfolk called themselves. When Wollerda had been a small boy, the king had been having trouble with the Kullvordi, and because Wollerda's father and grandfather had both been headmen, Wollerda and his mother had been taken to the palace as hostages. Wollerda had grown up there, he and his mother living in a small room in the servants' wing. As a bright, inquisitive child whom adults tended to like, he'd learned a lot about the flatlands, its government, and the royal court. And about the rest of the world, because the palace held a royal library with two or three hundred books, and the old man who looked after it took a liking to him.

When he'd pretty much grown up, he and his mother were let go, but after a few years of farming and herding, he'd returned to the capital, Teklapori, and set up business as a traveling salesman of books and jewelry. He not only traveled all over Tekalos, but east to the Great Eastern Mountains, west to the Great Muddy, and north to the Big River, buying and selling books, and fine jewelry made by the Sisters. He'd even been north of the river, into the Marches of the ylvin empire.

"How do you know so much about him?" Macurdy asked.

"We traveled together now and then," Kithro said. "I used to go from place to place making fine boots. And when you travel together and stay in inns together, you talk a lot. He and I got pretty close. I've made boots for him and his servants—traded them for books."

Macurdy nodded thoughtfully, not as tired as he had been. When his visitors were done, they left. By then the smell of smudge fires filled the camp, mosquitoes being out in force for the first time that spring. He'd killed several on his face and neck already, and decided to try a spell Arbel had taught him—one he hadn't had a chance to use before: creating a repellent field to keep them away. Briefly, as he muttered the formula, his hands moved, weaving something unseen.

It worked; the mosquitoes stayed too far away to hear. As he lay waiting for sleep, Macurdy thought about what Kithro had told him. He'd planned to get together with the commander of the other group anyway; now it seemed he had someone besides Wolf who could vouch for him.

A few hours later he awoke, slapping and scratching. The field had worn off. He wove another and fell asleep again, but the bites he'd already gotten still itched, troubling his dreams.

* * *

Macurdy spent another day helping the company get started in its new training mode. To his surprise, Melody was sharing a tent with the woman who'd changed from sex slave to recruit.

He somehow found that gratifying; he'd expected her to be sharing one with Jeremid. *Macurdy,* he told himself, *that's a lousy attitude. If she was with Jeremid, they'd both be happy.*

On the next day, leaving Jeremid in charge, he left to meet Wollerda, accompanied by Kithro, Wolf, and Yxhaft Vorelsson Rich Lode. He'd chosen them to make a good impression: Kithro was Wollerda's old friend, and Wolf one of his rebels, and surely he'd respect the dwarves. Recommendations, Macurdy felt, would be important; he was a foreigner with his front teeth missing or broken, and a face Melody told him still showed the pale green and yellow of old bruises.

A brawler, that's what I look like, he told himself. *Another thug like Orthal.*

The day had dawned to rain, not hard, but steady and cold, and they didn't talk much as they rode. Blue Wing had started out with them, but was seldom in evidence, flying high, and perhaps from time to time, far. Occasionally checking on their whereabouts though, Macurdy hoped, for the new leaves were almost full-flushed now. Men riding in the forest would be harder to spot from the air without a good idea of where to look.

They rode north awhile, then stopped at a small village where Kithro spoke to several older men, opinion leaders instead of potential recruits, telling them about Macurdy's Company. One called a son in, a well-built lad who Macurdy guessed at seventeen. Yes the boy was interested. He'd have joined up sooner, except his father disapproved of Orthal.

"Who do you know that can take us to the Saw Pit Road?" Kithro asked.

"I can," the youth answered. "I've ridden and hunted all through these hills with my friends. We know every creek and trail."

"That far east?"

"Sure. We hit it last fall, after a troll raided a farm over above Berol's Run. A bunch of us spent more than a week hunting him."

"Did you get him?"

"Nah. Struck his tracks a couple times though, his or some

other's the same size. Seems like he was just traveling through, instead of moving in. Maybe went on east to the Granite Range. It's really wild over there; no farms at all."

Kithro nodded to Macurdy. "Well, then," Macurdy said, "if you want to join us, get your rain cape and bow, and wrap something to eat. Your first job is to guide us to the Saw Pit Road."

The lad scrambled. In ten minutes he was saddling his horse. Then they set out more or less eastward through rugged hills, picking their way along trails some of which were little better than game trails. Here and there, a tree had been blazed with esoteric marks that meant something to the hillsmen, but nothing at all to Macurdy. Twice the boy swore and they backtracked a ways, but they had no real difficulty. It occurred to Macurdy that he himself had only a vague notion of how to find his way back, if it came to that.

The rain stopped late the first afternoon, so they didn't have to camp in it.

Soon after sunup on the third day, they reached the Saw Pit Road, an actual road with the tracks of wagons and carts. Kithro said it crossed over into the Big River drainage to the north, but they turned south. Now it was Wolf who took the lead. By late morning, the creek beside the road had grown considerably, and the draw it cut had become a narrow valley, with clustered farms. At one of these they left the road, riding eastward on a wide, well-beaten trail. Blue Wing came down then, calling to Macurdy, and they stopped to wait. There were men ahead, he said, "waiting with bows, in a place where many trees have been cut down."

Wolf nodded. "The commander had trees felled to block the woods," he said. "Any king's men can only come in on the trail. Men will stop us when we come to it, and ask questions, but there'll be other men watching us before we ever reach the woods."

They rode on. Shortly the trail left the cleared land, entering another forested draw. After a quarter mile, they saw abatises ahead, one on either side of the trail, presumably extending to the steep slopes that flanked the draw.

Macurdy had never seen or heard of an abatis before. Many trees had been chopped down, to lie on top of or diagonally across one another, their tops pointing more or less westward toward possible intruders. No one could ride through them. Even walking would be impossible, he told himself, for anything much bigger than a weasel. Anyone riding through the draw would have to keep to the trail, which could be defended by a handful of spearmen backed by archery.

When they reached the abatises, two men stepped out from behind trees; one of them ordered the travelers to halt. He talked with Wolf, whom he recognized, and got Kithro's name, then sent the second man trotting on foot up the road. A minute or so later, Macurdy could hear the dull thud of hooves ahead, galloping off eastward.

Half an hour later, a dozen well-armed men arrived on horseback, to escort and more or less enclose Macurdy's party. Six in front and six behind, herding them farther down the trail. *They're organized all right,* Macurdy thought, *and trained, by the way they do things.*

Less than a mile farther on the draw widened, and they entered an oblong basin. Three or four hundred acres had been cleared for pasture; some of it planted now to corn and potatoes, the rest a drill field. The grassy look of the surrounding woods told of livestock pasturing there, too. The rebel camp was at the near end, eight longhouses, and more under construction. Wollerda occupied an old log cabin, which served as both headquarters and living quarters.

The commander himself stood in front of it, waiting for them, and as they approached, Macurdy recognized him—the man who'd eaten with them once at an inn, and asked Tossi about dwarf swords. He was medium-sized and maybe forty years old, Macurdy guessed, and fit-looking, though not as physically hard as the escort he'd sent.

Wollerda recognized him, too, but it was Kithro he gave his attention too, pumping his hand as the two exchanged good-natured queries and comments. Now Kithro half turned, looking at Macurdy. "Pavo," he said, "I've brought someone I think you'll be glad to meet: Curtis Macurdy. He's taken over Orthal's band. We call it Macurdy's Company now."

Macurdy and Wollerda stepped up to one another and shook hands, Wollerda examining him. "Macurdy and I have run into one another before," he said to Kithro, then spoke to Macurdy. "How did you get rid of Orthal? From what I've heard, he wasn't someone who'd step down."

"He didn't. We rode into his camp to volunteer, and he decided he didn't trust us, so he made us prisoners."

Wollerda's eyebrows twitched. "And then?"

"Then I killed him, and his men made me their commander."

Wollerda cocked an eye. "Well. Best we go inside and sit down." He beckoned them into his headquarters, and seated them on split-log benches. "Now," he said, "there's got to be a lot of that story you didn't tell."

Macurdy shrugged. "It gets complicated."

"Excuse me, sir." It was Wolf who interrupted. "You might recall me; I was one of Minska's platoon. I've been with Macurdy since he cut me free from a hanging post in Gormin Town, and I guess I saw all of it."

Wollerda examined the hard-bitten rebel. "You're the one they call Wolf," he said. "Suppose you tell me what Macurdy left out."

Exaggerating only a little, Wolf told the whole story, beginning with the hanging posts. He included the campfires started with a gesture, Blue Wing, the slaying of Slaney, the tricking of Orthal, and the freeing of the captive women, ending with the organizing of the company and its training. "And we're giving chits to farmers when we commandeer food," he finished. "Good for payment when we've thrown down Gurtho."

Wollerda had seemed to enjoy the story. Briefly he grinned, a wry grin. "Well, that gives them another reason to want Gurtho gone. Now. You said '*we're* giving chits.' Does that mean you're staying with Macurdy instead of me?"

Wolf didn't flinch. "Sir, you trained me hard. Now Macurdy needs men to train his people, and it seems like I'd be of most use to him just now."

"Umm. So you would. Well, I leave it to you." He turned to Macurdy then, quizzically. "You sound like one of the heroes in the old folk tales. Did you ever kill a dragon?"

"Never even saw one."

"When I saw you before, I ignored you. Your face was more discolored then. I took you to be a large, rough young man who'd been hired by the lords in the mountain to tend their beasts and baggage. Someone who drank and got into brawls." He paused. "*Do* you drink and get into brawls?"

Macurdy grinned. "Water's my style, and buttermilk. And I generally try to stay out of fights, but sometimes—sometimes that's not so easy." He'd almost said *sometimes in this world,* and wondered if Wollerda would have made anything of it.

Wollerda turned to Yxhaft Vorelsson. "How did you lords in the mountain come to associate with this unusual tallfolk?"

The dwarf grunted. "That's a story to match the others ye've heard here," he said, and proceeded to tell what had happened at the fallen timbers, including the release of Slaney and his men.

"It still seems out of character for lords in the mountain to mix in tallfolk affairs."

"Aye. I can't imagine it of folk in the Silver Mountain. But we're westerners from the Diamond Flues."

"Hmm." Wollerda turned to Macurdy again, looking at him long enough to have made some men nervous. "I suppose I should show you some of our training," he said at last, then snapped his fingers as if remembering something. "After I've had you all fed! You and myself. Sometimes I forget to eat when I'm interested in something."

Lunch was a stew of potatoes, turnips, beef and carrots, and round hard loaves of bread they cut chunks from with their knives. Bread! Macurdy was impressed: Wollerda's commissary was obviously better than his. He made a mental note to learn more about it. Another broken tooth came out as he ate. His gums and teeth hurt from one side to the other, top and bottom, even the back teeth, which hadn't seemed damaged. It wasn't too bad yet, but he shuddered to think what it might be like in a month or a week. After they'd eaten, they witnessed the training of new recruits and of more experienced men. Macurdy couldn't help but appreciate the well-trained Ozian militia back at Wolf Springs, and wondered how good Gurtho's army was.

After supper he asked Wollerda about the Teklan army. It was made up of several levels, Wollerda told him. The best was the king's personal cohort, close to six hundred cavalry, whose training was sometimes a disaster to farmers whose fields they trampled in their exercises. Fortunately they trained mostly on their own reservation. Their pay and upkeep was a significant burden on the people, but they were the best troops in the kingdom; some of the best in all the Rude Lands. In addition, each of the six counties had a standing force of two mounted infantry companies—an even greater burden on the people. Each county had at least four shires—as many as six—each administered by a reeve with a platoon of fifty-five mounted infantry. Plus a reserve platoon, called on mainly at tax time. All told, Wollerda said, the king could call out more than forty-five hundred soldiers.

Most of the population were peasants, who fell into several categories. The highest was prosperous enough to hire help, or to contract with sharecroppers. The second class owned their own land and farmed it with the labor of their family. The third was sharecroppers, and below them day laborers who found paying work as they could.

The Kullvordi had a slightly different situation. One thing remained of their previous independence: they had no bailiffs. Local headmen, whom they elected themselves, presided over day-to-day life, but could be overruled and dismissed by the reeves, who also set and collected the taxes.

"And there you have it," Wollerda finished. "Our obstacles and our opportunities. We've got to work out ways to make use of the one and get around the other. What you did in Gormin Town showed me more potential in the flatlanders than I'd realized they had." He got to his feet. "Come ride with me," he said. "Just the two of us."

"All right," Macurdy said, and got to his feet. The invitation hadn't been casual; the commander wanted privacy. Wollerda saddled his own horse; he was not a leader who demanded to be waited on, though he might if his army grew enough to seriously tax his time. Unaccompanied by aides, they rode out of camp in the beginnings of dusk.

"There are things about you," Wollerda said, "that don't add up. First, you claim to come from Oz. I've never been in Oz, but I've known a few Ozmen in my travels. And you? You're different from any of them."

"All men are different."

"In details. But every people has its own ways, its own beliefs and viewpoints. Ozmen tend to be impulsive and more or less warlike. You fit there. But some of the things you've done…" Wollerda shook his head. "It's hard to imagine an Ozman undertaking what you did in Gormin Town. Or intervening at such risk in a fight between bandits and dwarves. And not keeping the horses?" He shook his head in rejection.

"Hmh! Interesting."

"Why did you do those things? What drives you?"

"I guess I'm an adventurous soul."

Wollerda grunted. "It goes beyond that."

Macurdy said nothing for a while, not consciously thinking about it, feeling the roll and shift of the horse beneath him as it walked, the animal's smell, the sound of tree frogs in the evening. And the hum and bite of mosquitoes. He wove a repellent field as he rode.

Finally he spoke. "If I told you, you'd think I was lying. Or crazy."

There was a short lag before Wollerda replied. "I can't commit myself to an ally whose motives I can't even guess."

Macurdy reined in his horse. "Are you telling me you'll turn down my help if I can't explain why I'm doing this?"

Wollerda eyed him calmly. "My friend, I admire what you've done—I'm even in awe of it—and I appreciate the guts and strength and ability it took. I wish you success in your efforts against Gurtho, and I'll move to take advantage of them. But unless I know more about you—why you've involved yourself—I can't exchange plans with you. Let alone operate under one plan, as the two hands of one body."

For a long moment, Macurdy sat his horse without speaking, reexamining Wollerda's aura. It told him this man could be stubborn, but offered no clue on what to do about it.

"I've been wronged and abused myself," Macurdy said, "been made a slave, and beaten, and my wife stolen from me. It's easy for me to see things from a Kullvordi point of view."

He felt Wollerda's eyes examining, and recalled something Arbel had said once in passing: That some people saw auras without realizing it, even learned to read them a bit without being aware of it. Was Wollerda reading his?

"There's more to it than that," Wollerda said. "The heart of it is something else."

Macurdy, looking for what else he might say, decided to try the truth. "All right," he said, "I'll trust you. I'm from Farside. I was a farmer there, and married a beautiful woman with red hair—and tilty green eyes." He paused, letting Wollerda absorb the words, examine them, realize their significance. He also watched Wollerda's aura, thinking to learn more about the indicators of disbelief, and maybe indignation. Instead he saw a flash of realization. "After a while," he went on, "she told me about Yuulith, and the gates, and the Sisterhood. Then one day, people from the Sisterhood found us and stole her. Took her through the Oz Gate. I followed them, but I had to wait a month before it opened again.

"Then I went through; that's when I was made a slave. And then a shaman's apprentice, because I had the talent. But not for healing, it turned out, so they made a militiaman out of me, and then a soldier in their Company of Heroes.

"I intend to get Varia back. My wife. Commanding an armed force is a beginning." He shrugged. "Sounds impossible, but I've made a start."

Wollerda's lips had pursed as if to whistle or blow. Now he frowned. "All of that! But your goal has nothing to do with ours—with the aspirations of the Kullvordi."

Macurdy's answer was not quick. He chose his words. "A hundred armed men won't get Varia back," he said. "A thousand won't. Dishonesty won't. But position might. Elevation.

Meanwhile I was raised to honor my responsibilities, to be loyal and respect the loyalty of others. When I accepted command of Orthal's Company, I committed myself to them. At least as much as they did to me."

Wollerda turned thoughtful a moment, then a smile quirked his lips, and he grunted. "The Sisterhood! Hmh! Would you like to know who sits on the throne next to Gurtho? He's got a new queen; a Sister. Something new in the world—the Dynast marrying Sisters to kings. They say she's quite beautiful."

* * *

By noon the next day, the two commanders had agreed in principle and writing on the coordination of military actions. Blue Wing agreed to be the courier between them; he was experiencing things his tribe would take great interest in. And after lunch, Macurdy and his party started back to his own company.

To be continued in *The Lion of Farside, Volume 2*

Books Published by Sky Warrior Books

Purchase them through online resellers and better independent bookstores everywhere. Visit us at www.skywarrior-books.com for news, upcoming books, and promotions.

Alma Alexander

2012: Midnight at Spanish Gardens (E-book, Trade Paperback)

Cybermage (E-book)

Embers of Heaven (E-book, Trade Paperback)

Gift of the Unmage (E-book)

Spellspam (E-book)

S. A. Bolich

Firedancer (E-book, Trade Paperback)

Seaborn (E-book)

Windrider (E-Book, Trade Paperback)

L. J. Bonham

The Debt (E-book)

Shield of Honor (E-book)

Wolves of Valhalla (E-book)

M. H. Bonham

Daemons and Shadows (E-book)

Prophecy of Swords (E-book)

Runestone of Teiwas (E-book)

Samurai Son (E-book, Trade Paperback)

Serpent Singer and Other Stories (E-book)

The Spirit Wolf (E-book)

Robert W. Brady Jr.

Indomitus Est (E-book)

Indomitus Vivat (E-book)

Bob Brown

The Dragon, The Damsel, and the Knight (YA E-book)

The Lost Enforcer (E-book, Trade Paperback)

John Dalmas

The Lion of Farside Volume 1 (E-book, Trade Paperback)

The Lion of Farside Volume 2 (E-book, Trade Paperback)

Signature of God Volume 1(E-book)

Signature of God Volume 2 (E-book)

Soldiers! Part 1(E-book)

Soldiers! Part 2 (E-book)

The General's President (E-book)

The Second Coming (E-book, Trade Paperback)

Deby Fredericks

Seven Exalted Orders (E-book, Trade Paperback)

Carol Hightshoe (Editor)

Zombiefied: An Anthology of All Things Zombie (E-book, Trade Paperback)

Gary Jonas

Acheron Highway (E-book)

Dragon Gate (E-book)

Modern Sorcery (E-book, Trade Paperback)

One-Way Ticket to Midnight (E-book)

Quick Shots (E-book, Trade Paperback)

Frog and Esther Jones

Coup de Grace (E-book, Trade Paperback)

Grace Under Fire (E-book)

Pat MacEwen

The Dragon's Kiss (E-book)

Rough Magic (E-book)

Christie Meierz

The Marann (E-book)

Michael J. Parry

The Oaks Grove (E-book)

The Spiral Tattoo (E-book)

Phyllis Irene Radford

Healing Waves: A Charity Anthology for Japan (Editor) (E-book)

How Beer Saved the World (Editor) (E-book, Trade Paperback)

Gears and Levers 1: A Steampunk Anthology (Editor) (E-book, Trade Paperback)

Gears and Levers 2: A Steampunk Anthology (Editor) (E-book, Trade Paperback)

Gears and Levers 3: A Steampunk Anthology (Editor) (E-book)

Lacing Up for Murder, A Whistling River Mystery (E-book)

The Lost Enforcer (E-book, Trade Paperback)

So You Want to Commit Novel (E-book, Trade Paperback)

Dusty Rainbolt (Editor)

The Mystical Cat (E-book)

Deborah J. Ross (Editor)

The Feathered Edge (E-book, Trade Paperback)

Laura J. Underwood

Ard Magister (Book One of Ard Magister) (E-book)

Ard Magister: Demon in the Bones (Book Two of Ard Magister) (E-book)

Dragon's Tongue (Book One of the Demon-Bound) (E-book)

The Hounds of Ardagh (E-book)

Steven E. Wedel (Editor)

Tails of the Pack (E-book)

www.ingramcontent.com/pod-product-compliance
Lightning Source LLC
Chambersburg PA
CBHW050409260626
47156CB00003B/935